DURABLE BEAUTY

STORIES

GARTH TWA

EPIPHANY
PRESS

A DIVISION OF PARISSOUND PUBLISHING

LARKSPUR, CA

"Explicit to the Idiot" originally appeared in *Kiosk*, issue 11/12, with modifications.

Epiphany Press
30 Tamalpais Ave.
Larkspur, CA 94939
(888) 544-5433
http://www.Parissound.com

Library of Congress Cataloging-in-Publication Data
Twa, Garth, 1962-
Durable beauty : stories / Garth Twa.—1st ed.
    p. cm.
  Contents: Thundra, awake! -- Explicit to the idiot -- Durable beauty -- Bingo Depue, the senator's wife -- Surviving in the Hollywood -- Pieces of Delores -- Going forth -- Repair -- Day job.
  ISBN 0-9648974-4-X (alk. paper)
  1. United States--Social life and customs--20th century--Fiction. I. Title.

PS3620.W3 D87 2001
813'.6--dc21

                                                                2001040220

ISBN-0-9648974-4-X
Printed in Canada

The paper in this book meets the guidelines for permanence and durability of the Committee on Production Guidelines for Book Longevity of the Council on Library Resources.

For my parents, Ernie and Jeanne, who gave me the fingers
with which to write

Advance Praise for *Durable Beauty*

"Garth Twa is dangerously funny, a subversive satirist in the grand and twisted tradition of Waugh, Amis, and Fielding."

—T. Coraghessan Boyle, author
World's End, The Road to Wellville

"Garth Twa writes like a Southern madwoman stoned on absinthe."

—Dick Wolf, writer/producer
Law and Order, The Wright Verdicts

"Garth Twa is naughty and should be spanked."

—Mink Stole, actor
Pink Flamingos, Hairspray

"Garth Twa introduces us to characters that are extraordinary and hilarious, a parade of misfits, oddballs, and grotesqueries that have in common what we all have in common: heart, innocence, and the simple need to find their places in a perplexing world."

—Curtis Harrington, director
What's the Matter With Helen?, Who Slew Auntie Roo?

"Garth Twa is a genius. He uses humor to reveal the human truths that we might prefer to avoid. Read any given page and you're hooked."

— Michael Donaldson, author
Negotiating for Dummies

"*Durable Beauty* is inventive, hilarious, and smart. But page 76 needs some work."

—Michelle Huneven, author
Round Rock

Table of Contents

If you do not understand poetry, perhaps it is better to leave it alone.

—Homer

Acknowledgements

I would like to thank the following people who, in their various and invaluable ways, made this book possible: for their tutelage, Peter Cameron, Michelle Huneven, Stephen Koch, Richard Locke, Carole Maso, and Robert Tower; for their friendship, guidance, and/or nurturance, Alvin Allen, David Bergesen, Art Brouillard, T. Coraghessan Boyle, David Chambers, Mark Davidson, Marc Desplannes, Natalie Dolishney, Michael Donaldson, Margi English, Curtis Harrington, Todd Harris, Paul Hester, Clive Hirschhorn, Elliot Jacobson, Seth Kanor, Clare Keon, Emily Keon, Joe Keon, David Kidney, Shane Liem, Matt Link, Lajuana Loy Twa, Elena McGhee, Richard "Mr." Parker, John Rennie, David Schweizer, Sidney Sproule, Mink Stole, Diego Taborda, Richard Tanner, Adrian Walker, and Dick Wolf; for her editorial assistance, Debra L. Eckerling; and for her artistry and hard work, Paula Doubleday.

Thundra, Awake!

THUNDRA BAUM, A STURDY WOMAN of staunch and illiberal convictions, paced her living room, steering her formidable frame like a barge across her antique carpet. She passed her writing desk (a dainty affair of fussy construction, made of blond wood and set primly with a pink blotter and several fine point pens); it was free of clutter, bereft of mementoes, save a tiny laminated card which read, simply, "Endure." She turned around and passed her desk again.

"My love is like a bird . . . My love's like the wind . . ." Thundra composed. Her muse had descended, and at a most inopportune time. "My love's like a rock . . ." No. "My love's like a flame . . ." Hmmmm. "My love's like a rock . . . within my breast." With a large sigh she sat down.

> "My love's like a rock
>
> "Within my breast
>
> "That makes breathing quite hard
>
> "And my food not digest."

Thundra smiled, pleased with herself. She lifted the piece of paper, on which she had written the verse in her most florid hand, and reread it aloud. It was one of her better ones, she thought. With a coquettish shrug of her shoulders she placed the quatrain in a drawer.

Enough indulgence. Her little diversions would have to wait. She had work to do. The annual update of her book on manners and hygiene, written in verse, was overdue. One day, perhaps, she would be able to pursue her long-harbored passion: a slim volume of romantic verse that she might entitle *Fancies*. But for now May Ellis, her editor, was waiting.

Thundra straightened her spine and pulled her chair up to her typewriter.

> "Though glorious be the spectacle
>
> "The pubescent bloom doth bring
>
> "There's no excuse, even chemical,
>
> "For behaving like livestock in Spring."

Yes. That would do nicely. Thundra found that she'd had to take a slightly tougher tack these past few years, the way things were headed, the way people were acting now. Young people.

For her hard work Thundra awarded herself with a little foil-wrapped chocolate heart. Heart-shaped not because of the maneuverings of some suitor, but because they had been on sale (it was March). Thundra ate chocolate compulsively. It was not so much that she had a sweet tooth but rather that she had a minor addiction to phenylethylamine, a chemical found in chocolate, and also made in the brains of people in love. As Thundra had nothing to compare it to, she assumed it was the chocolate.

Thundra took great pride in her work; she had composed probably the most apt rhyme for the word "fallopian"—"cornucopian"—of any poetess on record. But guidance could certainly be gruesome. Take, for example, the topic on which Thundra was currently focused: her chapter on coupling, entitled "Coupling—there is only one right reason." What was needed—and what Thundra provided—was a sensitive touch, a lyrical touch, one that could take the vulgar sting out of the necessary biology, a subject too often bruised by careless and mechanical handling. Thundra was well aware of these so-called modern educational tracts that were nothing less than legitimized smut. The owner's manual for a car was written with more delicacy.

The need for her guidance, she humbly felt, was never more acute than in these immodest and brazen times. It was a privilege for her to offer whatever moral assistance she could. In the old days—the good days—her verses served merely as a guide for distraught mothers, a mere addendum to proper parenting skills. Now, however, it was more like an all-out one-woman war. Or two-woman, actually. She and May Ellis.

Thundra Baum was a solid woman, solid of flesh and solid of ideals. She towered above most women—she had since puberty—and because of this her posture gave the impression of an apology. She always seemed to be folding herself inward so as not to be overly apparent. She jutted her shoulders forward uncomfortably to de-emphasize her ample bust, and her stance, with legs spread too wide in an effort to lessen her height, made her seem always ready to wrestle. Her hair was short and kept in tight, artificial curls. Throughout her forty-three years Thundra Baum had remained unbent by the wanton suggestions of men. She was inviolate.

She sometimes wished that her displeasures were less transparent—years of general disapproval had etched her countenance to such a degree that sharpness of expression had become a reflex—particularly since her displeasures were so extensive. Thundra pined for a more temperate time, a time when ladies were identified more by their behavior than by the public flaunting of their sexual apparati. She longed for more modest times, times of chivalry and deference, times of caution and respect. The current climate of disintegrating values and the adoption of standards more suitable to a kennel made her soul sick.

The fact that her books were slow sellers did not discourage Thundra. Instead she felt somehow vindicated, that her instruction—that her very existence—was all the more vital. With a single glance Thundra could tell that her books were not being read: harlots and slatterns roamed the streets, people bustled and jostled with less courtesy than headhunters from Borneo, and what had always best been locked behind bedroom doors was now paraded in shop windows. If one delicate blossom could be reached before it was too late, if one mother's worst nightmare could be circumvented, then her modest verses, Thundra felt, were not in vain.

May Ellis kept Thundra Baum, the poetess, alive. May ran the Vestal Press. May Ellis believed, as Thundra believed, that the world had sunk to a disgraceful state. Skirts were too short (if worn at all), lips were too bright, women too willing. Vestal Press had been the one and only publisher to whom Thundra had submitted *Restraint and the Modern Woman—a Guide to Behavior, Rhymed.* May Ellis had rejoiced.

Thundra had been an ongoing fan of Vestal's *The Impenetrable Miss Physs* series and so had felt a certain communion with the firm. It was no great surprise that May Ellis had leapt at the opportunity to publish Thundra's opus. May and Thundra breathed the same air. They were twin caryatids in the temple of decency.

May Ellis was decidedly less physically imposing than the formidable Thundra Baum, but she was Thundra's equal in moral stature if not circumference. They were linked by a shared dismay at a world spiraling Hellward. May was squat, that was certain, but otherwise she was most often described (when someone felt the need to do so) by her accoutrements, by that which covered her up. She wore thick-framed eyeglasses, a hair-do copied from the early suffragettes, and stiff, loose dresses that dulled all the angles of her body. She powdered her face into a mask and nervously covered her mouth with her hand whenever she spoke.

Thundra gathered her courage together so that she might endure the dislocated morality seething just outside her very door. May had called her on the telephone and she had been urgent, though unspecific. Thundra buttoned her collar to the jowl (in the heat of inspiration and the flurry of her fingers on the typewriter keys she had rather carelessly undone the top two buttons), pinned a hat to her bun, and stuffed her updated material into her folio. As well as a manifesto against flesh-piercing below the chin that was new for this year's edition, Thundra and May, after many heated discussions, had eased their stance on nylon stockings, causing some misgivings on Thundra's part.

With her hand on the doorknob, Thundra took a deep breath to steel herself. As much as she disapproved of it, she found the iniquity of the modern world invigorating. It was fuel to her fire.

She hadn't even walked all the way to the sidewalk when she saw that they, the dark forces, the Mass Disturbation, had been busy throughout the night. A little knot of hate curdled in her spleen. For all that Thundra Baum stood for, all that May Ellis stood for, there were rampant forces at work in the opposite direction. A bus drove by and the figures in the advertisement posted on its side were adorned with garish genitalia of incongruous proportion. The artwork was signed with the all too familiar logo of the Mass Disturbation—a bastard caduceus of twined, copulating serpents, their forked tongues kissing in the French manner. The headline of the newspaper lying on her neighbor's stoop announced, "Mass Disturbation Humiliates Foreign Minister."

The forces of Mass Disturbation had been at work for wholly a year, blazing into the public's consciousness by abducting a visiting princess, only to release her a week later covered from head to foot with tattoos of the logos of various motorcycle clubs.

No one knew the numbers of the Mass Disturbation. The press could only guess. Though annoyingly prominent, they had retained—cowardly, Thundra felt—their anonymity. At first their attacks on all that was decent had been sporadic. Now they had their own boxed update in the newspaper, as well as stealing the headline on more days than not. Their numbers were growing, judging from the increasing frequency, and the increasing geographic range, of the assaults. They were also getting more sophisticated, though, evidently, tyros in the movement were still reared on genital graffiti.

"Thundra! Quickly!" May Ellis said, grabbing Thundra's hand and pulling her into the entrance hall of her apartment. May was flushed and her eyes were frantic behind their lenses. Her face was so unnaturally rosy that Thundra wondered if she might have forgotten the powder that morning or if, in fact, her disquiet had reached such a degree that it actually shone through. Once safely behind the closed door, May released Thundra's hand. Thundra took out a handkerchief and discreetly wiped off the clamminess that was left on her palm.

"May! Please! This is most unbecoming! Pulling me about! Please. Sit down before you dislodge something."

"Thundra I could think of only you! Only you would understand!"

A thin line of moisture formed on May's forehead and, to Thundra's horror, went unchecked. Thundra considerately looked away.

"Oh, where can I begin? This whole day has been awhirl." May Ellis was wringing a fold in her dress. Thundra knew that it would take more than one washing before the wrinkles would come out.

"Thundra, you know of the Mass Disturbation?"

"Oh, May! Please! Don't tell me they got your car, too!"

"No, Thundra. It just might be worse than that." May Ellis was betraying an uncomely excess of emotion. She was talking far too quickly, fairly sputtering, and her eyes were unable to rest on anything for more than a few seconds at a time. "You can understand that someone of my standards and bearing is a perfect target for their crimes. As are you, dear. And you should be proud of that, too. They loathe what we stand for because they lack our strength, our fortitude. They want nothing more than to see our ruination, and the ruination of all that we represent."

Thundra was relieved to see May finally pull out a handkerchief and tug on that, letting her poor dress hang unmolested.

"May, you're in a state. Please. Sit down. What could possibly be causing all this frenzy?"

May remained standing, making no motion to sit.

"Well," May said. She seemed on the verge of saying something. She pulled harder on the handkerchief. She took a deep breath and looked straight into Thundra's eyes, judging their temperature. "Come with me," she said at last.

May led Thundra over to the hall closet and when they were in front of it she checked Thundra's face for all the trust she could find there. She reached for the handles and pulled open the double doors. She stood back with a sheepish smile.

Struggling on the floor of the closet were two bohemians, both bound at the wrists and ankles, both gagged. Rather severely gagged, Thundra thought. One was a girl with long hair, although that was not the index by which Thundra had divined her sex, as both hooligans had long hair. The girl's immodest T-shirt left little doubt as to her gender. What was even more appalling to Thundra than the obvious absence of a bra was the absence of sleeves on her shirt and the furry patches underneath her arms which were therefore displayed. Also, the girl was wearing blue jeans, always a source of consternation for Thundra that had never dimmed. She had a pretty face, this girl, though grimy. There were sticky, matted places in her blond hair where blood had dried.

The male had longer hair than the girl. He was evidently older. His filthy beard, as well as his hair, had prominent streaks of gray. He was skinny, pale, and also wearing blue jeans, which was fine for a man, provided he was employed as a laborer. He was struggling, but he was doing so with less enthusiasm than the girl.

The pair looked like animals: roped, wriggling, a primitive panic in their eyes. When May had opened the doors they had begun to grunt frantically and stamp their feet on the floor. Their struggles were not as successful as they might have hoped due to the expertly tied seafarer's knots that bound them. Scattered around them on the floor were the fragrant contents of a sachet that had fallen, due to their thrashing, from the clothes in May's carefully tended closet. Thundra thought immediately about suggesting to May that she might wish to relocate some of her more delicate apparel for the time being. She could already see the discoloring on a lace house dress where the two had leaned their heads.

"I caught them," May Ellis said, kneading her hankie. The two captives escalated their thrashings with renewed zeal.

Thundra raised her hand to her throat and fingered the border of her collar. "Yes, but what are they?" she asked.

May grabbed Thundra's arm. She seemed astonished that Thundra needed to ask. "Thundra, dear, they're Mass Disturbation!"

Thundra gasped and reflexively took a step backward. She grabbed back at May's arm for balance.

"Do you need to sit down?" May asked. Thundra nodded. Her face was becoming a dangerous red.

May led her to a chair and went to get her some water. Thundra thanked her with a helpless wave and sipped with great flourish. May stood waiting, watching Thundra anxiously and then she remembered her prisoners. She crossed the room and closed the double doors. Thundra had regained her composure by the time May had returned.

"May, dear, how did you get them?"

"They broke in! Here! What they had planned, I don't even want to think about." Thundra tightened her grip around her collar. She glanced nervously around at the closet.

"I came out of the powder room—I was washing my hands—when I heard them in the living room. The one with the beard was trying to get into my bureau."

"How did they get in?"

"Through the front door, if you can imagine!" Thundra looked at the front door. It was undamaged as far as she could tell. May followed her gaze. "They broke in without so much as a splinter!"

"May, how did they get into the closet?"

May reached behind the couch. "I used this," she said and held up a can of mace. "Then this." She lifted up a ballpeen hammer. "I had plenty of time to tie them up. They were out for over two hours. Lands! Hauling them across the carpet didn't do my bursitis any good!"

Thundra was stunned. "Dear, we must call the police immediately."

"No!" May said in horror.

"No?" Thundra was puzzled.

May shifted quickly into a reassuring smile. "We can't. We simply can't."

"May, we must. They break the law. They're criminals." Thundra spoke softly, as though explaining to a child. May must have had a frightful shock. "May, none of the Mass Disturbation have ever been apprehended. This could be momentous! This could be the end."

"Thundra, that's just it. It would be momentous. And all over the newspapers and on the television! My name would be on the cover of every magazine on every horrid street corner. It would be frightful!"

"You'd be a hero!"

"I'd be notorious! Cheap sensation would be a scandal. I'd be recognized in the streets, be stopped cold by who knows what psychopath or deviant." May settled back. "The very idea of it makes me nauseous."

Thundra set her jaw. Granted, publicity of this sort was hardly desirable, but it would be a small sacrifice. Think of the legions of delicate sensibilities that would be saved with the forces of Mass Disturbation finally behind bars. Thundra regarded May. May, still wringing her handkerchief and with eyes unfocused and deep in thought, snapped her attention to Thundra. Thundra squared her shoulders.

"Then what are they to be?" Thundra asked. "Pets?"

"Thundra," May admonished, "I thought you, of all people, would help me."

"And I will. I'll call the police."

"Thundra, that's not the kind of help I need." May thought hard for a new, more convincing approach, but came up with none.

"May, they no doubt have their battalions waiting somewhere. Probably somewhere close. We have no time to waste. We're flirting with untold danger!" May let out a little whine. Thundra could not fathom her hesitation.

Both women jumped at the sound of the doorbell. They looked at each other and were frozen. At the second ring May was startled into mobility and ran to the door.

Thundra knew the voice in the hall. It was Noah Stella, a suicidal cook whose books were Vestal Press's biggest sellers. Thundra heard May's hurried tones, but these were answered by Noah's unabashed sobbing. May returned shortly to Thundra.

"It's Noah. I have to get rid of him. I'm taking him down to the lobby to talk." May locked Thundra with her most trusting look. "Thundra, you're my best friend."

"Come right back."

Thundra was on the phone as soon as she heard the door catch shut. She was barely two digits into the phone number of the police when she was stopped by the unmistakable sound of a gasp coming from the direction of the closet. She silently replaced the phone in its cradle and held her breath. The gasp was soon followed by a definite whisper and a series of grunts. Thundra stood up, smoothed her dress, and crept over to the closet doors.

Oh Lord, she thought. What if they're wired with grenades like the airport types? What if they've got cyanide pills tucked into some bodily crevice and are maybe even at that very moment choking their last breaths? Two contorted Mass Disturbation corpses in the hall closet. How distasteful.

Thundra leaned and put her ear to the crack in the door. She heard little grunts from the girl and then, "Hold on, Serge, I've just about got it."

Thundra grabbed the handles and yanked the doors open. Both terrorists recoiled, eyes wide. The remnants of the girl's gag rested on her shoulders and her lips were lavender from the dye in May's scarf. She had gnawed her way through it, and, judging from the moist spot on the side of the man's gag, she'd been working on his as well. Thundra stared down at them and they stared back. Thundra's reluctance was evident and her resolve was obviously as flimsy as one of May's scarves. She bit her lower lip, looking from one captive to the other. The girl, perceptive as a trained guerrilla ought to be, leapt at the weakness she saw in her opponent.

"Please help us," she said in a small voice, widening her eyes in what she hoped would pass for innocence.

Thundra sized up the waif, and then the man. She doubted that even their combined weights equaled her own. She could not imagine that these two could have been responsible for shaving the First Lady's head.

The girl leaned forward and glanced in both directions into the room. "Your friend has a past," she whispered confederately.

Thundra squeezed her collar into a knot and drew back. The girl's sincerity had made the words shock. But Thundra quickly regained her balance. The logic of the cockroach, as the boot descends, is bound to be desperate.

"Oh?" Thundra said, attempting flippancy.

"She's not what she seems."

"And just what does that mean?"

"Well, first of all, before today, did you think she was a kidnapper?"

"Kidnapper? She is no kidnapper! You're thieves! And terrorists! What did you expect her to do when you broke in here? Serve you her best tea?"

"Broke in!" the girl laughed. "We were invited!" The man nodded his head vigorously and made assertive grunts. Thundra again grabbed her collar.

"The Righteous Forces of Mass Disturbation have enough on this so-called 'May Ellis' of yours to smack her back into the gutter for good. Her prissy little act, her retrograde morality, she's fooled some of the people for a long time . . ."

Thundra let out an involuntary growl. Blood filled her face and little tears of rage gathered in the corners of her eyes. How *dare* they?

"You filthy little beasts! You are no better than livestock in spring! You're out to destroy all that has made this society great—restraint! Restraint and temperance! What exactly do you think the free-for-all that you and your type advocate will lead to? Collapse! Collapse of all that is decent! Leaving you all to wallow in the smut and the muck that you seem to be so proud of!" Thundra gasped. She hadn't inhaled in quite some time. She delicately plucked her dress away from the inelegant moisture that had formed on her bosom. The girl was smiling deviously.

"Your friend, *May*, might have some insights into wallowing."

That was it. Thundra would not have her friend slandered by such a noisome whelp any longer. She lunged forward and slapped the girl across the face and there was a resounding crack. Thundra immediately jumped back. "I'm so sorry," she said. The words slipped out before she could check them. The girl continued to smile even as the pink outline of Thundra's hand appeared on her cheek.

"Did that make you feel better? Do it again if you like, but it won't change the fact that your friend, 'May Ellis'—better known as 'Rhoda Silk'—was a fluffer for porno films back in the early seventies."

"What nonsense!" Thundra boomed, though she had no idea what a fluffer was, but it sounded rather pretty. May Ellis would never have been something as common as a "Rhoda."

"We have the film out-takes from *Auto Body Repair* and *The Head Waitress* and countless others. In fact, outtakes from Serge Stone's entire career. We're highjacking the Disney Channel next Sunday to broadcast them. We told Rhoda, your Miss May, so that she could set her VCR," the girl said and let out a raucous laugh. "Then she invited us here." The girl shrugged. "We came. We're not going to say no to a little extortion."

"I've never heard of anything so silly! 'Rhoda'! How ludicrous!"

A deafening screech stopped Thundra and all heads turned toward the door. May Ellis came running at the closet with alarming speed, her mouth open in a mindless bellow. Thundra winced as she approached.

"What is this?" May screamed. Her jaw was pumping and her eyes floated loose in her head. Thundra considered reaching out to comfort her but thought better of it.

"May. Please," Thundra said. "Just breathe!"

"Why is she not gagged?" May shrieked, thrusting a knotty finger at the girl.

"May, let me get you a chair."

"Gag her! Gag her now!"

"May, really! You are being rather inappropriate." Thundra shook her head, scolding.

"Hey, Rhoda!" The girl was leering. "You look a little rusty, but Serge here wouldn't mind a hand job for old time's sake."

May leapt on the girl, the high-pitched cry that tore loose from inside of her seemed hardly human. May's hands targeted the girl's neck and landed there tightly.

May was no contest, considering Thundra's bulk, but still Thundra had some difficulty prying her fingers from the girl's throat.

Once disengaged, May suddenly seemed more aware of herself. She sat down heavily in a nearby chair and looked slightly lost. The girl lay on her side choking.

Thundra was confused. She put her hands on her hips and pursed her lips. She looked from May Ellis to the girl and back again. The man had slid back into the closet and was hidden behind a flocked salmon tea dress. Thundra finally fixed May with a stern glare.

"May, this girl is a victim of a dreadful misunderstanding."

"What?" the girl exclaimed in a raspy voice. "How can you say that? After she just—"

"Quiet!" Thundra commanded and the girl obeyed. Thundra returned her attention to May. "As I was saying, these people, in their reactionary, low-bred stupidity, have confused you with some Rhoda who is apparently a poofer or tosser or something. They think you invited them here."

"Hey, Rhoda, why don't you tell this old buffalo what a fluffer is?"

"You little bitch!" May screamed and leapt again.

"May!" Thundra was horrified. She had never before heard language of that sort coming from May. What could have prompted her to such depths? Thundra stopped May's attack with a prudently outthrust arm that caught May under the chin. This took May's feet out from under her and she land-ed flatly on her back with a solid thud. May remained there, stunned. Both Thundra and the girl gaped down at her.

"A fluffer," the girl said, her eyes never leaving the motionless body of May, "is someone on the set of porno movies who keeps the actors aroused between takes. Someone who is in charge of continuity, you might say."

This was lost on Thundra. Pornography was not in her realm.

"Let's kill them," May said levelly from where she was lying. Thundra could not respond immediately.

"May, dear," Thundra said after a moment to break the silence, "you've hit your head. Now hold still and I'll fetch some ice."

"You'll go under, you stupid throwback." May still hadn't moved. She spoke from the floor, staring straight up at the ceiling. "Who else would publish a book that sells maybe one copy a year? If these bastards show that film I'm through and so are you." Thundra felt her knees go weak but she caught herself before she fell.

"No! You can't be this Rhoda!"

"Yes, of course I am. Was." May sat up. She rubbed the back of her head. "But that was decades ago. I was an idiot and poor. You can't imagine the tortures that I dreamed up for that worthless slug . . ." May pointed vaguely in the direction of the man, this Serge Stone. The man made himself even smaller by pulling his knees up into his chest.

Thundra could not look at May. "All the things that we shared, all the things that we talked about . . . they're all lies?"

"Of course they aren't! Knowing scum like Serge here was the most convincing argument I could ever imagine for wanting him and the likes of him eradicated. Thundra . . . they must be killed. They deserve to die. No one will even miss them."

"What?" the girl sneered. "You think they won't broadcast if we don't come back? Of course they will."

"You stupid girl!" May said, pulling herself up onto her feet. "I've known that man since before you were born! Those films are the most valuable things in his life. He's actually proud of them! He's got them locked up in his apartment. I know. If he dies, no one will be able to find them. If you broadcast without Serge's films, it would just be weightless slander."

"Stop! This is insane!" Thundra's limit for comprehension had been surpassed. How could people behave so poorly? "May, no matter what has occurred in your admittedly vague past, nothing can be that bad. Please. Let's just call the police. These people can't touch you. You're an upstanding woman, a paradigm of clean living. Whatever might have occurred will be forgiven and forgotten. We must hand these two over, rid ourselves of them, so that we can begin to understand our lives again."

"Okay." May pulled out a large carving knife from a hidden pocket in her dress. "Good riddance!" She launched herself at the man in the closet.

Thundra jumped in front of her and blocked her way. May continued to scramble, fighting her way around Thundra in order to gain access to the cringing Serge. As she fought, her arms and legs flailing, the knife caught the shoulder of Thundra's dress and tore it open. Thundra, with a force born of panic, heaved May away. May reeled backward, tripped over an end table, and, without slowing, went crashing through her fourth-story window.

Thundra, the girl, and Serge froze. Thundra, in some still-functioning region of her brain, was glad that the noise of the traffic swelled up from the street below. She did not care to hear her friend land.

"Untie me! Quick!" the girl said. Thundra moved without hesitation. She didn't feel capable of coping with the moment alone. She did not want to have to be the one to go to the window.

The girl ran to window but withdrew immediately, flattening herself against the wall. The sound of a voice amplified by a bullhorn came up from the street.

"We've seen you," it said. "The building is surrounded. Go immediately to the main floor and exit through the front doors with your hands above your heads. All other exits have been sealed. You have three minutes."

"Yes!" the girl said gleefully. "Fender tipped them off! This is perfect! This is front page!" The girl grabbed a pistol that was tucked in the back of her jeans and with a laugh she leaned into the window and fired two wild shots. Before she could withdraw a bullet hit her squarely in the forehead. She spun around once from the impact and landed on her face on the carpet.

Enough was enough for Thundra. This was getting ridiculous. This had nothing to do with her world. She picked the gun up from between the girl's limp fingers and walked to the window to toss it out, to let the police know that the situation was over, that noble, upstanding citizens were again in charge.

No sooner had she entered the window frame—to signal in a way that she was sure would be interpreted as meaning that order had been successfully restored—than a bullet grazed the sill, not an inch from where she stood. Thundra heard a faint "Damn!" come up from below. She took a lesson from the deceased girl and flattened herself against the wall. She swallowed hard once before a hail of automatic weapon fire shattered what remained of the window. Thundra was livid! How careless! Didn't they do their research? Didn't they know who was in the building? Didn't they care?

From where she stood, Thundra heaved the pistol. If they saw that all weapons were relinquished perhaps that might convince them. The gun hit the concrete ledge outside the window and it fired. There were screams and then a roaring murmur. Thundra heard one voice through the din. It said, "The captain's been shot!"

Thundra was bereft of hope.

Anxious grunts coming from the closet snapped her out of her descent into shock. She crossed over to Serge and ungagged him. He took deep breaths and faced Thundra. "Hurry! Get my ankles! Our van is downstairs."

"You're not going anywhere, you hoodlum. Except jail."

"Snap out of it, you silly bitch! They're on their way up here by now. You've seen that they don't ask questions. Now come on!"

Thundra leaned down and untied the man.

"I'm staying here," she said when the man was freed.

"Suit yourself." The man ran to the door. "Adios!" he said and slammed the door behind him. Thundra stood up and walked slowly to the couch and sat down. She heard helicopters flying by outside the window.

The front door opened. It was Serge.

"Come on, lady," he said. Thundra didn't move. She just looked at him. "Lady," he said, "they're going to shoot you. You shot the captain! Come on. We'll give you a lift home."

Thundra sat on a roll of canvas between two reeking, unshaven teenagers dressed like soldiers. They drove down a bumpy road. Serge sat across from her looking absently out the window. He no doubt felt badly, Thundra thought, because they hadn't had the time to drop her off.

She felt a nudge from the boy to her right.

"Sardine, Comrade?" he said. Thundra looked down at the proffered tin. She wrinkled her nose and shook her head weakly. She turned her head and through the window she saw that the road was lined with trees. She pressed her legs together tightly, the space not allowing her to cross them.

"High hems are eschewed, wide footholds are rude," Thundra thought, unable to stop herself, "and are hardly befitting a woman who's sitting."

She fought gallantly to keep from crying.

Explicit to the Idiot

BRENDADA FUCKOFF HAD CHANGED her name. Brenda Lynne Whitherflor, she'd concluded—and justly—was hardly a fitting name for an Assaultive Artist of the stature that she hoped to achieve.

"And what's the new name?" the woman behind the counter said.

"Brendada Fuckoff," Brenda Lynne Whitherflor said.

The woman's eyes darted to the security guard seated by the door. "Piss," she muttered when she saw that his eyes were closed and his head was lolling forward, a bridge of saliva trailing down to his chest. The woman lifted her pen from the paper and looked, fed up, into Brenda's eyes without blinking.

"What?" she said.

"Brendada Fuckoff." Brenda adjusted her weight and looked down at the floor.

"Spell it."

"B-r-e-n-d-a-d-a F-u-c-k-o-f-f." Brenda swore at herself when her voice cracked on the second "d."

The woman set down her pen without writing and pushed herself away from the counter. "Someone must've left the gate open this morning," she mumbled as she turned. "Roger!" she hollered. "Roger! I'm gonna be needing you!"

"Please!" Brenda said, hushed and urgent, "I'm absolutely serious. This is for my work." The blood pulsed hotly in her cheeks. But Roger was shortly there.

"What seems to be the problem?" the security guard—Roger—said. He smiled, but his smile was official: trained to comfort, yet firm enough to make it clear just who exactly was boss here. The woman looked at Brenda.

"All right, honey, tell the man what you want your name changed to."

"I don't see what all this fuss is about," Brenda said through a constricted throat. The man at the head of the line that had formed behind her began to cough irritably. The woman behind him loudly tapped her foot. "Brendada Fuckoff. I'm an artist."

Roger's grin didn't change. He picked up Brenda's paperwork and glanced at it.

"Come with me, Miss, uh, Whitherflor."

"Next!" the woman behind the counter said.

Her name was not the only thing that Brendada Fuckoff had changed.

"Lose the flowers," Angry Helen, her friend, had said. Brendada was sinking behind her third chi-chi in the Parasol Room. Angry Helen was referring to Brendada's canvases, as well as to Brendada's wardrobe, which favored large floral prints in muted colors adorned with what Brendada dreamily referred to as "little touches," and Angry Helen referred to as "all that Goddamned frilly shit." Brendada, sadly, liked pretty things.

"I *like* pretty things," Brendada said, sort of to herself.

"Nah. That whole natural, earth-birthing, lunar princess, mother-healer crap is so *yesterday!* It's so *the day before* yesterday! Lose it." Angry Helen took a long draught from her beer, getting most of it in her mouth. She belched.

Brendada's eyes were beginning to glisten and she could only respond with a sigh.

Angry Helen had brought the crestfallen Brendada to the Parasol Room after yet another third-rate storefront gallery had refused Brendada's work.

Angry Helen was an enormously successful artist, and arguably the most assaultive in the Assaultive Art movement. She was so successful because her paintings (subject matter aside) were offensive in a complex and layered way. Angry Helen painted only with animal products. She'd done a series of ill-humored works—using several gallons of pigs' blood that she'd procured from an abattoir—that had quickly become collectors' pieces, but her main claim to notoriety was with the murals she had completed in her medium of choice: rancid lard on canvas. She would use ordinary spoiled lard, dyed. She quite incensed the animal rights activists and the vegetarians, and her paintings, especially after a week or so, were assaultive not only on an aesthetic level, but on an olfactory one as well.

Angry Helen was large and adorned herself with endangered species just to annoy. Her hair was colored a flat black and shorn close to her wide, soft head. Her eyes were warm and her smile was easy. She was slow to anger and always composed, qualities that only served to further infuriate those who took exception to her art and were looking for a fight.

Angry Helen had taken Brendada, as part of her education, to an opening at the Harrington Harris Gallery to show her how a true artist rankles. After draining the better part of a bowl of punch, Angry Helen caught sight of Vincent Havoc, the noted art critic who had once derided Angry Helen's *oeuvre* in his column. He had praised in print the reception following her last opening, yet claimed that viewing the attendant paintings, the work for which the celebration was being thrown, had "put him off the canapés and exquisite French terrapin dip."

"Ho, ho," she chuckled. "Watch this." She placed Brendada behind a pillar, out of harm's way.

"Hey!" Angry Helen bellowed across the crowded gallery. The crowd immediately hushed. "Oh, Christ," Havoc muttered from deep within a clique of plastics magnates, donor industrialists, and a North African potentate. Angry Helen, drawing up her shoulders, stomped her way through the apprehensive crowd with the taurine grace that was her trademark and that made small children cry.

She elbowed aside a New Jersey philanthropist and bent down into Havoc's face, "So ya don't like my paintings, huh?"

"Frankly," he said, "I find your work—your public persona included—sick-making."

"Yeah?" she said, grinning and taking a step back. "Well, try on this feedbag!" At which point she hiked her skirt up past her waist.

"Pretty is nauseating," Angry Helen said, gently taking Brendada's hand. "But it's my way."

Angry Helen took pause. She liked Brendada. She honestly did. But sometimes she wondered if a good cuff on the head might perhaps yield quicker results.

"But it doesn't sell. Assaultive sells."

But pretty was, indeed, Brendada's way. Brenda had attended the Edengreen College of the Arts, deep in the woods, and had been indoctrinated in the values of purity and harmony. Rousseau had been exalted, adored, and emulated. The noble savage was nowhere held so nobly than in the minds and curriculum of the Board of Trustees of Edengreen. Millet had been attended to likewise. And Monet! Well, no amount of slavering was too much slavering for Monet, and Brenda's instructors had dwelt rapturously on the geography of Giverny for fully half of a semester. Pollock, Warhol, and Rauschenberg (and those of similar ilk), on the other hand, had been dealt with, in hushed tones, in a perfunctory addendum. As had the futurists. An abstract expressionist was not something one wanted to be at Edengreen.

"Paint what you feel," had been the persistent entreaty. And what was there to feel at Edengreen but the dappled sun on rosy cheeks, dewy breezes through the healthy hair of non-smokers, and the reflective solitude of walks along birch-lined paths? So Brenda painted verdure. She painted hillsides dotted with flowers, flowers so bursting, so fecund, that they would have been lewd if they had not been flowers. She painted pastorals, sometimes adding distant figures (with blurs for faces; they could have been milkmaids, shepherds, or country virgins) but most often not. She liked the simplicity of the green pelt of a meadow. She liked the play of purples and yellows in the bud of a gladiola, the dense and vibrant overstatement of the lilac, the impudent curves of the snapdragon. She adored the dignity of the dandelion.

Brenda Lynne Whitherflor had worn billowing blouses and long, flowing natural-fiber skirts. She was drawn towards clothing that bespoke a freedom of movement. "Flowing" and "freedom"— and, for that matter, "billowing"—were *de riguer* at Edengreen. Brenda had kept her long blond hair tied simply with a cotton ribbon and her skin free from make-up. It did not matter what color your hair or your skin were, as long as they were natural. At Edengreen, natural was beautiful.

Competition, though arguably natural, was not beautiful. Competition, the Board of Trustees of Edengreen stoutly believed, encouraged base dispositions. Regimentation, they also believed, encouraged militarism. The Board strove instead for a more nurturing environment than the harsh strictures of academia might ordinarily allow. The Board therefore eschewed attendance records, assigned classrooms, and grades.

Instead of grades the students received happy faces, the curvature of the smile indicating the student's progress. In the year that Brenda had dropped out, she had received four ebullients and a dispassionate (she never was very good at math).

It was not, therefore, because of any scholastic disappointments that Brenda Lynne had left. She had begun to feel an itch that maybe there was something more to art than merely art's sake. Like commercial success, perhaps.

At Edengreen her ravishing tableaux had met with great praise. And Brenda was nothing if not a sponge for praise, and the praise had been superlative. She had basked in the adoration and encouragement heaped upon her and her work, and this sparked something deep within her that was less than noble. As was the policy at Edengreen, the pupil next to Brenda, and those down the line, would receive equal helpings of adoration and enthusiasm, whether they deserved it or not. This dampened Brenda's pride of accomplishment, though she knew that it shouldn't. The gnawing that overtook her ran counter to all that she had learned in the Generosity and Abundance Workshop that all students were required—or, rather, fulsomely encouraged—to take in their freshman year. Brenda had become guilty and frustrated (more frustrated, though) about her situation at Edengreen. Eventually, and after much moral deliberation, she packed up her brushes and left for more competitive climes.

The city. The scoffing art galleries and clawing artists of every stripe. The starvation and dreams of unfettered success. And Angry Helen.

"What you try to sell, darling, is what sells." Angry Helen sat back, rather pleased with herself for the quip. She would have to remember it for later.

"But," Brendada said, disconsolately, "Blake said, 'that which can be made explicit to the idiot is not worth my care.'" She held her breath. She looked up at Angry Helen.

Angry Helen pursed her lips. Her brow contracted. "They're not referred to as 'idiots,' Brendada. They're called 'patrons of the arts.' They're called 'the market.'"

"But . . ." peeped Brendada.

"And besides, Blake was a nut job. He couldn't be explicit to idiots. He couldn't be explicit to anyone. Except other nut jobs."

"Hello, dear, it's your mother."

"Yes, Mother, I recognize your voice."

"How are you?"

"Hold on." Brendada ran around the sofa untangling the phone cord. "I'm fine."

"That's good."

"How are you?"

"I'm fine."

"Mom," Brendada blushed and pushed her bosom flat, "I changed my name." She listened. Her mother was still breathing.

"Your father's fine, too. The circumcision went well. He's home now."

"I changed my name to . . ." Brendada held the phone away from her mouth to let out her breath, "Brendada Fuckoff." She winced.

"He's making a fuss, of course, wants to get back out to the shop! Can't stand just lying around, he says. But you know Dad!"

"Mom, did you hear me?" Brendada heard an angry pause.

"Do you *need* more money?"

"No! No, I'm fine. And thank you for the check. It's an artist's name. I need it . . . to do art."

"Dear, no one's actually going to believe you're a Russian."

"Mom! It's . . . it's not Russian. It's . . . assaultive."

"I'll send a check."

"What else do we need to take care of?" Angry Helen said.

"I'm not getting rid of Daisy." Brendada was firm on that.

"A what?"

"My kitty. I'm not getting rid of her."

"Oh, my dear, no!" Angry Helen patted Brendada's hand. "Heaven forbid! A kitty! If you must keep a pet, make it a snake or something. Something poisonous would be best. Or a lizard. Lizards haven't been done in years."

"No! A lizard might hurt Daisy!"

"Marvelous! Then you could keep a dead Daisy for a pet." Angry Helen took a sip. "Wait a minute. I don't think I'm kidding." Her grip tightened on Brendada's hand and her eyes widened in blossoming inspiration. "Yes! It's brilliant! A dead cat for a pet! They won't be able to write enough about you!"

Brendada turned to Angry Helen. Her face had gone limp, her eyes on the verge of spilling. Angry Helen realized that perhaps they had made enough progress for one night.

"Don't worry, dear, we'll get you all set up. Finish your drink and I'll take you home." Angry Helen smiled warmly and kneaded Brendada's hand.

They rose to leave. Angry Helen paused. "So you don't think you're going to use the dead cat idea?" she said. "I wouldn't want to see it go to waste. And besides, it really is more me, anyway."

So Angry Helen took Brendada to her beaver-draped breast and set forth to guide her on her journey to commercial success.

"Black, dear, is in. It always will be."

Brendada's hair was clipped to a mangy shortness, the length and shape of moss, and dyed to match Angry Helen's flat black. Angry Helen led Brendada through an endless stream of second-hand boutiques, wrapping her in black apparel of every description and for every occasion. Angry Helen showed her how to powder her face to a ghostly white and how to apply eye shadow and mascara so that it didn't look so much like make-up as it did poor nutrition.

The kitty went to a neighbor and the lizard went under the sink. Brendada had attempted to transfer it from the cardboard box to its tank without touching it, but it had tried to smell her with its tongue and she'd dropped the box and squealed. She never saw it after that, though she lived in fear.

Brendada purchased a dozen large canvases from Rembrandt's Bargain Garret and placed them around her apartment—on her dresser, on her bed, on the tank behind the toilet. She felt invigorated and alive surrounded by so much possibility; $174.50 worth of emptiness needing her to fill it, worlds waiting for the creator's hand, buds seeking her pollination.

Angry Helen opened the door without knocking. Brendada thought she had locked it.

"I thought I'd locked it," she said.

"You did," Angry Helen said, setting her seal pup handbag down on the kitchen table and throwing something that looked like a dead cat into a chair. She walked into the middle of the room and pirouetted majestically, marveling at the new canvases.

"Marvelous!" she said, beaming. "Blank canvasses. How dada. How Duchamps. And leaving the price tags on was a stroke of Marxist genius."

Brendada flushed and looked at the floor. "I'm not done with them yet."

"Of course not, darling, you have to sign them."

"No," Brendada said, "I want to paint them. I . . . I kind of like to paint."

"Oh." Angry Helen stopped smiling and stopped being exuberant.

Brendada sensed that Angry Helen was somehow disappointed. She was. "I see," she said.

With a flourish Angry Helen brought her exuberance back up and crossed to Brendada, taking her hands in her own, "Then paint you shall!" She patted Brendada on the shoulder. "But I do think blank canvasses was an inspiration." Angry Helen pursed her lips and paced around Brendada.

"Penises," Angry Helen proclaimed. "Big, ugly penises." Brendada shook her head. Angry Helen, the outer envelope of her patience fastly being approached, said, "Car accidents. Cruel, violent car accidents." A tiny moan escaped from Brendada's little mouth too quickly for her hand to stop it. Angry Helen snorted. "Well, *something* with wounds."

Angry Helen was suddenly distracted. "Where's . . ." she winced, "Daisy II?" Daisy II was the lizard, a fire-banded gecko. Brendada had named her.

Brendada's hand went protectively to her throat. She looked quickly around the perimeter of the room. "I don't know," she said softly.

Brendada knew that to be a success she would have to ride the trends, yet she was wary to cast her lot so irrevocably with the tide of fashion. Fashion, by its very definition, was transitory. Brendada wanted to maintain some credibility, and she stubbornly held onto the notion of timelessness.

Brendada went to the library. Perhaps she didn't have to be Assaultive. Perhaps she could be Post-Assaultive.

She carefully opened up the massive *The Treasures of the Louvre*, looking for direction. She was drawn to Watteau, Fragonard, and, well, all the rococo painters. To a fault. She had been since Edengreen. Poussin gave her *frissons*. Boucher's unfortunately named *Toilet of Venus* charmed her beyond measure. She found herself getting misty, so she quickly and randomly flipped through the pages.

She stopped at Rubens' *Triumph of Truth*. Brendada rather liked Rubens. Angry Helen had told her to paint penises, big, ugly penises, but Brendada would rather, like Rubens, paint rosy-bottomed nymphs. But Rubens did, perhaps, take things a bit too far. Really, did he actually need corpulent women writhing naked in *Apotheosis of Henry IV*? Did he really need to add ripe sets of loose breasts to *The Majority of Louis XIII*? Brendada admired Rubens when he stuck to the allegorical innocent cherubim, but when he couldn't resist the post-pubescent allegories Brendada was made decidedly uncomfortable. The man could certainly paint a leaf, she'd give him that, but his maidens' thighs unnerved her. They looked to Brendada like butter in a cheesecloth bag.

She flipped through the pages. She stopped briefly at Jean-Baptiste Pater (Brendada always did favor paintings where the trees were larger than the people), and then paused nostalgically at the Dutch. All the Vans had that certain sublime, unspeakable something that she so admired. Van Dyke, Van Ruisdael, Van der Neer. That crepuscular, distant mists sort of thing. She moved on to Jacques Louis David, who, Brendada felt, displayed that admirable restraint that Rubens so crudely lacked. He always managed to drop a sword or a dagger—depending—right where a scabbard ought to be placed.

Brendada's breath was caught at Gericault's *The Derby at Epson*. Gericault! Gosh, his very name, with all its excessive letters—its vowel cluster and silent consonants—was so ornate, so rich . . . so *riche!* But she must resist. She closed the book and took a breath.

On a whim Brendada pulled out a slim volume called *Divine Inspiration*. She opened the cover and the frontispiece was *The Ancient of Days* by William Blake. Brendada happened to disagree vehemently—though vehemently to herself—with Angry Helen. She liked Blake. She quickly put the book back.

"Hold on," Angry Helen said as she set a box of dusty condiments—well past their shelf date—on Brendada's couch. "I've got one more in the trunk." She dashed out of the door without closing it.

Brendada tugged on the front of her smock. She took a baby step toward the box and looked inside. On top was a jar of reduced-price sandwich spread. It was hard and brown inside near the lid, with cracks.

Angry Helen was slapping the steps with her thongs and breathing loudly through her mouth. Brendada smoothed the underside of her chin with her hand.

"That's it!" Angry Helen said, dropping the box on the floor. "Good. Now I have room for beer."

"But . . . what?" Brendada said.

"Darling! Your medium!" Angry Helen held out her arms expansively.

"Old sandwich spread? With mildew?"

"Hey! Food products got me a Volvo!"

"But . . ." Brendada said. How to phrase this politely? "But you already do that. I mean, food stuff. It's been done. I can't—"

"No, honey, it's great! You can homage me! It's great!"

"But . . ."

It was dark. Brendada had a candle lit and a glass of wine poured. She had placed a canvas on her easel and now sat in front of it. She held her brush in her teeth and gripped the lid of an antediluvian container of mustard. She grunted as she used all of her strength but it would not budge. She was on the verge of giving up when the lid sprang free in a burst of yellow dust. She looked into the jar. She looked up at the pristine canvas. Brendada took the brush from her mouth and tapped absently on the fissured brown crust. With a little more effort she broke through the dried shell and scooped out a dab of mustard. She threw it in the middle of the virginal whiteness.

She worked the mustard by tentatively poking at it. It took shape, primitively speaking. She smiled. It was quite gay, actually. A little runny, perhaps, a little pungent, but, yes, quite gay. She poked with a bit more enthusiasm, risking insouciant curves and sweeps. The consistency was certainly not what she was used to, of course, but she felt that she was getting the hang of it. She was beginning, actually, to like it. The way it separated into its component ingredients added unexpected textures. She dipped into the mustard for another scoop when something moved near the bottom of the jar. Brendada yelped and flung it from her. It rolled under the bookcase. What could it have been? What could live, and apparently thrive, in the harsh environment of ancient, spoiled mustard? Something in the phylum of those alien tube-creatures that live in the volcanic vents at the bottom of the Pacific Ocean, no doubt.

Brendada got a broom from the kitchen and tried without success to grapple the jar. Chagrined, she sealed off the bottom of the bookcase with a bath towel.

She looked at the canvas. Her experimental strokes had, unbeknownst to her at the time, turned out to be a rather skilled rendering of a jonquil. It would never do. Angry Helen would be furious.

She decided to get her paints from the kitchen table. She rummaged through the mess that Angry Helen had made on her last visit but, apparently, Angry Helen had taken them to save Brendada from temptation. With much hesitation, and against her better judgement, Brendada reached into the dusty box of condiments and pulled out a bottle of time-thickened steak sauce. She held the bottle up to the light and shook it. She turned it slowly at an angle, scrutinizing the murky interior for life. Safe, she thought, she unscrewed the cap and dashed the contents onto the canvas. The effect was hideous and disturbing. Brendada hauled it out to the curb so that she would be able to sleep, but she still couldn't sleep because she was so annoyed at how much the wasted canvas had cost.

Angry Helen stood behind Brendada like an unpleasant man. Brendada was on her stool. She held her brush nervously.

"Okay," Angry Helen said, "paint."

Brendada's breathing was shallow, her shoulders squeezed together in front of her. She looked at her palette and panicked.

"Go on!" Angry Helen said, and gave her a little shove. "Feel the hate!"

"But I don't feel the hate," Brendada said, which was true.

"Think hateful thoughts," Angry Helen said gently, "and then *throw* them at the canvas!"

Brendada twirled her brush in the red paint. Red, she'd heard, was an angry color. Angry Helen, actually, had told her that. To Brendada, red had always been a lovely sunrise. The color of innocent children's lips. A poppy.

Angry Helen came around and stood between Brendada and the easel. She looked stern. Her nose wrinkled and unwrinkled furiously. She moved her face abruptly to Brendada's bosom. She darted over to Brendada's underarms and sniffed. She drew herself up and faced Brendada, eyes narrowed contemptuously.

"Are you wearing . . . *scent?*" she asked crossly.

Brendada bounced along the cobble-stone path, trying hard not to smile, her flushed face seeming even brighter between the black turtleneck sweater that was drawn up to her throat and the non-reflective black of her hair. Angry Helen, wearing sunglasses, was trudging along behind her.

"I swear, if you start skipping I'll brain you."

Brendada turned around and offered Angry Helen her hand. Angry Helen was having a difficult time negotiating the root of an oak tree. "Isn't this lovely?" Brendada asked.

"I thought this was a short cut."

"It is. Maybe we should take the path behind the pond."

"The *pond*? You've got to be kidding. Ponds have no place in cities. That's why we build cities and that's why we live in them. To get away from ponds. And trees."

"But it's Spring . . ."

"Fuck Spring."

Brendada surreptitiously admired a patch of purple wildflowers to the left of Angry Helen. She longed to bend down closer, to sniff them. She longed to skip.

"God, I need a drink," Angry Helen said. "I thought I needed a drink before, but, God, do I need one now."

Brendada pointed to the top of a knoll. "How about we walk up that way, up by where that honeysuckle is blooming."

Okay. Now she was getting carried away. "Brendada," Angry Helen said firmly. She took off her sunglasses and turned Brendada around to face her. "This is not good. You are never going to learn if you don't make the effort."

Brendada went home, deflated, alone, leaving Angry Helen to go to the reception of A. Arthur Bowling, the sculptural paste pioneer, by herself. She sat on the bed, kicked off her clogs, and was preparing for a good weep when she noticed her gecko, Daisy II, lying lifeless under the coffee table, its head wedged hermetically in the mustard jar.

Brendada dolefully thumbed her way through *Treasures of the Prado*. She averted her eyes from the Titians and Raphaels. It was hopeless. She was hopeless. She sighed when she came to the corpulent, roseate Rubens tableaux and was about to toss the volume aside when something stopped her. It was Rubens' *Saturn Devouring His Children*. Something struck her. She turned back several pages. There it was again: Saturn eating his children, this time by Goya. It was certainly assaultive, yet who could deny that it was also painterly? It was certainly a subject respectable enough for the likes of Goya and Rubens. It was something with wounds.

Brendada smiled.

Brendada Fuckoff, dressed in a black spandex leotard with a bicycle chain for a belt, pulled down the black blinds in her loft and approached the vast, empty tundra of her canvas like its enemy. She clamped her lips and tightened her eyes in concentration, in an effort to stifle any tendrils of floridity that might try to forge their way into her creative psyche. Her knuckles were white around the handle of the brush and on her palette were messy, bleeding dollops of harshly-colored paint, not a hint of pastel among them.

Brendada lunged at the canvas and a primal cry was loosed from her diaphragm. Her brush scythed along the canvas like a Hun's blade. Swaths of paint clustered and coalesced like storm clouds mounting on the horizon.

Sweat broke out on Brendada's pinched forehead as she dived and swept like an ecstatic. Slowly, ominously, emerging from the turmoil of the churning flows of Brendada's paint was the blackened, scaly musculature of the titan Saturn. He seemed to heave himself up through the vortex of pigment, struggling, gaining strength. The tendons of his thick neck pulled, his massive shoulders gleamed and roiled.

The red-rimmed eyes shone out through a nightmare shadow. But they had no Goyan hollowness, no Rubenesque preoccupation with the matter at hand. These eyes seethed and stared directly ahead, beyond the world of the canvas; they hypnotized and paralyzed like the poison of a spider. Saturn's maw was slightly agape in both mid-mastication and the start of a malevolent grin. His serpentine teeth were layered in the warm red froth of his infants' blood. In each of his gnarled claws he held the limp remnants of a ragged and torn child.

Brendada leapt back from the painting. She only then noticed that she was gasping for breath and that her hair was snug to her head with sweat. She didn't bother to pull up a chair but instead sat directly onto the floor. Pride inflated her as she stared, frankly surprised, at her success. She had always shied away from painting people, but painting Saturn had unleashed a force that had taken her talent to a place well beyond what she'd ever attained at Edengreen. Angry Helen would be delighted. Or even jealous.

She slowly traced Saturn's rippling outline with her gaze, admiring the dexterity of her work, the lumpy details of his flesh, the play of light and hue against the background of deep, fathomless black.

Brendada felt the twinge of something absent. She got up and stepped backward. He was indeed gruesome, and the enveloping black void hinted at unspeakable, unacknowlegable places, but he seemed somewhat detached. Ungrounded, really. Working instinctively, Brendada grabbed a tube of green paint and with delicate, loving flicks enshrouded one of Saturn's barnacled toes in tufts of grass. She stood back and smiled. Yes. Of course. This was a primeval world, a world before man, a world unspoiled. She approached the canvas again and did the other foot. Then, with a meticulous movement of the wrist, she wrapped a delicate green tendril (of the sort indigenous to Edengreen) around the ankle of Saturn. And then up the calf.

Durable Beauty

KINGSLEY TOTBOTHAM SAT FIDGETING with his papers in the hallway outside the Council's chambers. He was preparing to present this year's recommendations and he was troubled, wrestling with a conundrum the nature of which he would never have suspected. He was a solitary man, a bit pouchy now, with ear hairs; his thinning blond hair less blond now than gray; his pale blue eyes less blue than drained of blue, and now framed by eyeglasses without which he would be forbidden to drive a car, if he chose to drive a car. He was less contentious—as many believed—than simply unaware that others had opinions; less inscrutable than merely unconcerned. He ate simply, eschewed public gatherings unless forced, and had a cat at home called Slippers.

Kingsley Totbotham was a professor of Durable Beauty at Peake University, on the cape. He was essentially the head of a committee of one (originally there had been eight, but death, scandal, or ineptitude had winnowed the ranks) whose mission was to assess history's outstanding works of artistry—from fresco painting to soliloquies, from orchestral symphonies to embroidered armchairs—and select those that ably demonstrated Durable Beauty. Every year, as new works became eligible, Kingsley would present his scholarly opinions to the Council of Five (appointed by the board of trustees) for final ratification.

John Milton was in; Clarence Jawbry, the comic librettist of *The Knockabout Shepherd Maid*, was out.

Kingsley Totbotham had been chosen for his finely honed discernment (a Master's degree in Flemish Painting, 1426-1644; a Master's degree in European Rhyme Schemes, 900-present; and a doctorate in Comparative Secular Iconography) and his impeccable intuition. It was a delicate occupation deciding which works of art had lasting value (and thus gain entry into the official canon) and which works should be relegated to the slag heap of misguidance, paucity of talent, or mere shameless pandering. Da Vinci, of course, was in; Pepe de la Sante, the Breast Painter of Toledo, was out.

Moliere was in as well, as, of course, was William Shakespeare (although not the twenty-second sonnet). Francis Tiffany, the poet who experimented— unsuccessfully—with trying to write poems using only algebraic equations, was out. Practically just being born during the Enlightenment ensured that you got in, should you be Bacon, Voltaire, or Pope. Of course, if you were J. Helmut Trotter, the Deist and Prussian wag, then it didn't.

Peake University and the Council of Five had taken a great chance because there was always the possibility that no one would care. But the world did care, and the University had become firmly established as the nucleus of aesthetic circles worldwide; the Council of Five, and Kingsley, had become the prime cultural and academic force in formulating public taste. Thus, and the world agreed, Frederic Chopin was in; Kut Christen, the foot percussionist of Jutland, was out.

Because the vagaries of taste and the Doppler effect of current affairs might taint objective discernment, the true weight of timelessness (it was arbitrarily—though perspicaciously—decided) could only be fairly judged after a window of one hundred years had passed between a work's creation and its assessment by the Council. This would allow for the settling of emotions and afford a clearheaded discussion. Some zealots on the Council had proposed a mere fifty-year hiatus, but Kingsley had steadfastly held out. Thus, Monet's Rouen Cathedral series was in, but his *Blue Water Lilies* were still rhetorically questionable, at least for sixteen more years. John Rodd, the tenacious pamphleteer and caricaturist most noted for his series of anti-Chartist babooneries, was out, and always would be. Staunch adherence to the hundred year rule had been beyond question for Kingsley. He was only too happy to avoid the tumult of shunning a living artist, no matter how generously the term was employed. With any luck he would be dead or retired before he would have to torture himself with the durable unbeauty of da-da, or the pseudo-beauty of the cubists or pop art or Soviet Constructivism. Yes, the moratorium was fine by Kingsley Totbotham if for no other reason that it would save him from Duchamps with his bicycle wheels and "fountains." Certainly a urinal, as art, made a statement, but Kingsley was in the business of pulchritude, not sociology. And God help his successors who would have to deal with the movies (but, really, could commercial arcade amusements—even accidentally—be art? It was paralyzing to even consider the question. Kingsley had always held films to be culturally suspect, and film studies even more so).

Kingsley Totbotham knew his job and loved his job; his uncertainly this year alarmed him because such an emotion was a novelty. Kingsley was a dispassionate man and ruled over his handsomely appointed research library (endowed by not one but two international pharmaceutical conglomerates) with an iron fist; arguments and hesitation were strangers to him. (Well, there was that one moment several years ago when he briefly anguished over the mosaic allegories featuring priapic goatherds that were unearthed under a convent outside Avignon, but he concluded that the simple fact that he would even question their suitability automatically disqualified them.) He needed to focus; up for consideration this year were Puccini's *Tosca*, Cezanne's painting with the onions, and two-thirds of triptych by Pissarro (the final panel would not be eligible until next year). There was also a small portrait by Renoir of and for his dental surgeon; though never considered an important work (a confection, really), Renoir could doodle on a train schedule with lip rouge and it'd be a shoo-in. And most pressing, to Kingsley's malaise, this was the year that they would have to start considering the Fauves as it was one hundred years ago that they had first starting making an appearance.

What was tormenting Kingsley, however, was not the emergence of the Fauves. Instead it was an item that had caught his eye as he was leafing through the newspaper. It was a personal ad, an ad from a male seeking female. The author of the advertisement (as well as including such pertinent information as "br/br, mustache, 6' 4", 210 lbs., likes league bowling" and "seeking swf, long hair a + but not essential, no flakes") had taken time to compose a poem, a mere quatrain of questionable metric integrity (and a rather puerile use of masculine rhymes) but of undeniable beauty. The earnestness, the simple elegance of the lines astounded Kingsley, moved him in a way that he had never been moved before. Not by Donne, Wordsworth, or even Dickinson (before she got all maudlin). The poem had stuck with him, in his hair, in his shirt, like love; blinding him when he tried to read the eligible works of Dreiser, Colette, and Shaw; sang in his head in the shower, on the bus, during conversations with student interns in the cafeteria. He was unnerved.

Miss Manly (an unfortunate moniker for one so lithe) opened the hewn oak doors and smiled at Kingsley. Kingsley adjusted his eyeglasses.

"They're ready for you," she said.

"Thank you, Miss Manly," Kingsley said. "You've been well?"

"Thank you, Professor Totbotham, I have."

"Good."

Miss Manly held the door open as Kingsley gathered together his folios and files and crammed them into his satchel.

"Rather an anxious year for you, I would imagine," Miss Manly said, "what with the Fauves and all."

"Yes," Kingsley said, "it is."

"I admire your work, Professor Totbotham," Miss Manly said. "It takes a great deal of courage."

Kingsley fumbled with the latches on his bag, one of which had to be secured with a paper clip. At last he stood up and proceeded through the doors.

"Good luck," Miss Manly said, closing the doors behind him.

The Council of Five sat high up in thickly cushioned black leather armchairs at a semicircular podium of polished mahogany. The chambers were decorated in the late Georgian manner, with columns carved from old-growth redwoods, 17th Century Portuguese tapestries hanging between these, and a high series of stained glass windows commissioned in the style of Raphael. This extravagance, however, was for no one's benefit but the Council's as the Hearings on Beauty were strictly closed. Kingsley's place was in front of them at a long table spacious enough so that he could comfortably organize his papers so as to be handy. He did this.

"Learned Sirs," Kingsley began, "I trust that you have all received my recommendations and have had a chance to give them due consideration."

"That we have, Learned Sir," said Dr. Bitumen, Professor Emeritus in the Department of Cryptoeconomics; a rarefied field and the University was lucky to get him. Dr. Bitumen didn't much care for students as a whole and held the University's record for sabbaticals. He was 52.

"We've long known the unpleasant day would befall us when we'd be faced with the difficult question of the Fauves," said Dr. Wesley Lorraine, "and we wholeheartedly support your opinion, Professor Totbotham." Dr. Wesley Lorraine was chancellor of the School of Ethnopharmacology and holder of the coveted Hormel Chair of Medieval Balladry. A pleasant man who, because of his fondness for Lisbon wines and the complete disregard for his physician's entreaties to cut down on rare beef, would be dead in five years at the age of 68. He'd be sorely missed, not least for his consistently amusing take—with which he invariably won over his freshman classes—on Sebastion Cabot's hijinks with curare during his 1527 expedition to Paraguay.

"Yes," Dr. Bitumen groaned, "the Fauves."

Kingsley did not hold much ken for the Fauves. Certainly some of the paintings themselves were, well, *bright,* and some—particularly Matisse—could be amusing in a certain *naif* way. But beautiful? Sanctionably beautiful? That would be a loosening of all criteria of mastery and skill, and a sharp slipping of the standards of which they—the Council of Five—championed. Impressionism had been enough to try their patience, but *post-*

impressionism? The Council of Five concurred.

"But the problem, as you've anticipated, Professor Totbotham, is the public," Mr. Tobor said, "and their tastes. Matisse and Braque are pop stars. And the masses will rally if we don't give them what they want." This was Mr. Tobor, an adjunct professor in the Classics Department whose singular expertise on parsing Old Greek infinitives was unequaled. He was 42 and the author of an historical novel on the early life of Homer called *Ease Now, My Flaming Love.*

"Yes, we'll be discredited," Professor Nicolai Luft said, "if we discredit the paintings that adorn the lunch pails and refrigerator magnets of the common folk." The Council of Five and Kingsley chuckled. Professor Nicolai Luft, 60, was interim Chair of the Department of Applied Indo-European Languages and the author of a ground-breaking two-volume study on the practical use of earthenware in the Ch'ing dynasty. His wife left him for a postman.

"So, Learned Sir, it is your considered proposal to be selective," Mr. Tobor said to Kingsley, "to be inclusive enough to sate the pedestrian mob yet discriminating enough to retain our credibility in history?"

"Yes, Learned Sirs. I propose that we look the other way as far as Matisse is concerned, at least while his fad is at a cyclical high. We might instead vent our collective disgust on Auguste Norin, who's far less admired right now, and censure his entire body of work."

"That would help me sleep at night," said Dr. de la Coule, Professor Emeritus of Tools and Weapons in pre-feudal Europe, and of Weaving and Dance in the post. He was 63, father to three children, grandfather to two, and shared a birthday with Claudia Cardinale, the voluptuous international film star.

"Capital idea," Dr. Lorraine said. "Again, Professor Totbotham, Learned Sir, you've done an exemplary job with your research, your unassailable good taste, and your commitment to Durable Beauty."

"Thank you, Learned Sirs," Kingsley said.

"What about Derain and Braque?" Dr. Bitumen asked.

"Would anybody miss them?" Professor Luft said.

"That's the Fauves done with, then," Mr. Tobor said. "And now what's this about Renoir's dentist?"

As was usual, Kingsley's recommendations went unchallenged, with only cursory discussion for appearance's sake. The Cezanne, the Puccini, the Shaw, and the Dreiser were all officially ushered in, as were the Pissarro, the Colette, a Gaugin, and Tolstoy's *The Living Corpse*. Monet's so-called "ugly paintings"—little seen but much discussed—were more problematic. This short-lived phase in the artist's career (where the artist had let his sleeve drag through the paint) was attributed to the last week before the prohibition of absinthe in Giverny. The "ugly paintings" were dismissed, as were *Ma Toilette*, a farce in four acts by Eugene Vachette, *Oratorio With Bells* by Faroud Sik, the Bellsman of Yemen, and a volume of light verse by the proto-communist Ygor Chekhov (no relation). Sargent's *Sitwell Family* was, however, duly sanctioned, as was *Lord Jim* by Conrad.

"Well, this should conclude our—" Dr. de la Coule started.

"Wait," Kingsley said. The Council of Five was surprised. Dr. de la Coule reached into his waste basket and fished out Kingsley's report to make sure two pages had not stuck together.

"Yes?" Dr. Bitumen said, checking his watch.

"There's one more thing," Kingsley said.

"Another thing?" Dr. de la Coule said. "But what else is eligible?"

"Surely not Freud's *Interpretation of Dreams*?" Professor Luft said. "You know where we stand on Freud, Professor Totbotham."

"And I thought we'd all agreed that science wasn't beautiful," Dr. De la Coule said.

"Except Newton," Mr. Tobor pointed out.

"Except Newton," Dr. Lorraine said.

"Now there was a yarn!" Dr. Bitumen said.

"No," Kingsley said, "it's a poem."

"A poem?" Professor Luft said. "A Yeats? But wasn't Yeats into his theatrical phase by then? I don't think we need concern ourselves with Yeats for another ten years or so."

"No," Kingsley said, "not Yeats."

"Harding?" Mr. Tobor said, "Zola?"

"No," Kingsley said. He paused. Perhaps he should just go home. "A new poem. A current one."

"*Current?*" Dr. Lorraine said, astonished.

"Yes. I know it's highly irregular—"

"To say the least."

"But . . ." Kingsley faltered. He reached into his satchel and brought out five photocopies of the poem he had read in the newspaper and distributed them.

"I'm sure I don't have to remind you, Learned Sir," Dr. Bitumen said, lowering his voice, "that our mandate here—one which I, personally, cherish—is Durable Beauty. How can something that has just been written prove durable? We're not in the business of faith, Learned Sir, nor are we in the business of promotion. I am not sure that you have not an unclouded perception."

Professor Luft turned to Dr. Bitumen and smirked. "Was that a double negative, Dr. Bitumen?"

"It was used for effect, Professor Luft," Dr. Bitumen said.

"Oh?" Professor Luft said. "The vernacular, is it? And is the council now resorting to low humor?"

"I hardly consider litotes to be low humor, Professor Luft."

"I suggest that Dr. Bitumen reacquaint himself with the proper usage of litotes."

"I'll let the Chaucer scholars know of your misgivings."

"Gentlemen," Dr. Lorraine brought his hand down loudly on the table, "please."

"Learned Sirs," Kingsley said, "just read it for yourselves."

"Who's the author?" Mr. Tobor said.

"He's, uh, I don't know." Kingsley knew nothing of the man (except his weight, his penchant for league bowling, and his aversion to flakes) and hadn't bothered to track him down because he hadn't decided to present the poem until he had opened his mouth moments before and the words had come out.

"You know we frown on anonymous works if at all possible," Mr. Tobor said. "Unless, of course, for reasons of religion."

"Or, say, fires. That sort of thing," Dr. de la Coule added.

"And I support that with zeal," Kingsley said. "I just haven't found him yet."

"Well, where did you find this mysterious poem, then?" Dr. de la Coule said.

"It's . . . it was a personal ad."

The room went silent and heavy. The Council of Five watched as Kingsley became red. Dr. Lorraine didn't smile, but Drs. Bitumen and de la Coule, Professor Luft, and Mr. Tobor did.

"A *newspaper* personal ad, Professor Totbotham?" Dr. Bitumen asked at last.

"Really, Professor Totbotham, it's not what we *do*," Mr. Tobor said.

"I know. I know. It's just . . . please. Just read it. I ask for your indulgence."

"This willfulness is most uncharacteristic, Professor Totbotham," Dr. Lorraine said.

But indulgence was granted and the Council of Five read the poem. It did not take long, being a mere four lines. One by one the council members looked up, astonished.

"Learned Sirs," Kingsley said, "if I could content myself to know that I might leave this poem in the certainty that in a hundred years hence it would be joyfully discovered by one of my successors, I would. But, Sirs, *it's a personal ad from a newspaper.*"

"It's remarkable," Dr. Lorraine said, "quite . . . beautiful."

"Is it really an advertisement for a sexual union?" Dr. de la Coule said.

"I should think it an effective one," Mr. Tobor said.

"It sounds like Barrett Browning," Professor Luft said.

"You recognize it?" Dr. Lorraine said.

"No. No, it's not specifically familiar, but it has the ease of Barrett Browning."

"Well, if it's Barrett Browning, it's in," Mr. Tobor said.

"No, it's definitely not Barrett Browning. He was never fond of masculine rhymes," Dr. Bitumen said.

"Barrett Browning was a she," Professor Luft said.

"Oh. I thought you meant Edgar Barrett Browning."

"Who?"

"Never mind."

"No, I agree," Dr. de la Coule said. "It's not Barrett Browning. But it could be Swinburne."

"Swinburne my balls!" Dr. Bitumen said. "This poem could never be Swinburne! Swinburne wrote by leafing through a thesaurus wearing mittens!" This had gone on for some time, this disagreement between Dr. Bitumen and Dr. de la Coule, ever since Dr. de la Coule had won a Certificate of Merit from Georgetown for his paper on Swinburne and the poetry of mid-Victorian flagellates, narrowly inching out Dr. Bitumen's treatise on Shelly and the question of Atheism versus Pantheism after the British occupation of Java. Dr. de la Coule, though a weaponist by disposition, was—as were all the others—expected to be well rounded, well versed, and well published.

"Well, it's certainly not Shelly," Dr. de la Coule said. "It doesn't have that understink of alcoholic pederasty."

"That's never been established!"

"Are you sure it's original?" Dr. Lorraine asked Kingsley.

"I'm sure," Kingsley said with a tremor in his voice.

"Well," Dr. Lorraine said, "I, for one, am moved. If, in fact, it has been appropriated from some heretofore overlooked work of Barrett Browning—or Swinburne—or anyone else, then it should be duly granted admittance under the name of the rightful author. But before we can even discuss abandoning our prime criterion and taking such an unprecedented action as including a contemporary poet, especially one who shops for mates in newspapers, we must have all the facts. Its inclusion is moot until it can be authenticated."

"Shall we meet again in a week?" Mr. Tobor said.

"Make it two," Dr. Bitumen said.

"Will two weeks be enough?" Dr. Lorraine asked Kingsley.

"That shouldn't be a problem. Thank you, Learned Sirs, for your patience."

Dr. de la Coule, Dr. Bitumen, Professor Luft, and Mr. Tobor filed out of the doorway behind the podium as Kingsley gathered his papers together.

"Remarkable development, this," Dr. Lorraine said. He got up from his chair, unsnapped his black robe, and unclipped his bow tie. He came through the swinging door and down the steps to Kingsley's table. "Are you all right?"

"I'm fine," Kingsley said, "just as surprised as anyone at my reaction to the poem. I'm not used to this sort of thing."

"Yes. It's not like you."

"No. It isn't."

Dr. Lorraine honestly liked Kingsley, though he thought that Kingsley could definitely use some loosening up. Kingsley had first been brought to Dr. Lorraine's attention when he—Kingsley—had become the butt of all jokes in the department; then, serving as a convenient release, the target of all derision, a veritable sponge for all of the faculty vitriol (which flowed freely as it was brewed copiously in the frustrated academic ambitions of the Department of Humanities). So, as was his nature, Dr. Lorraine had taken Kingsley under his wing. He was amused at Kingsley's humorlessness and unmalleability. But amusement had evolved into affection and they had become friends. Dr. Lorraine had invited Kingsley up to the house, had invited him on the faculty elk hunt (which had subsequently proved disastrous, particularly for Dr. Bitumen, though through no fault of Dr. Lorraine's), and had even chosen Kingsley to write the forward to his book detailing the romantic verse of the eugenists.

"This could prove a bit messy, you know, the strictures of the Council notwithstanding," Dr. Lorraine said. "Really, Kingsley, not only a modern writer, but a living one as well. Are you sure you're up to it?"

"Believe me, Wesley, this is important. It's remarkable that I even stumbled onto the poem in the first place, and then when I read it, well, it was like a physical blow. It felt . . . eternal. It's like I was born to champion it. Because if not me, who else? It'll be forgotten in another week let alone a hundred years. The author is . . . well, no author. Just a lonely newspaper reader."

"That's all well and good, but our mandate is to preserve and glorify the greatest works of art in history. It's not a talent contest."

"I'm sure I don't have to convince you that no one is as dedicated to that as myself. I've always placed the utmost importance on what we do. But it's never before felt, I don't know, *vital*."

"I think it's vital."

"Perhaps I should modify that. It's never felt passionately vital. This poem is passionately vital. Presiding over the sanctioning of Michaelangelo and Verdi and Goethe has been an honor, but it's sort of hollow. Really, Wesley, a hairdresser in Newark is qualified to give the thumbs up to the Mona Lisa. But to get this poem recognized would justify my tenure, my life's work. My life! I'll have done something that no one else could do. I'll have done something honest and good."

"I see," Dr. Lorraine said. He cleared his throat. "Now, Kingsley, you don't have to tell me if you don't want to, and I only ask because I'm concerned, but what were you doing reading the personal ads?"

Kingsley blushed. "I was on my way to the used car section."

"But you don't drive."

"Because I don't have a car."

"But you hate to drive. You hate to be a passenger."

"I . . . well . . . groceries . . ."

Dr. Lorraine walked around the table and put his arm around Kingsley's shoulders. "You know, Liz is very active and has a lot of friends." Liz Lorraine was Dr. Lorraine's wife; broad-shouldered with a deep laugh, she had been the Head of Fundraising for the Department of Endocrinology but had given it up to concentrate on closing down zoos. "She's always pestering me to invite you over so that she can fix you up."

"That's very kind, but I hardly think it's necessary."

"It's not too late, you know."

"Too late for what?"

"You know. Pair bonding. It's not that bad. Sometimes it's even quite nice."

"I really ought to be going. Mid-term assessments due tomorrow."

"All right. But think about it." Dr. Lorraine slapped him jovially—if forcefully—on the back. "Good luck with the poem."

Kingsley went home to his one-bedroom faculty lodging across the road from campus. It was small, but it was enough for him. There was room for a dinette table and a chair, and plenty of room for his books if he used the floor. There was little room for extraneous decoration or mementos, which was fine since he had none and had no plans of acquiring any. He hadn't opened his curtains in at least two years.

He put the kettle on as Slippers hungrily twined through his legs. After making a mug of tea he went to the table and laid out the newspaper he had saved. He picked up the telephone and dialed the number he found under the masthead of the Personals section.

"Personals," the woman's voice answered. Rather coldly, Kingsley thought, considering.

"Good day," Kingsley said, "I wish some information regarding an advertisement that was placed in your newspaper Thursday last."

"What?"

"An advertisement. A personal advertisement. In last Thursday's paper."

"What about it?"

"I need information pertaining to the gentleman who wrote it."

"Why don't you write the guy yourself?"

"Because time, dear woman, is of the essence. I must meet him promptly."

"Oh, I get it. What was he? An Escort/Model?"

"What?"

"Look, I don't give a rat's arse what you guys get up to in the privacy of your own bathhouse, but don't bring me into it."

"Madam, I'm an academic."

"I ain't a dating service."

Kingsley paused. "But I thought that's precisely what you were."

"Look, I answer the phones, I take the information, I do the billing. After that you guys are on your own. Got it?"

"I just need the name of the fellow who wrote the poem that—"

"The poem?"

"Yes. There was a poem in the advertisement, and—"

"I know the poem. Talked to the guy myself. Now, poems and shit just ain't my thing, but I gotta tell ya, I kinda liked it. I went all sort of loose, you know?"

"Yes! I know! That's the poem! I'll just have the name and address of the gentleman who wrote it, please."

"What, are you kidding? I can't give you that. That's confidential. I could get fired." The pertinent question to Kingsley was, how could she get *hired*?

"Ma'am, it's of vital academic importance—"

"You're chasing the wrong train, pal. That guy ain't looking for no guy. He's after a woman, which you ain't. Why don't you look in the back, in the 'Escorts/Models' section?"

Kingsley realized that he was failing to reach a communion with this woman. "I feel that I have perhaps underrepresented myself. My name is Kingsley Totbotham, and I am a professor of Durable Beauty at Peake University."

"Oh, now I getcha."

"Good. Finally."

"You're one of them naughty types, ain't ya? Like to get smacked around a little, don't ya?"

Good Lord! "No! I'm a respected theoretician with credentials from the finest—"

"You know, I got caller I.D. on this phone, you know. I know exactly where you're calling from."

"May I offer you a piece of advice?"

"Oh, Christ!" The woman hung up.

Kingsley had many pressing matters to attend to—mid-term evaluations of his students, Slippers needed a distemper booster, and he really ought to get to work at polishing the article on Artaud's brothel odes that he wanted to submit for the autumn issue of *Letters and Lore*. But if writing a letter was what it would take, then he would just have to write the letter.

Dear Sir, he began. It seemed a little dry, however. Although he was an academic, he was not insensitive to recognizing ardor, and felt he should, after all, appeal to the man's poetic soul. Excessive formality didn't sit well with poets. Consider Blake.

Dear Scribe. No. Some people, Kingsley realized after many hard lessons over the years, confused archaism with sarcasm, and he couldn't risk that the man would appreciate that Kingsley Totbotham didn't have a sarcastic breath in his body.

Dear Poet . . . too unctuous . . . *Dear Troubadour* . . . not technically correct, though he liked the sound of it. But Kingsley thought that poetic license ought not be used except with someone that one knew well. If even then. . . . *Dear* . . .

Dear Sir;

I am writing in response to the quatrain included in your personal advertisement for a companion. It struck me immediately as a rare and exceptional instance of Durable Beauty. Although it is highly unusual for me to say so, after anguished consideration I strongly feel that official ratification is not out of the question. Please respond to—

> *Professor K. Totbotham,*
> *Peake University*
> *Cape Swell, ——————*

The reply came by regular mail four days later. It read:

Dear Miss Totbottom [sic]*;*

Thanx [sic] *for you're* [sic] *replay* [sic] *to my ad, but I* [sic] *allready* [sic] *met someone special. Glad you liked my peom* [sic] *and tho* [sic] *you want to ratificate* [sic] *me (and I appreciate the offer but I have to say I'm not quite sure what that is. This whole scene is kind of new to me), its* [sic] *only fair that I tell you I'm a one woman man. Good luck finding the right guy. I'm sure you will. God bless.*

Best Wishs [sic],

Frank

Oh dear, Kingsley thought, he's not only misapprehended my sex but my intentions as well. Kingsley dashed off another letter, more to the point this time, explaining exactly who he was and emphatically clearing up any issues of gender confusion. He also made sure that this Frank was made quite aware of the eminence and respectability of his—Kingsley's—position, and to the honor bestowed on him by Kingsley's correspondence.

Kingsley waited a week. No reply came. Time was running short and, as he was already treading precipitously on the patience of the Council, asking for any extension would no doubt burst the envelope of their good will.

Frank was a much cagier quarry than he'd originally anticipated. Kingsley considered writing another note, only this time risk the abandonment of propriety and get terse. But what good would it do to scold the man?

Kingsley sat at his table with pen in hand, deciding which was the best approach to take. Politeness obviously hadn't worked. He supposed he could fawn, but the very idea gave Kingsley a cramp in his side. Appealing to the man's sense of aesthetic duty seemed fruitless, judging from Frank's precarious grip on English grammar.

Suddenly, unbidden, a light dawned within Kingsley's soul. He knew
how he must approach Frank. He would woo him, lure him with his own
bait. It was so simple and so logical that Kingsley wondered why he hadn't
thought of it before. He would compose his own poem.

Not ever having written a poem before, Kingsley considered which form
to employ. An ode? Always a popular choice and with a fine historic pedi-
gree. A lyrical ballad? These worked to great success for Wordsworth. A
mock heroic saga? Something nice and iambic, to be sure; that was always
accessible, at least for himself. He briefly debated using the noble pentame-
ter, but opted instead for tetrameter, though, because he was in a bit of
hurry. Perhaps he ought to tackle a haiku; that would certainly save time.

Kingsley decided on the sonnet. Keats certainly managed to pump out
the sonnets in a rush before he died, and as Kingsley had to cram as much
poetry into one afternoon before, well, not before he died, but certainly in
enough time for the next Council meeting, the sonnet seemed an ideal vehicle.

He began with an invocation to the muse Erato, who guided all poems
of love: it was good luck, classically admirable, and it also gave Kingsley the
chance to rhyme "beloved muse" with "may love infuse."

Kingsley wrote feverishly, borrowing a couplet from Nashe (but who,
today, would know? Besides, if he got caught he could just pass it off as
homage), breezing through an extended reflection on Hellenic devotion,
and even throwing in some alliterative poetry in the manner of the four-
teenth century, just for spice.

By the time his wrist buckled and he was forced to stop to rub it, he saw
that he was on the fifth page and realized that he was no longer writing a
sonnet. Indeed, he was entering the territory of the Spenserian epic. But
Erato had authoritatively descended and was clutching Kingsley firmly by
the back of the neck and not letting go. Kingsley didn't worry, though;
revision of one's work is not only necessary but a virtue, as he always told
his students.

He got stuck on the seventh page, fourth stanza, when he was unable to locate a rhyme for "chanterelle" (used in the sense of the highest pitched string on an instrument, not the edible fungus). It occurred to him that he could reference the nonsense verse of Carroll or Lear and just make something up. Like, say, "snaffer-bell." If it was good enough for those other two eminent Victorian bachelors it should certainly be good enough for Kingsley Totbotham. And, after all, Eliot had once managed to rhyme "window-panes" with "windowpanes." A perfect example, thought Kingsley, of the virulent laziness of the modernists and their insistence on mucking up all boundaries of what is acceptable. Note to his successors: eschew Eliot.

With breath held and brow moist, Kingsley scrawled hurriedly to the finish, dangerously courting bathos with his penultimate couplet, where he indelicately joined "vanity" with an anthropomorphism on the "restraint of the manatee."

He sat back and took a sip of cold tea. He had completed fourteen densely written pages. He'd have to whittle it down, even if just a little. He re-read.

He thought he could spare the seven stanza argument on the subjugation of carnal pursuits for the cause of a more perfect democracy, which, to be fair, was something of a digression. But he was rather proud of the couplet "the Phoenix fled on wings persimmon / Like Plato did the arms of women," and it needed those stanzas to set it up. He could perhaps rework the lines into his reflection on Bathsheba's obsession on page six, and still manage to get the effect that he wanted. After several hours of anguished work, he trimmed his poem down to eleven and a half pages. He took the envelope to the post office himself and made sure to include his home address because Frank obviously harbored an uneasiness towards academia. He also signed it, simply, "K."

Kingsley went about the campus for the next four days inflated, as though with helium, walking on the balls of his feet, his lips tugged into a reluctant smile, his eyes behind his glasses reflecting the bright spring sky. He felt victorious, bloated with pride, a suitor who had bested his rivals. A stag in full rut, a knight returning from Antioch with the forefinger of a saint while all his compatriots lay slain on Saladin's fields, a movie star for whom all things are possible. Unaware that he was even doing it, he began to whistle when he walked across the quad, some pop tune that he'd heard in the cafeteria and had disparaged. This frightened his students. They thought that he'd gone insane or taken up drink. One biopsych major, who'd been forced to take Kingsley's class to fulfill a humanities requirement, opined to those around her in the back row that Kingsley's sudden, violent mood swing was a textbook case of Mature Onset Psychotic Bipolar Disorder. No one could disagree.

On the evening of the fourth day, however, the pendulum swung back. The response from Frank had arrived and was waiting under his door when Kingsley got home. He tore open the envelope, letting it fall to the floor, and read the letter like he was eating it. His face fell slack, then hard. A vein in his temple grew alarmingly full. Tiny beads of perspiration gathered in the creases of his forehead.

Frank had written:

Dear Miss K:

You were nice to send your peom [sic]. *I guess it was good. But did you mean to send it to me? I mean, I dont* [sic] *know who your* [sic] *talking about. I dont* [sic] *know any Dianna* [sic], *or Orpeus* [sic], *or Dimeter* [sic]. *And I dont* [sic] *mean to be rude, but you mispelled* [sic] *EAR. You wrote E'ER. Plus I think you could make it more simple. I dont* [sic] *think big words are really good. There* [sic] *just confusing. And its* [sic] *kinda long. I got pretty lost by page 2 and had to get a beer. Keep trying tho* [sic]. *If you practise* [sic] *you can only get better.*

Yours truley [sic],

Frank

P.S.

I allready [sic] *met someone.*

P.S.S. [sic]

Isn't halcyon a sleeping pill? Why would you want to write about that?

P.S.S.S. [sic]

I allready [sic] *met someone.*

With trembling hands Kingsley placed the letter on his dinette table. How dare he, the desperate swain? *Kinda long?* And not the least hint of admiration for the effort and inspiration that had gone into its writing; certainly more effort and, one could even say, more talent than it would take to jot down a mere four lines. Kingsley supposed that he had asked for it by violating his long-held tenet never to engage philistines.

Just then the phone rang. Kingsley grabbed it out of its cradle.

"What?" he barked.

There was a pause. "I suppose the answer to your question is that I'm calling to speak with you," it was Dr. Wesley Lorraine, "that's what."

"I'm sorry," Kingsley said. "I just . . . it's been a disappointing day."

"Hmmmm. How's the research going on the poem?"

"Uh, very well. Very well indeed. I just received a letter from the author."

"Oh? I'm intrigued. Some unrooted wayfarer, perhaps? Some lovelorn sophomore?"

"No, a . . . a gentleman of primitive intelligence, but of honest passions, however coarse."

"And is the poem original?"

"Indisputably. I'd wager the man has never been within fifty feet of *An Ode to a Grecian Urn*. The only poems this man would know would be those that could fit comfortably in a tattoo."

"This is all good news. Challenging, but good." Dr. Lorraine paused to take a sip of his daiquiri. He was calling from his lanai. "And how are you doing, Kingsley? On a personal level."

"I'm fine, Wesley. Your concern is starting to concern me. I'm fine."

"All right, all right. I just want to make sure you're happy."

Kingsley was surprised. "I'm surprised."

Dr. Lorraine slurped. "That I would want to see you happy?"

"Well, yes."

"Perhaps I'm being effusive. Forgive me."

"It's all right."

"Are you free this evening?"

Kingsley thought quickly. "Unfortunately not."

"Oh?"

"Yes. My article on Artaud's venereal poetry . . . you know."

"Take a rest, Kingsley. Liz is preparing ostrich, and she's invited Wanda from primatology."

"No, really. I have to work. You know how it is when the muse descends."

"The *muse?*" Dr. Lorraine said, "The muse of academic periodicals? I didn't know there was one."

"Can I take a rain check?"

"Why don't you pop over for coffee later, and dessert. Liz is preparing a flan."

"That sounds good. I'll try to do that."

"Yes, Kingsley, do try. Wanda's a terrific girl, and has a bright future ahead of her."

"Sounds good."

"You need to break out of your shell, Kingsley."

"Goodbye, Wesley."

"Sorry. Goodbye."

Kingsley picked up Frank's letter. What had he gotten himself into? What had he been thinking? He crumpled it in one fist and was about to throw it away when he noticed the envelope on the floor. He reached down and grabbed it. The return address said, "GAS CIGS SNAX," with a crude icon of a large breasted woman engaged in frottage with the capital letter "G."

GAS CIGS SNAX. It shouldn't be too difficult to find.

Actually, there were three listed in the phone book.

And, luckily, Kingsley guessed right on the first one. It was in a part of town that Kingsley had never visited: low, windowless buildings with fleets of forklifts parked at loading docks; houses with ill-tended yards and bed sheets for curtains; outlets for major department stores that sold their defective merchandise at greatly reduced prices. Boarded-up bakeries, boarded-up stationary shops, boarded-up maternity wear boutiques. Bail bond offices, however, seemed to thrive, as did storefronts with white-washed windows offering private screenings of adult-oriented movies for a mere 25 cents.

The GAS CIGS SNAX was on the corner of an intersection, bordered by two vacant lots. Kingsley paid the cab driver and told him to wait, that he wouldn't be long. The driver nodded and Kingsley got out of the back seat. The driver sped away as Kingsley was shutting the door.

Kingsley adjusted his tie, put his wallet in the inside pocket of his jacket, and walked past the gas pumps to the service bay where a sedan with a cracked windshield was suspended on a hydraulic lift. Under this was a man in coveralls, either prying something off of the car or forcing it on. He was bulky, thick-featured, and had black sludge under his unpared fingernails.

He also had the name "Frank" embroidered on a patch sewn onto his chest. Kingsley's poet was a mechanic. How Byronic.

Kingsley coughed into his fist. The man looked up.

"Are you Frank?"

Frank stopped what he was doing with a tool that Kingsley had never seen before and looked at Kingsley with tired eyes. "What can I do for you?"

"I'm Professor Totbotham. I wrote to you."

"Oh," Frank said, and went back to work under the car, "Mr. Totbottom."

"I hope I'm not intruding, but it is very important that I talk to you. The Council on Durable Beauty is meeting the day after next, and I need to verify some information so that I can effectively argue for the inclusion of your poem into our archives." Kingsley smiled magnanimously, expecting to be thanked.

"In your archives?"

"Yes."

"Is there pay?" Frank asked.

Kingsley stopped smiling. "No! Of course not. But there's something better: immortality. This will ensure that your poem will not be lost and forgotten."

Frank wiped his hands on a greasy rag. "You know, I don't think so. I don't want the guys to know, you know, that I wrote a poem or anything. I don't want them laughing at me or anything."

"But you'll be entered into history alongside Shakespeare, and the Brontës, and Dante!"

Frank thought about this for a moment. "Can you put in there that I'm a specialist with vintage Mustangs?"

"You don't seem to grasp the import of this honor . . . may I call you Frank?"

Frank shrugged. "I don't know what else you'd call me."

"Well, then, Frank, perhaps you're unaware," Kingsley said, though it hardly seemed possible, "of the renowned work we do at Peake University. We legitimize for the entire world—and not just for now but for generations to come—only the most deserving and valuable works of beauty mankind has ever known. And it's highly unusual for me to even be talking to you about—"

"Look," Frank said, "I wrote it to find a girl, and I did." He held Kingsley's eyes for a moment, then turned and rummaged through a box of greasy metal things.

"Well, who is she?" Kingsley himself was startled at the accusatory tone that had somehow crept into his voice. "A woman of letters? A Guggenheim recipient? A poet herself, maybe?" She couldn't possibly have the refinement that Kingsley himself had. He was a scholar, beauty was his life's work, there was no one alive who could appreciate Frank's poem more than he himself did. It was wasted on a woman who would actually comb through want ads to find sex with a man. And Kingsley's own poetry was wasted on a man who would place one.

"No," Frank said, "she's a product tester. She actually doesn't much like reading. Especially poems. I figure now I could've saved the twelve bucks on those four lines. She read my ad and liked the 6'4" part. She likes her men tall."

Kingsley felt deeply, spiritually, sick. It was like discovering a gloriously patterned butterfly only to find that it feeds on dung. "But that's a waste! No, a blasphemy! It's a slap in the very face of beauty, of *durable* beauty!"

Frank stopped and looked puzzled. "They're just words."

"No! They're not! You've touched the sublime! You've ventured into the realm of the transcendent. Your poem is—"

"Just words, Mr. Totbottom. Just words I made up."

He obviously hadn't struggled. If he'd struggled, he'd be able to appreciate the lot of the poet. All true art requires a struggle.

This man was a travesty.

"As this ordeal is unprecedented," Kingsley said, barely keeping his voice under control, "I suppose I don't really need to procure your enthusiasm. All I need is your consent."

"I'm sorry, Mr. Totbottom."

"It's Totbo-*tham*."

"Yeah, well, no offense, but I don't think so. Sandy wouldn't like it. That's my girl. She'd think it was kind of, you know, fruity."

"Fruity," Kingsley said and nodded. "I see. Fruity. Thank you for your time, Frank."

Frank cocked his head. "Wait a minute. Can I ask you something?"

Kingsley sighed.

"What's your first name?"

"Kingsley."

"That's with a 'K'?"

"Yes. That's with a 'K.'"

Kingsley turned and left. He crossed the street to the Rowdy Rick's ALL NUDE! ALL NUDE! and called a cab.

Kingsley sat on the bench outside the Council chamber. He was humiliated, but felt that he deserved it. He'd never surrendered to emotional blindfolding or flights of whimsy before. It served him right. How messy and contradictory living people were. From now on he would confine himself to the straightforward—and, quite frankly, more focused—talents of dead people. He had been foolhardy and now he was penitent. He would ask for the forgiveness of the Council and promise never to do it again.

Miss Manly opened the door.

"Professor Totbotham."

"Miss Manly."

"You've put some color in their cheeks, I dare say. What on earth have you done?" Miss Manly smiled. She was a sly one, Miss Manly was.

Kingsley's eyes left hers and he frowned. "I can't imagine," he said and walked past her without looking up.

"Do keep it up," Miss Manly said from behind him.

Kingsley walked to his table and set his satchel down beside his chair. "Learned Sirs, I'm afraid I've been errant in my duties—"

"We've thought long and hard on this poem," Dr. de la Coule began, "and though it may defy all policy established by our position—"

"We want it!" Professor Luft said. "We love it!"

Dr. de la Coule turned to Professor Luft. "May I finish?"

"*Will* you finish?" Professor Luft mumbled.

Dr. de la Coule continued: "And we would be remiss in excluding such a durably beautiful piece of work merely because it happened to have the misfortune of being written contemporarily with ourselves."

"Why the passive voice, Dr. de la Coule?" Professor Luft said.

"Please, Learned Sirs," Kingsley said, "we cannot allow this to happen. It is simply not worth sacrificing our beliefs and established ideals, not to mention the high regard of the people, to succumb to the passing infatuation of such a trite, flimsy . . . bon-bon!"

The Council was astonished.

"But, Learned Sir," Mr. Tobor said, "it was you who brought it up."

"It was a momentary lapse in judgment," Kingsley said, then added, "I haven't had a vacation in five years."

"But," said Professor Luft, "we've already voted to admit it in."

Dr. Bitumen turned to Professor Luft. "Learned Professor Luft, was that a preposition I heard before your interrogative signifier?"

"Oh, dear Dr. Bitumen, must I remind you that the old saw about not ending a sentence with a preposition is a fallacy based on the fact that in Latin grammar there is no such construction? I was not speaking Latin, Dr. Bitumen."

"Well," Dr. Bitumen said, "rules are rules, Learned Sir. If Mr. Webster didn't allow for it—"

"Might I also remind Dr. Bitumen that Mr. Webster beat his wife? I suspect that Mr. Webster's judgment should not be overvalued."

"And may I remind Professor Luft of the necessity for proper hygiene when one insists on wearing the same woolen suit two weeks running?"

"Gentlemen," Dr. Lorraine said, "please! I only have five years left, tops." He turned back to Kingsley. "Professor Totbotham, your duty is the recognition and preservation of Durable Beauty. And you have done that. Admirably. The one hundred year restriction, at your instigation, has been superseded in service of a higher purpose. The rule, Professor Totbotham, has been bent. We like the little poem and we want to sanction it."

"Can we go now?" Dr. de la Coule asked no one in particular.

"I was mistaken," Kingsley said.

"I think you're mistaken now," Dr. Bitumen said.

Dr. Lorraine leveled his gaze at Kingsley. "Kingsley . . . Professor Totbotham . . . why the sudden reversal?"

Was it spite? Kingsley didn't know. It was probably spite. "Because," he said, "it's not original."

"Aha!" Dr. de la Coule said and elbowed Dr. Bitumen, "It's Swinburne!"

"No," Kingsley said. He could never pass that off. "The real author was heretofore unknown. I only stumbled on him while researching the plagiarist with the newspaper ad. This is truly groundbreaking, Learned Sirs, a Jacobean discovery."

"Jacobean?" said Professor Luft. Professor Luft had a soft spot for the Jacobeans. "What, pray, is his name?"

Kingsley faltered. "Sam . . ."

"Sam?"

"Yes. Sam. Josiah Boorhead . . . Sam . . . " Kingsley said, "two 'm's' one 'e.' Samme."

"Samme?"

"Are you sure about the pronunciation?"

"Yes. I found a folio containing seventeen odes, three sonnets, a villanelle, and two false starts on an epic concerning Hero and Leander."

"Predating Marlowe's aborted attempts?"

"Quite possibly."

"Well!"

"Why haven't we heard of this Samme before?" Dr. Bitumen said.

"He has never been published. It was pure luck that I found a reference to him in an appendix by Rosenbach. He was born into illiterate Yeoman stock in west Herefordshire. His father was a dissolute sheep breeder and his mother was a dismayed and nervous woman who took in laundry. No siblings survived. Instead of seeking his fame in letters he chose instead a life with traveling players. But his poems are his true glory . . ."

"May we see one?" Professor Luft asked.

"Uh, yes," Kingsley said, "I've transcribed one." He took a tattered copy of his own poem and handed it to Mr. Tobor, who was the nearest.

"It's rather long, isn't it?" Mr. Tobor said.

Dr. Bitumen reached over and grabbed it. He flipped to the last page and read. "Well," he said, "just going on a cursory glance, it seems to me that the penultimate couplet approaches the bathetic."

"Remember Pope and Byron, Dr. Bitumen, remember Pope and Byron," Dr. de la Coule said and grabbed the poem. He began reading. "The use of tetrameter is bracing."

Professor Luft and Dr. Lorraine leaned over and read as well.

"The alliteration is most affective in Minerva's rumination," Dr. Lorraine said.

"Are we going to get to page two?" Professor Luft asked Dr. de la Coule.

"I was absorbing, Learned Sir," Dr. de la Coule said. "Don't you absorb?"

Dr. Bitumen stood up, as did Mr. Tobor, and rushed over and stood behind Dr. de la Coule and read over his shoulders.

"Rather astute simile with regards to Plato," Mr. Tobor said.

Dr. Lorraine agreed. "Quite ahead of its time."

Kingsley watched as the five huddled and read. He took out some papers from his satchel and arranged them over his table, shifting them, stacking them, folding and unfolding them.

"A 'snaffer-bell'?" Professor Luft said. "Could he possibly be anticipating the nonsense verse of the nineteenth century?"

"Not at all," Dr. Bitumen said, "Snaffer bells were forged by S. Snaffer and Sons Foundry in County Donegal between 1150 and 1262 using a rare ore rich in titanium. The business folded, however, when the vein was depleted. Only three of the Snaffer bells are known to exist today."

"Extraordinary!"

After half an hour had passed, Kingsley heard the creak of the door behind him. He turned and saw Miss Manly's shapely torso leaning in. He pushed his chair back and went to her. She stepped outside and Kingsley followed, closing the door behind him.

"I wanted to make sure they were still alive," she said.

"Yes," Kingsley said, "it's been a harrowing session this year, I'm afraid."

Miss Manly laid a hand on Kingsley's arm. She nodded sympathetically. "Oh, yes," she said, "the Fauves."

"Yes," Kingsley said, "the Fauves."

Miss Manly leaned back and scrutinized Kingsley. "Have you done something with your hair?"

Kingsley patted his head. "Uh, no, I—"

"You seem taller."

"Taller?"

"Would you like some tea?" she said. Her hand was still on his arm.

"No, thank you. I'd better get back inside."

"Maybe later?"

"Later?" Kingsley said as though he was unable to translate the word.

"Yes. Later," she said.

"I'd better get back in." Kingsley quietly opened the door and slipped inside. He hadn't been missed.

Kingsley sat with his hands clenched into fists as Dr. de la Coule turned over the final page. All five Council members looked up at Kingsley.

"You've done a remarkable job unearthing this Samme fellow," Dr. Lorraine said, beaming. "You're a credit to Peake University. This will definitely put us on the map, as far as grants go. I think you might have even earned yourself a Georgetown Certificate of Merit."

Kingsley flushed. "Thank you, Learned Sirs. Thank you very much."

"Nice work," Mr. Tobor said. Professor Luft mumbled his assent, as did Dr. de la Coule. Dr. Bitumen got up without a word and left.

"Are we adjourned?" Mr. Tobor.

"I gather we are," Dr. Lorraine said. He turned to Kingsley when the others had left.

"Stop by the house later. This calls for a celebration."

"Thank you, Wesley, but I've got plans later."

Dr. Lorraine grinned. "Plans?"

"Oh, yes," Kingsley grinned back.

Dr. Lorraine looked past Kingsley. "Thank you, Miss Manly," he said. "See you Monday." He winked at Kingsley and left.

Kingsley turned and saw Miss Manly at the door. "Five o'clock?" she said. "I get off at five."

"That's fine," Kingsley said.

"Good," she closed the door.

Kingsley gathered his papers together. Softly, liltingly, he recited his poem. Imagine, the first poem by a living writer ever to be sanctioned as Durably Beautiful! Frank was a moron.

Kingsley abruptly stopped what he was doing and turned pale. What had he just done? His poem was a forgery. It had taken so little to deceive the Council and, in essence, alter the history of letters. Just a minimum of extemporaneous lies. He had demolished the very foundation on which his life had meaning. He had turned the whole concept of Durable Beauty into a fallacy.

Oh, well, he didn't have time to think about that now. He had to go home and freshen up for Miss Manly. And then he had to get started on seventeen odes, three sonnets, a villanelle, and two false starts on a epic concerning Hero and Leander.

Bingo DePue, the senator's wife

BINGO DEPUE, THE SENATOR'S WIFE, bit harshly on the inside of her lip and awaited the worst. Watching, she stood on the first landing of the marble staircase that was directly across from the grand entrance of the Millard Fillmore Ballroom. This vantage afforded her the optimal view to survey the roiling throng that moved below her. She wasn't greeting; she wasn't granting audience. No one felt slighted. They respected her preoccupation and sympathized. They knew—oh, Lord, did they know!—what intrigues festered at affairs such as this.

Bingo had locked her mother in the hotel room, but now she sensed her imminent arrival. She couldn't explain why. It was simply like the whiff of ozone one gets before a thunderstorm has breached the horizon.

Rence DePue, the senator, was sedated and positioned on a stool at the wet bar—like a marble bust on a plinth—charming, politicking, and never further than arm's length from the scotch. He was a large man with thick fingers who carried himself gracefully (that is, in the brief windows when he was still in possession of his sense of balance). He was a kind man. He was good-humored. He was tolerated. He took up space, both politically and socially. Not unlike a paperweight, or a vase, his wife thought. He was amiable and had many friends. And why not? He posed no threat, either politically or socially.

Bingo continued to canvas the crowd, to mentally divide it into a manageable grid. Her husband was fine for now and could be forgotten until morning. She scanned each quadrant methodically, noting the fur, cringing at the unfortunate profusion of vermillion chintz this year (the result of an upstart designer from Soho who'd traded sex for a cover story in Vogue) and stopped when she caught sight of Richard Mentor, D-Illinois. Richard was surrounded by a cabal of Balkan representatives, judging by their taste in shoes. No one important. Bingo could tell by the way Dick was focusing over their heads when they spoke.

But Bingo's gaze could not rest there; not yet. Her breath caught in her chest and the brie brioche curdled heavily in her stomach. She watched the entrance with accelerating anxiety. Ted, or Tom, was one of the security guards on duty. A good boy, but easily distracted. Bingo, without even trying, tended to distract him a lot. He had a crush on her that charmed Bingo, and she always let him escort her to her car. He had even volunteered his services to watch over her whenever Rence was out of town on business.

Bingo began to chew the index finger of her white glove. She felt—at the most basic, primal level—that within moments the blond dome of her mother's hair would glide into the ballroom carried along by its corseted torso, like the princess of some parade riding in on the final float. She just *knew* it.

"Binny! Darling!" Bingo jumped. Felda Brooks had sneaked up behind her. Bingo tried to regain her composure and her breath.

"You look positively quintessent!" Felda said. She liked the word "quintessent" and used it often. Felda could barely maintain the appearance of congeniality, however, when she noticed the gnawed, lipstick-smeared tip of Bingo's index finger. Bingo noticed her noticing and tugged her glove down and hid it behind her back. She laughed politely and looked demandingly at Felda.

"I'm sorry. What did you say?"

Felda Brooks was a columnist of the lesser sort. And unfortunately for her she had misapprehended Bingo's position when Bingo and the senator had only just started courting. Considering it her social duty, Felda had investigated Bingo and was delighted with the colorful past that she had unearthed: she had uprooted Bingo's mother. Thinking herself the intrepid journalist, Felda tracked her down to interview her. She'd been astonished at the bawdy stories of the still-reigning Queen of Burlesque (no one had ever dared challenge the throne). She was thrilled with the scoop that this newest

deb had decidedly un-grand beginnings, and that Bingo had actually attended American University *on a scholarship*. She was especially surprised to find
out that Bingo's mother had had no idea where her daughter was, and was
very excited to know that her daughter had done well. Felda had arranged—
very publicly arranged—their reunion after their long separation. Bingo's
mother was definitely *not* the churchwoman and ardent gambler that Bingo
had described.

Rence had quashed the article after, thankfully, only a very few forgiving
souls on the paper's editorial staff had read it. But Felda Brooks was hence-
forth forever banned from the DePue register, which turned out to be quite
influential, not so much through the senator's actions but rather through
those of his wife. Felda had been attempting to curry favor ever since.

"Quintessent. I said you look quintessent."

Bingo merely grunted, though she maintained her smile. "Really, Felda,
charm doesn't suit you. I think your talents are better suited for something .
. . I don't know . . . something a little more obvious."

Bingo heard a murmur coming from behind her, coming from the
entranceway. She froze. She dropped her smile and forgot about Felda. No
doubt she alone perceived the subtle shift in room dynamics (her mother
changed magnetic fields, reversed the polarity of ions), but that was because
she was tuned to it after years on the front line. Bingo spun around. A
bright mushroom cloud of blond hair bobbed into the ballroom.
Underneath it was the liquid face of Xavia Jamais, Bingo DePue's mother.
Her loose, bright red smile kept reshaping itself. Her eyes—wet little beasts,
each with its own hunger, and punished with so much make-up that they
looked like bruises—glared without humility at whatever fell into their individual paths. To her utter horror, Bingo DePue saw that her mother had
hauled out her 1957 Mardi Gras outfit—a garish affair of crinoline run
amok, with flounces and patches and festoons of primary colors, and rusty

baubles, lewdly cut to reveal more of her artificially pitched bosom than was
decent. Her shawl consisted of a garland of slightly dusty plastic fruits with
leaves. In 1957, when Xavia Jamais had been named Miss Big Easy, the outfit had rightfully been a success. There was always room for bawdy excess in
Burlesque. But Xavia had long since devolved from parody to self-delusion.

Bingo's mother had always been a woman of unsurpassed vanity and a
startling professional acumen when it came to the exploitation of her own
fleshy skills. She had never been of a particularly maternal bent—had never
pretended to be—but instead was, at least in her own eyes, an eternal
gamine. She hadn't wanted a child (much less a daughter) because that was
what she played at herself. She was an enterprising woman whose capacity
for spite was a marvel to all those who had been stung.

"Bingo," Xavia had muttered at the christening, and then giggled. The
minister gaped. Major Lamar Faith, Bingo's father, turned in surprise to his
new bride. "*Bingo?*" he said. They'd agreed on Patricia.

"Oh, Sweetie," Xavia said to the Major, smiling shyly. She turned to the
minister. "It was my grandmother's name. An ardent churchwoman, and
something of a gambler." Xavia's doting was solely for the benefit of the minister. It was not necessary to pretend with the Major anymore. Xavia could've
christened *him* Bingo that day and he wouldn't have put up a fight.

Xavia was still chuckling in the car on the way home. "Bingo, Bingo,
Bingo," she cooed, and chuckled some more. Let's just see how far you get
with a handicap like that!

Major Lamar Faith had officially been Xavia's manager. In fact, he was just
a sex-blinded fan whom Xavia had chosen more for his malleability than for
any business sense he might have had. Xavia was the one who made the deci-
sions, managed the business, and meted out the discipline. But in those days, in
the business of Burlesque, the Major had been necessary luggage. The circuit

consisted of a lot of tiny towns and a lot of disreputable venues. The Major's robust presence assisted in the smooth running of Xavia's accounts on many occasions.

Though lurid to a fault with her own appearance, especially in her decline, Xavia had been close to cruel with Bingo's femininity. She dressed Bingo like a boy—an ugly boy—and insisted on cutting Bingo's hair herself, usually downing a bottle of tequila first for inspiration. When the Major passed on, Xavia was forced to put Bingo in a home for girls and wondered why she hadn't thought of it years before. She sent Bingo occasional birthday cards for the sake of appearance, but never on the same day year to year, seldom the same month. One year she sent her three birthday cards, one in May, one in July, and one in October. Bingo's birthday was in March.

Before Felda brought the two together again, Xavia had fallen to waiting on tables in Oklahoma City. She'd been forced to retire—after decades of flogging her revue around the South—because the Burlesque circuit had dried up, giving way to coin-operated porno movie booths in strip malls. Xavia might have considered porn if she'd been asked, but she wasn't asked. Needless to say, she'd been delighted to find out that her daughter had achieved some prominence. And Rence had been more than happy to welcome his future mother-in-law into the family. He had been a fan since his overeager adolescence when he had traded a pack of cigarettes for a tattered copy of *Beavers and Boobs*. Rence DePue had spent many formative hours with that particular issue. The confession had made Bingo quite ill. And it was Rence who had secretly financed Xavia Jamais' comeback tour (at Bingo's insistence; the only way to get her mother out of town was to provide her with a tour of back-water saloons and a steady supply of drooling winos). Bingo was distraught that Xavia had found her way back to Washington, having fully expected her mother to be arrested once she'd hit Kansas and that would have been the end of her.

Bingo watched as Xavia drifted into the ballroom. Heads turned, initially shocked, but Xavia quickly deployed her rough charm and all social fears
were vanquished. From her staircase, Bingo kept her mother in sight at all
times. She held her position for the time being to see what direction Xavia
might take. That she had escaped the hotel room did not surprise Bingo.
She had expected it. That she had found the ballroom, that she was even
aware of the ball, also did not surprise her. Xavia had a frightening ability to
sense exactly what would make Bingo the least happy.

Though Bingo far surpassed her mother in beauty—especially now that
Xavia was in a physical free-fall—Bingo's cultivated grace was no match for
Xavia's sheer will. Xavia was used to years of unchallenged indulgence. No
man could weather such a force. Xavia Jamais had had Senator DePue. He
had been an easy catch, and Xavia delighted in the fact that she could ply her
feminine wiles with the assurance that her daughter was still a rank amateur
in comparison. But now he was yesterday's bucket of fish; to both women.

Bingo gradually maneuvered herself away from Felda by ignoring her.
Her heart was pumping frantically and her muscles were poised for action.
For now, Xavia was just generally leering and effusing randomly. But
suddenly Xavia jerked her head, slightly, and gained a focus as though she
had just been slapped out of a drunken stupor. Her course began to take a
direction. She seemed to have found a purpose. Bingo drew a bead between
her mother, the Queen of Burlesque, and Senator Richard Mentor.

Bingo sprang, effortlessly taking the marble stairs two at a time. On the
floor, she negotiated her way fluidly, avoiding gesticulating potentates and
doyennes trailing fox stoles. Bingo would head her off. Xavia was none too
swift these days—even nude—so, outfitted as she was with a picnic basket for
a purse, she would be hindered all the more. Bingo was also sure that her
mother didn't yet realize what she wanted. She was guided by some animalistic
drive, some deep force that moved her and that she merely obeyed.

With a quick move Bingo managed to sidestep a band of roaming pundits. She was barely squeezing by a covey of Libertarians in order to skim past a particularly dense clump of lobbyists when out from behind an ambassador stepped Frankie Winger, the wife of R-Delaware, blocking her way. She caught Bingo's eyes and hooded her own seductively. She spread her full lips into a flirtatious leer. She stepped slowly toward Bingo, who only offered her a series of quick, polite little nods. Bingo looked anxiously past Frankie. Frankie advanced, luxuriously shifting her weight with each step. In each hand she brandished a skewered cocktail sausage.

She stopped in front of Bingo. "Weiner?" she said, after a pause. Bingo absently took the plastic sword.

"You look absolutely delicious," Frankie said, staring baldly down into Bingo's cleavage. "Say, how close is that lush of yours to being sent home in a cab? Some of the girls are having a pajama party over at the Holiday Inn on Q Street when this thing winds down. I'll probably head over there right after dinner and skip the square dance. You can ride with me if you want."

"Thank you, Frankie, but no. Not tonight."

"You really ought to try it one of these nights. You don't know what you're missing."

"Thanks, Frankie. Maybe one of these nights," Bingo said, patting Frankie's shoulder and pushing her out of the way.

"You still have my number, right?" Frankie called after her as Bingo wedged her way into the crowd.

Xavia had migrated to the edge of Senator Mentor's circle. With delicate but persistent baby-steps she managed to part the wall of Eastern Europeans. Bingo watched from a short distance away. She saw the hypnotic beacon light up in her mother's eyes. She saw that the senator was initially repelled, but then, almost immediately, as though by black magic, he warmed to her.

"Why, I don't believe we've met, Senator . . . ?"

"Senator Richard Mentor, D-Illinois." He took Xavia's hand and gently kissed it.

Bingo could see that her mother's talons had landed firmly on target. Xavia used her wiles like a machete. She leaned toward the senator to force him to stare at her valise of a bosom. Granted, there was some archeological fascination to be had, even Bingo could concede that.

"And I'm Xavia Jamais. You may have heard of me. I'm quite renown in some circles. Entertainment circles."

Senator Mentor squinted thoughtfully and turned fully towards Xavia, concluding his business with the Balkans.

"Yes . . . yes . . . Xavia Jamais . . . that name is so familiar . . ."

Xavia pushed out her big red lips in what Bingo supposed her mother supposed would pass as a seductive pout. Bingo cringed when she heard the hoarse rattle escape from her mother's throat. This was her stage purr. Xavia then arched her back—the senator was getting the full twenty-dollar treatment—and rocked back and forth.

Senator Mentor snapped his fingers and smiled deviously. "Miss Jamais . . ."

"I believe it's coming back to you."

"I believe it is. You didn't by any chance, um, you weren't by any chance featured in . . . in print, were you? You didn't do any *magazine* work, did you?"

Xavia returned his smile. "Well, I must say, and I do so with the utmost humility, that some of my earlier work is now considered quite collectable."

"Well, *Mother*, there you are!" Bingo dove forward between the two of them. Xavia abruptly scrutinized her daughter's face and then—just as abruptly—turned to read the senator's face. She turned back to Bingo and slowly nodded in comprehension.

"Senator Mentor," Bingo said, "is my dear old mother bothering you?" Bingo smiled cheerlessly and before the senator had a chance to respond,

Bingo was leading her mother away, firmly gripping her elbow.

"Mother, I have some friends your own age that I'd like you to meet."

"No, thank you, I've already met people like them." Xavia yanked her arm away and stepped back toward the senator.

"I say, Senator," Xavia said, "would you do me the biggest favor?" Senator Mentor nodded his head like a schoolboy. "By the way, Senator, must we remain on such formal terms?"

"Please. Call me Richard."

"I'll call you Dick," Xavia said. "Oh, yes. I like that. 'Dick.' It just sort of feels right on the tongue. 'Dick.' Well, Dick, I'm about as parched as the Gobi Desert on the Fourth of July. Would you be so kind as to escort me to a highball?"

"It would be my honor." Senator Mentor offered Xavia his arm and she graciously took it. They headed off without a word when the senator suddenly remembered Bingo.

"Oh, Binny, please excuse us. We'll be right back."

Bingo was left alone, pale and mute.

"Bingo!" Senator DePue said with a relaxed tongue. Bingo turned and saw her husband stumbling toward her. He smiled broadly and sloppily. He looked down at the cocktail sausage that Bingo held in her hand. She looked down as well. "Where's an ashtray?" she said. Senator DePue shrugged. "Mother's here," Bingo said.

"Oh!" the senator exclaimed in a drunken mock-up of surprise. With clumsy, exaggerated gestures the senator took a swig from his drink and made to lead Bingo away to find Xavia. Bingo, disgusted (he was heading for the ladies' room), turned from him and parted the crowd. Senator DePue followed in her wake.

Xavia and Senator Mentor were surrounded by a rapt group of congressional freshmen when Bingo arrived, dragging her husband. Xavia was holding forth. " . . . and so you can imagine my surprise when the Judge's wife said she *didn't* want me to leave but instead . . ."

"My darling!" Senator DePue sputtered when he recognized the varnished blond wig of his mother-in-law. "My cream tart! My D-cup angel!"

Xavia went rigid at the sound of his voice. It looked like she was still smiling, but she wasn't really. She turned to greet her daughter's husband.

"Rence! Dearest! How lovely to see you again!" She stood back and weighted her voice. "My, but you look positively unwell! Positively medicated! I know it must be difficult with no one to look after you properly. Now, Sugar, you get that little wife of yours to get you cleaned up a little." Xavia had her hands planted firmly on Senator DePue's chest, her arms stiff to keep him at bay. "Rence, you go on now. You go get that handsome face of yours into a sink." Xavia turned and glanced back at Senator Mentor and the others waiting. She rolled her eyes confederately. This aside, however, allowed a breach in her defense. Senator DePue fell forward and seized Xavia in his ursine arms and pushed a kiss squarely on her mouth. When Xavia finally managed to heave him off, after an unduly long struggle, his mouth had a wet, bright red corona which mirrored Xavia's.

"Why, no, Baby! I don't wanna be cleaned up. I wanna dance!" Xavia involuntarily grunted as Senator DePue roughly pulled their bodies together and began to sway to his own atonal humming. Xavia, trapped, looked past Senator DePue's bicep at Bingo. Bingo stood with her arms crossed and smiled at her mother. Xavia tried to kill her with her eyes.

"Senator," Bingo said, crossing over to Senator Mentor. She took his arm and held it tightly. "Have you met the Fletcher-Simmeses?" She led him away. He went willingly, grateful to be diplomatically disengaged from a potentially unpleasant scene.

But Xavia had dispatched leaner, younger, and more sober adversaries in her day, so dislodging herself from her son-in-law was really just a matter of elementary judo. It took five broad steps to catch up to Senator Mentor and Bingo. Xavia stomped down heavily onto the train of Bingo's gown and kept her foot planted firmly. Bingo's dress was a creation—expensive and well made—and the material did not give. Bingo had been moving quickly and was yanked backward with considerable force. Xavia side-stepped the trajectory of her flying daughter. Bingo, arms and legs flailing like a freshly mounted insect, knocked several people out of the way like bowling pins as she landed on the floor on her back and slid six feet into the crowd.

"Oh, my little baby, have you had another accident?" Xavia was the first to reach Bingo's side. "She's prone, you know," she said, addressing the crowd. She bent down over Bingo and cradled her head. She looked straight into her daughter's face. Her eyes were glittering triumphantly. Her face was cut with a huge, vicious grin that she only allowed Bingo to see.

"Oh, my poor little princess," Xavia said, "you'd better get on home now and pack yourself in ice. Senator Dick is in good hands with your dear old mom. You should know that I have a special way with senators. They can't seem to resist me."

Bingo's humiliation seared her cheeks. She hated the glee in her mother's puffy face. She realized that she was still holding onto the plastic sword that impaled the diminutive sausage. Without consideration of consequence, blinded by malice, Bingo flung her arm straight up with all her strength and plunged the skewer into her mother's thigh. Xavia's mouth dropped open. Her eyes went wide and emptied of everything except shock. She didn't utter a sound. Bingo brusquely withdrew the saber, leaving a greasy oblong stain on Xavia's haunch, in the middle of which appeared a tiny dot of blood.

No one saw the impaling. Senator Mentor took Xavia by the shoulders and lifted her away, allowing access so that someone could attend to Bingo. Rence filled the void, suddenly looming over her. In his misguided enthusiasm he leaned a little too far when he went to pick her up. "Hups," he said as he fell on top of her. Those standing closest heard the ribs crack.

"I'm fine," Bingo said, wincing, after Bradley Dyshe, R-Wyoming, and Simmon Dooley, I-Vermont, had hauled Rence off of her and Frankie Winger had swooped in. Frankie helped Bingo get to her feet. "Please. I'm fine." She swatted Frankie's hand off of her buttocks and hobbled to the ladies' room.

Bingo stood in front of the mirror and gently poked at her ribs. The pulsing ache became a sharp stab when she touched them. But she didn't feel them move, so that was good. She brushed off her gown as well as she could, though she was unable to get Xavia's footprint off of the train; Xavia had apparently trod in tar. She pulled her necklace around to the front again and tucked her hair back behind her ears. She checked her face and was alarmed at her eyes. She considered touching them up, but her make-up was fine. It was something else, something in the eyes themselves. She heard the outer door open and quickly ducked into a stall.

"Yeah, well, if you're born in the gutter, you stay in the gutter, I always say." It was Felda Brooks.

"But who was that other woman? The frightening one?" That was Veronica Foam, the anchorwoman of D.C. Today.

"You haven't heard of Xavia Jamais?"

"I must've missed that luncheon."

"She was an 'entertainer,' and let's just say that her stage work would hardly qualify for an government grant. More like prosecution for moral turpitude."

"Oh, my god! She's not the one who showed up two years ago at that tea given by Bunny Ghent? The one wearing candyapple-red hot pants?"

"That's the one."

"How ghastly! I thought that was one of those novelty Strip-O-Gram things."

"Nope. That was Bingo DePue's mother."

"Where's she been? Jail?"

"Bingo tried to get her out of the picture by having Rence ship her out to the midwest to work Teamsters' conventions."

"But she's back?"

"Oh, yes," Felda laughed. "She's back."

Bingo stayed in the stall until all was clear. Unable to bring herself to return to the reception, she instead went to the dining hall to rest before the other guests arrived.

She gingerly made her way up the back staircase holding her side. She was stopped cold, however, when she reached the doorway of the dining room. Her mother was at the far end of the table. Xavia was rearranging the place cards. A waiter stood by, watching her. When she was finally pleased with her arrangement, she handed the waiter a crumpled bill. The waiter bowed, and, without smiling, left. Xavia looked around, searching for something. With sudden relief, she walked over to the sideboard and picked up her half-finished cocktail. She rubbed her thigh where she'd been stuck. She took two steps, drink in hand, and stopped. She bent her head back and emptied the glass. She straightened, blinked several times, and belched loudly. She stood motionless for a moment as though unsure of where she was. Abruptly she narrowed her gaze like a bird of prey. She sniffed the air. She snapped her head around just as Bingo silently yanked herself back from the door jamb and held her breath. Finally, she heard Xavia leave.

Bingo went to the far end of the table. Not surprised, she found Xavia's place next to that of Senator Mentor's. Poor Sissy Mentor was again mysteriously relegated to the distant end of the table, far from her husband. Bingo picked up Senator Mentor's card and, looking around, saw the card bearing the name of Senator Thuesan, the Grand Ol' Dad of the Senate. Bingo picked this up and set it next to her mother's place. Someone from her own epoch would be nice for a change. Senator Thuesan was by far the oldest man in the Senate. Possibly the oldest man ever. Bingo left her own place where it was, across from her mother. She placed Senator Mentor, rightfully, next to his dear Sissy.

"So, Mrs. Jamais . . ."

"Miss."

"I'm sorry," Senator Thuesan said, "*Miss* Jamais . . . so I understand that you're involved in the show business."

Xavia had known who was responsible for the counter-espionage from the moment that she had sat down. Who else? But she had taken her place without faltering. She was a trouper. You just have to play to the house that you're in.

"Yes. The second oldest profession, though sometimes the line has been blurry." Xavia smiled magnanimously to those all around her, especially across the table at Bingo. Xavia was delighted that the spotlight had been turned on her without her even having had to take the initiative herself. She sat slightly angled to the right so that her bosom favored the senator. Senator Thuesan's failing eyesight kept him bobbing very closely above it.

"Were you a . . ." Senator Thuesan started, but Xavia interrupted him here to wipe up a bit of food that was caught in the patch of stubble on his chin that he had missed when shaving. Bingo could hardly contain her joy. ". . . a dancer?" the senator finished, unfazed by Xavia's ministrations.

Xavia drew in a huge breath and straightened her back to its full height. She cast a nostalgic glance to both her left and her right, and began expansively: "Oh, my dear Mr. Senator, *vraiment, vraiment*. I was a member of the noble and loving family called Burlesque, the true and humble heart of the theater. Some even dared call me its queen, though those words are not my own." She smiled pensively to herself for a moment, looking down, working up some tears. "I am sad to report," she bravely raised her head, "that it is truly a dying art."

"Dead." Bingo looked straight at her mother.

"What?" Xavia asked.

"Dead. It's a dead art." People stopped eating. Xavia let the moment linger.

"Ah, the very young, how foolish they can be. Senator, have you met my daughter? Senator Thuesan, this is my daughter, Bingo. You know, I always expected Bingo's father to go into politics. Unfortunately, he went the way of the bottle instead. It's not easy raising a girl."

"Very pleased to meet you, Miss Bingo," the senator said. Bingo had been introduced to the senator several dozen times, the last time being at the DePue's own house during a celebration for the vetoing of the Welfare Bill. "Miss Bingo, are you an entertainer, too?"

"Oh, heaven forbid!" Xavia laughed. "Bingo is a housewife. Unlike me. I never could keep a house." Xavia reached over and patted Bingo's hand. "But like I always said, if you lack talent, it's always good to have a predisposition."

The senator grunted his assent. Frankie Winger, seated next to Bingo, reached over and squeezed her knee.

Bingo knew that left to her own bestial ways Xavia would sooner or later secure her own banishment. Bingo noted regretfully that sooner had already passed.

"There's a Shriners' convention in town," Bingo said too abruptly, offering bait. Xavia's Shriner jokes had made sailors blush. No one spoke. Xavia looked at Bingo, waiting. "It's funny, but I just thought of it," Bingo went on, "and it reminds me of a funny story I once heard about a Shriner and a Shetland pony . . ." No one budged. "Actually, Mother, wasn't that one of your stories?"

A pause.

"I don't think that this is the place for it, dear," Xavia said, and grinned. She didn't continue. The spotlight was now temporarily on Bingo, but that was all right, considering. The silence was too delicious.

"But I'm sure the senator would love to hear one of your stories," Bingo scrambled, "something from your repertoire. One of the stories that made you famous." Or got you run out of town.

"Well, now, Bingo, I thought I raised you better than that. Only common people tell smutty stories at the dinner table."

"No, please," the senator said, "I would greatly love to hear one of your stories."

"See, Mother? Don't disappoint the senator. Tell the one about the Irish traveling salesman who meets the three priests in a bar."

"Oh, yes!" cried Senator Thuesan. "Priests in a bar!" All ears were on Xavia. She cleared her throat. It would take a lot more than a few cuss words to undo Xavia; and besides, hadn't her very livelihood been based on making the vulgar amusing? She began to tell the joke with gusto, not scrimping on the details or the language. No one moved. No one uttered a sound. Bingo's excitement grew. She wrung her napkin underneath the table, not even caring that Frankie's hand had moved up her thigh. Xavia got to the part where the second priest finally goes for the olive in the martini and Bingo grinned maliciously.

And Xavia finished her joke.

The senator sat as though stunned. Everyone at the table waited for his reaction, not daring to breathe. Could this be it? Bingo thought. Could this be the grave, the joke the spade? The senator made a small, rasping sound. Xavia grabbed her water, hoping to prevent the asphyxiation of an elder statesman. But he made another rasping sound. Then another. He wasn't choking. He was laughing. Soon the entire table was laughing, uproariously, and applauding. Xavia beamed.

Bingo pushed her chair back, the throbbing of her ribs suddenly being too much for her to handle. She wasn't paying much attention, nor was the waiter carrying sixteen cruets of cheddar-baked bouillabaisse with whom she collided.

Bingo's gown was ruined beyond redemption, but while toweling off in the kitchen she purloined a chef's apron, a bartender's cummerbund, and a floral dress left on a hook by a maid. With the help of a few bobby-pins from a cocktail server she managed to fashion together a startlingly effective ensemble. On her way out of the kitchen she grabbed the chicken scissors.

In the ladies' room mirror she saw that the left side of her face and neck were scarlet from the second-degree burns. But that didn't concern her. What concerned her was her hair. She dried it as best as she could, but the molten cheese had clumped together and couldn't be pulled out. She went into a stall and stood over the toilet and hacked off the larger knots. She heard the door open.

"Well, it's not surprising, really"—it was Veronica Foam—"I spoke with her mother . . ."

"Oh, really?"—and Cindy Koteck, the daughter of the notoriously illiberal Supreme Court Justice—"The Jamais woman? She has a certain, I don't know, *élan* that just sort of grows on you."

" . . . and she told me that Bingo isn't really her own daughter. That she felt sorry for her when she was touring Georgia and took her in to help with the laundry."

"And look at her now."

"Yes," Veronica Foam said, "look at her now."

"You know, I never really trusted Bingo. Never really liked her."

"Something sneaky in the eyes."

"Yes. And I've always thought her mouth was too hard."

"I heard from Felda Brooks that she'd blackmailed Rence DePue into marrying her by threatening to pay an unwed teenager to claim that the baby was his."

"You know, I heard the same thing . . ."

Bingo opened her stall door and walked up to the mirror. She'd missed some strings of cheese but it was all right; they were the same color as her hair and blended in. Veronica Foam and Cindy Koteck were mortified, alternately gawking at her outfit and at her butchered hair. Bingo turned around. She wrinkled her nose and looked concerned. "Veronica," she said, "have you rubbed yourself with cat shit again?" She left.

When Bingo arrived in the ballroom the string octet had already launched into a partita, setting the mood, generally assisting in digestion, and allowing spouses the opportunity to optimally distance themselves from each other. Bingo noticed that the people in her immediate vicinity stopped talking. Although they were too polite to stare, they did sneak glances. Gradually, successive concentric rings of silence spread out from where she was standing.

She saw Richard Mentor's back across the room and trotted toward him.

"Richard, I need to talk . . ."

He turned and saw her. He looked angry. "Not now, Bingo."

"Richard. I need to talk to you." She reached out to touch his arm.

"Bingo!" he hissed. "Please!"

She grabbed his forearm and he pulled back. "Bingo, you're embarrassing yourself."

"It's not me!" Bingo couldn't believe what she was hearing. "It's her! She started it!"

"Bingo, go home. You look like a clown!"

"*I* look like a clown? *I* look like a clown?" This was too much! "What about her? Dressed like a—"

"Go home!" He turned and stiffly walked away.

Bingo threw up her arms and looked around her. She saw Frankie watching her, but then Frankie quickly looked away when Bingo caught her eye.

"Frankie . . ." Bingo said. But Frankie was gone.

Bingo couldn't understand it. Wherever she turned, senators and their wives, representatives, delegates, upwardly mobile pages turned their heads.

Except for Felda Brooks. Felda was smirking. This did not portend well. Felda was standing across the room, by the punch bowl. She swaggered. She looked—could it be?—smug. Felda had a new bravura that alarmed Bingo. Bingo was used to Felda's toadying. Haughtily, Felda looked Bingo up and down and turned, without so much as a wave or a nod, and gave the liqueur tray her complete attention.

Bingo heard a sudden burst of excited whispering and noticed the crowd splitting apart. Through the center, coming toward her, were two security guards. One was Ted, or Tom. She usually had to thwart his advances, but he didn't seem very moony at the moment. He was frowning and coming at her with his shoulders bunched up and his hand on his holster. Bingo was at a loss to explain his odd behavior, and why everyone was now looking at her. She lifted her hands in a stage shrug and realized that she was still holding onto the chicken scissors.

A lone, stifled cackle broke the silence. It was Xavia. She had moved to the front of the crowd, her arm linked with Senator Thuesan's. Bingo watched her as she mouthed the words, "I *win*! I *win*!"

Perhaps Bingo could have given the situation some more thought, perhaps she could've carried herself with more aplomb, but the way the evening had progressed had really worn her down. She ran at her mother with the scissors raised.

She didn't get very far, though. Ted or Tom had broken into a run, diving at her and grabbing her ankles. Bingo fell forward in a slide, Ted or Tom still holding her ankles, and she hit a chair but kept going; past the steam tables offering *crêpes framboises*, past two dumbstruck waiters, past a fine eighteenth century French divan and a later Brancusi on a marble base, and finally—as Felda Brooks leaped out of the way—into the folding table which held the punch bowl. Next to the punch bowl was a 200-pound block of ice which had been sculpted into the form of a courting albatross to commemorate an environmental bill championed by Lance Sutcher, D-Oregon. The bill had been summarily squashed, but the ice sculpture had been paid for in advance, so there it was. The punch bowl—unfortunately just refilled— landed directly on top of Bingo's left femur. The albatross hit her squarely in the chest and—being of a rather elaborate design, and, after all, being an albatross—also hit her left shoulder and collarbone. Oddly enough, Ted or Tom escaped without injury.

Bingo's body cast started just below the chin and went down—encasing both of her arms just above the elbows, her chest, and her pelvis—to mid-calf. Rence came to visit for the first week, thoughtfully bringing magazines and newspapers. He would read them to her as she was unable to lift them herself. He liked to start with Felda Brooks's column.

"No," Bingo said, "please."

Rence cleared his throat. "' . . . and what sauced-up senator whose wife has been so recently indisposed has been seen in the company of what quintessent blond representative? He must be a glutton for gold diggers!' Gosh," Rence said, honestly perplexed, "do you suppose she's talking about Dart"— R-Iowa—"Dillon?" Bingo just closed her eyes. Perhaps if she was really quiet he'd forget that she was there and go home. Rence continued: "'And *La Jamais* has pulled yet another social coup, this time decked out in a smashing sequin tube-top and leotard ensemble, stunning the entire economic conference of the G7 Nations . . .' Gee, Binny, aren't you proud?" Bingo could no longer bear it.

She didn't see Rence anymore after she got a room on a different floor without telling him.

The nurses and interns were a little peevish, particularly Nurse Busk, a tight woman whose harsh ways left Bingo to ponder which came first, her bitterness or her spinsterhood. She couldn't understand why Bingo would want to move; after all, she *had* the nicest room in the hospital. And didn't she know, and didn't she care, how inconvenient it would be to move her in her condition? But Bingo insisted, and so she was moved, Nurse Busk at the head of the gurney, huffing and snorting as she pushed Bingo down the hallway, aiming for the loose tiles.

Her new room was smaller, and had no light, but it did have a television set. She switched it on. It was D.C. Today, with Veronica Foam. Bingo, unable to turn her head, fumbled with the T.V. remote. It slipped from her fingers and fell under the bed.

"At the Four Seasons today," Veronica Foam reported, "the League of Disappointed Mothers held its annual luncheon, honoring this season's gal-about-town, Xavia Jamais." Bingo was held hostage by the plaster, unable to throw anything at the television, unable to plug her ears. "Let's cut to the tape we shot earlier today." On the television, Xavia walked up to podium in a huge red wig and a boustiere of peacock feathers. She waved graciously, waiting for the standing ovation to sit back down. Bingo frantically felt around her for the nurses' call button. Xavia cleared her throat. "The psychotic break of a child is nothing compared to the breaking of a mother's heart . . ."

Bingo's new room was without a television, without a phone, without windows, even, and was next to the furnace room. And though she was alone with the constant throbbing, the heat blisters, the rashes, and the complete annihilation of all compassion from the nursing staff, she was relieved. At last, solace.

But her solitude did not remain undisturbed for long. Perhaps it was a change in the weather—perhaps it was a sudden change in the ionosphere or a magnetic shift—but after several restful nights her pins began to hum, the metal pins that they'd put into the bones in her legs. She didn't believe it herself at first, but after the second night she could distinctly feel the vibrations course through her body. Her doctors scoffed, but Bingo insisted that they were picking up a Top 40 station.

It was late one night, Bingo was lying stiff and itchy and wide awake. "And today on the local front," the pins sang through her body, "the Vice-President served as the best man to the oldest living senator, ever, on this, his fourth marriage, to a former carnival stripper once considered the Queen of Burlesque . . ."

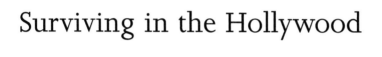

Surviving in the Hollywood

IT WAS MARV WHO HAD insisted that Jeremy go to Rondo, North
Dakota, to attend the America's Bread Basket Film Festival. Not only would
they be screening Jeremy's latest movie, *Dead Man, Dead Woman* (his next
to latest movie had been fifteen years before that), but they would also be
honoring him with a retrospective of his life in films. And that could only
be good.

"Making small independent films will kick your career in the ass," Marv,
his agent, had said. "Small independent film festivals are the wave of the
future, Bubby, Sweetheart!" And Jeremy Hatch was a realist. He knew that
his career could use a jump start. Here he was, sixty-two years old in a business that valued youth over wisdom, looks over intelligence, and novelty over
talent. And even in his prime he had never been one of the pretty boys. But
he had never had to be. Jeremy had had something else; he had touched a
cultural nerve. So he trusted Marv—which went against all Pavlovian behav-
ioral theory—and accepted a humiliating role (and for deferred pay, no less)
in a derivative and sophomoric movie called *Dead man, Dead Woman,*
which had been nominally directed by Maxwell P. Dressler, an acne-scarred,
malnourished, culturally illiterate sociophobe just out of high school or film
school or whatever. Marv had told Jeremy that the movie would refresh the
drug-addled memories of casting directors, letting them know that he,
Jeremy Hatch—a former Academy Award nominee—was still alive and willing to work for free.

Unfortunately, there had been no retrospective at the America's Bread
Basket Film Festival. Marv had lied, although Marv never called it lying. He
called it "creative visualization." And there hadn't even been anyone to meet
him at the airport to drive him into town. Nor had there been a hotel room
booked for him. Jeremy had even had to buy his own ticket to see the
travesty that was *Dead Man, Dead Woman* and had been forced to sit
through it because his ulcer was flaring so badly that he couldn't move, let
alone walk out.

And after the screening the director, Maxwell P. Dressler, had taken the opportunity to regale the audience with lurid, barely accurate tales of Jeremy's misbehavior during the making of the movie, capping off his litany with a vow never to work with Hollywood has-beens again. Dressler then had the nerve to invite Jeremy up on stage, but Jeremy, with nerve of his own (and sufficient scotch in his circulatory system) had yelled out, "Fuck you, Pus-Face!" and stumbled out of the theater clutching his stomach.

When Jeremy had returned to Los Angeles (via an unscheduled three-day stopover in New Orleans after he'd boarded the wrong plane, none of which he could later remember) Marv had suddenly and unexpectedly begun to act like an agent. He had feigned outrage at Jeremy's poor treatment at the hands of the gap-toothed townsfolk of Rondo, North Dakota, and thought he'd scored a coup by screaming at them until they relented and arranged a special One-Night-Only seminar for Jeremy, giving him the chance to share the secrets of surviving in Hollywood with a roomful of Weight Watchers and tractor salesmen. And then Marv had actually expected to be thanked for it. And when Jeremy hadn't thanked him, Marv had gone all pouty, then all huffy, had walked out on Jeremy in the middle of dinner at Le Dôme and left him with the bill. Marv had even suggested that Jeremy might want to start looking elsewhere for representation. So Jeremy agreed to attend the seminar just so Marv would start returning his phone calls again. All Jeremy wanted to do was to leave the humiliation of Rondo behind. The surest way to survive in Hollywood, as far as Jeremy could tell, would be to fire Marv.

Jeremy Hatch looked out of the window of his reasonably priced room at the Good Nights Inn on Airport Road, bolstering himself for his seminar on "Surviving In The Hollywood." That's how they wrote it on the brochure. Apparently typeset by someone whose mother tongue was one of the romance languages. He looked down onto the dumpsters that lined the parking lot, and, beyond them, at the carefully pruned shrubs and the foot-path that followed the sad little creek that the good people of Rondo liked to call the Rondo River. The hotel was near the airport, but not near enough for him to walk there, which was what he felt like doing. Had it come to this? Jeremy had thought he'd hit bottom when he signed on to be the voice of Sheldon the Toad on *Bulrush Corner*. He had once been the first choice for *Kramer Vs. Kramer* (but because of agency politics and the fact that the studio owed Hoffman a picture—and the fact that Jeremy had acci-dentally called Robert Benton an "a-hole" at a party—Jeremy wound up doing *Diablo Six-pack* instead, which wasn't bad, except it was for cable). Good Christ, he needed a drink.

Jeremy knew that he couldn't have a drink because, a), if he got drunk out here in the middle of goddamned nowhere without Marv around to clean up after him it would surely make the local newspaper. Just his being in Rondo was big news. After all, what did he have to compete with? A shortage of binder twine? A big sale on chaffing lotion down at the tack shop? And from the Rondo Herald-Register it would hit the wire services and that's all he needed at this juncture in his life was another goddamned scandal. And, b), he was already hungover and if he did have a drink he probably wouldn't be able to keep it down anyway.

Jeremy planned to start the seminar by talking about his wife, Susan Roman. Ex-wife. Defuse that topic, get it out of the way right off just to shut them up. Because they *all* wanted to know about Susan Roman. Susan Roman was a superstar. Susan Roman had fan clubs in all fifty states and twenty-three foreign countries, including Libya. Susan Roman was her own industry with twelve full-time bodyguards. One could even buy shares in Susan Roman if one wanted to. Meanwhile, Jeremy could walk into a mall and get a Hot Dog On A Stick and no one would bother him. There was a time when Jeremy had been on the cover of Time as "The New Unsexy Face of Sex Appeal," back in the early 70s when having a personality disorder was considered erotic. Back then people got suspicious if you were glamorous. But times had changed and Jeremy hadn't; he had instead held onto his ideals. Susan had been luckier, of course, being unhindered by ideals. And it was luck. It had nothing to do with talent. A lot of people were talented, but not everyone was Susan Roman. But Sid—Sid Poppity, his old agent, before Marv; before he'd been *reduced* to Marv—had kept Jeremy bogged down with assignments in Italy and France and Jeremy rode the wave of failure of bloated European art films. Meanwhile, pandering to the masses with trite romantic comedies and vacuous musical fare had been a shrewd career move on Susan's part. And the woman was certainly shrewd, if nothing else. By the time Jeremy had quit drinking a newly hatched gaggle of less complex actors had gnawed their way to the top, leaving Jeremy to guest star in ensemble roles, supporting Burt Reynolds in cross-country car chases. A new era of greed and bloodthirsty ambition had dawned and Jeremy had failed to adapt. Susan, on the other hand, had managed to adapt quite nicely. But she had left him long before, back when his star was only beginning to fade. She was far too cunning to risk getting caught in the downward suck as his career went under. One would think that her vanity and arrogance would have worked against her, but no. Even though she had chosen roles that were well beyond her range as either a singer or an actress, instead of destroying her career (as should have been the case) these films had become a favorite of the gays, who liked that sort of thing. Susan's foundering performances—caricatures, really—had inadvertently inspired a cult, and every album she recorded had gone gold, if not platinum (with the single exception of *Susan Roman sings Lech Stivech*, a serious misfiring aimed to capitalize on the polka craze that never happened). Jeremy, however, was despised by the gays; after the divorce they hated him, like spiteful children. He wasn't sure why. Were they jealous? Or did they think he had somehow sullied Susan by bringing her down to a carnal level? Maybe they assumed that all their divas were martyrs to love like they were themselves, and that he was responsible for making her suffer. He didn't know. All he knew was that no one was making floats for him every Gay Pride Parade. All he knew were the sneers he got every time his son, Alexander, took him to dinner in West Hollywood.

Jeremy left the window and went to the little refrigerator and got a can of diet cola. He tried the door of the mini-bar, just to see what was in there, just to pass the time, but it was locked. He pulled harder. There was no key in the lock, like there always was. How did they ever expect to move any liquor if a person couldn't even get to it? If one chose to get to it, that is. Not that he was. But *if* he was. He yanked again, purely out of annoyance. It didn't budge so he kicked it. It still didn't open.

The Oak Room was off of the lobby and was smaller than Jeremy had imagined. Much smaller, actually. It was a windowless rectangle formed by cutting up a larger room with sliding wall partitions. It should have been called the Acoustic Tile Room if accuracy instead of romance had been topmost on their minds. The hotel staff had placed an easel outside the door displaying his head shot pasted onto the middle of a piece of red cardboard. His face was surrounded by stars hand-drawn with a silver felt-tipped pen and at the bottom, also by hand, was written, "Jeremy Hatch Presents Surviving In The Hollywood! Tonight! In Person!" There was a time when his name had been above the title on the marquee of the Chinese Theatre. Inside the room what looked like forty folding chairs had been set up, though it could've been more. Seated in the front row was a desiccated old man with no hair wearing large-framed glasses and a jogging outfit. Jeremy thought he looked more than qualified to host his own seminar on surviving. Beside him was what was probably his wife because she was wearing a matching jogging suit, only in pink. This exercise-wear was evidently someone's idea of seniors' fashion in Rondo, because the woman had obviously never jogged in her life, and just as obviously didn't let her husband have any of the food. They weren't talking, just waiting, each staring at his or her own individual middle distance. Perhaps they were left over from the last seminar; perhaps they hadn't realized it was over. Jeremy ducked back out. The placard outside the door led him to believe that he was where he was supposed to be, but maybe they'd put it up outside the wrong room, outside the room for the less important seminar. Forty chairs? He went up to the front desk to ask.

"May I help you?" said the robust girl with blond hair who stood behind the desk. The fact that she didn't recognize him as an actor didn't upset Jeremy, even though he had once had lunch with Orson Welles on the Warner Lot. But she wouldn't have known who Orson Welles was, either. After all, she hadn't even been born when Jeremy received his Golden Globe for *Brother Jones and the Preacher*, back when he'd been voted "Person of the Year" by the American Association of Retailers and Exhibitors. What bothered Jeremy was that she didn't even recognize him from when he'd checked in two hours earlier. He remembered *her*, for Chrissakes, even though it was doubtful that Johnny Carson had ever called her "possibly the most bankable man in Hollywood."

"Yes," Jeremy said, "I'm here for the seminar on Surviving—"

"In the Hollywood?"

"Uh, yes. But I believe Hollywood is a proper noun so the definite article isn't really necessary."

She tapped her pen on the counter. "So are you taking the 'Surviving in the Hollywood,' then?"

"No." Jeremy used his special smile, the smile that Marv only allowed him to use with drunken reporters or psychotic fans. "I'm Jeremy Hatch. I'm giving it."

"Oh," the girl said. She dropped all pretense of civility. Apparently she'd had some unpleasantness with these seminar people in the past. Jeremy could sympathize, but not at the moment. "That's in the Oak Room," she said.

"Is that the Oak Room?" Jeremy asked, pointing in the direction of the room where he hoped the two pretend joggers were still breathing.

"It is," the girl said.

"But there must be a mistake," Jeremy said.

"Why must there be?" she said. Jeremy sensed the girl was getting surly, which he thought was completely unnecessary. If she had been her mother, she'd be at his feet by now, begging to pleasure him.

"There can't be more than forty seats set up in there."

"Why don't you take it up with Amanda Larch," the girl said, pointing over his shoulder. "She's the one who booked the room."

Jeremy turned around and saw a harried woman in an ill-fitting pant suit trotting past carrying a weathered manila envelope and a metal cash box.

"Miss Larch," he said, taking a step toward her. She drew back, frightened. He stopped. "I'm Jeremy Hatch."

Amanda Larch relaxed and extended her hand. "Oh, Mr. Hatch! Welcome! I loved you in *The Sting!* Is your room all right?" He hadn't been in *The Sting*.

"Fine," he said, "just fine. Listen," he drew her aside, a tactic which always worked; it gave the fans the illusion of intimacy with an actual movie star. "I wanted to talk to you about the lecture hall that—"

"Oh, yes," Amanda Larch said, "the Oak Room."

"Yes, the Oak room, it's—"

"Over there."

"Yes, I know it's over there, but it's . . . it's a little cramped, don't you think?" Marv had promised him 20% of the door, which wasn't much, but it wasn't nothing, either. Jeremy had worked at a time when actors weren't pampered the way they are today. When actors acted because they loved the craft, when they were actually expected to have talent and didn't jump at the first opportunity to hawk diet soda or hair dye.

"Oh," she said, "it'll be a cozy affair. People around here like cozy. And I'm sure it'll fill up."

"Fill up?"

"Give it time."

"How many people are expected?"

"We have seventeen so far!" Amanda Larch said.

Seventeen? There were more people than that making coffee when he'd filmed *The Idiot Woman of Borneo*, which the studio shelved because, well, because it was *The Idiot Woman of Borneo*. But even Susan agreed that it was the role that would have finally won him the Oscar.

"Excuse me," he said. He walked across the lobby to the bathroom and doused his face with cold water. He went into a stall and crouched, holding his head in his hands. Lord have mercy, could he use a drink.

At five minutes after eight he left the bathroom and went back into the lobby. Amanda Larch was at the table beside the door to the Oak Room.

"So," he said brightly, "how many do we have?"

"Sixteen," Miss Larch said.

"*Sixteen?* But I thought we had at least seventeen."

Amanda Larch hooded her eyes. She leaned forward and said in a low voice, "Laure-Luda isn't here yet."

"Laure-Luda?"

"Hmmmm." Miss Larch nodded slowly. Apparently she assumed that Jeremy was well acquainted with the social intricacies of Rondo, North Dakota.

"*Laure-Luda?*" he asked again, making sure this time to raise his inflection so that Miss Larch would be absolutely certain that he was asking a question.

Miss Larch looked cautiously to either side and leaned even closer. "Laure-Luda came to Steve Allen's seminar when he was in town." She sat back and shook her head sadly.

Jeremy stood at the back of the room. Beside him, sitting in the last row, were two teenagers in matching polyester uniforms probably belonging to the Good Nights Inn. Jeremy looked down at his watch. It was 8:11. He took a deep breath and strode through the folding chairs and up to the podium. The modest gathering clapped excitedly and sat up straight.

Jeremy smiled magnanimously and quieted them by holding his palms up. The applause died down. In the front row, across from the senile joggers, was a pretty woman in her early thirties who was already scribbling furiously on a yellow legal pad. She was dressed in a tailored suit and kept her back unnaturally straight.

"Hello," he said, "Welcome. My name is Jeremy Hatch"—a large grimy man, holding a plastic bag stuffed with neatly folded, yellowed newspapers on his lap, clapped violently and then abruptly stopped—"and I'm here to talk to you about surviving in Hollywood . . . surviving in *the* Hollywood." Jeremy chuckled. No one seemed to get it. He continued: "I have to say I love this business; it's been my whole life. I feel blessed to have had even a small part in it. But I won't kid you; it can be tough. It takes a lot of hard work, courage, stamina, and a whole lot of luck. But it's worth it." In the third row, three middle-aged divorcees in knock-off Gucci blouses and with their make-up applied with a sandblaster whispered approvingly among themselves. The businesswoman in the front row scribbled on her note pad. Two seats over from her a man in his early twenties, wearing a plaid shirt that he had ironed and buttoned to the collar, nodded vigorously. Jeremy was pleased; he was doing well. Avuncular, accessible, humble. "Take my ex-wife and myself," he said. Once Susan was out of the way they could all keep their focus on him. A thin, pale man in the back row who was wearing a Susan Roman T-shirt from *Baltimore Down* frowned and crossed his arms. "I'm sure that some of you might have heard that I used to be married to Susan Roman—" Damn! He phrased it wrong; he should've said, "When Susan Roman and I were married." Now it seemed as though he was *Mr.* Susan Roman, like everyone wanted to think, anyway. Damn.

"Back when I discovered her"—he lied, but what did it really matter? Who was he really hurting by it? People were here to see his seminar, anyway—"she was hardly out of high school and working nights at a laundry in Queens. She'd take the train every morning after her shift to audition for the chorus." Another fib. It was actually Jeremy who had worked briefly in a laundry in Queens, but he'd been fired after a month when he got caught sleeping in one of the bins. "I'd been cast as the lead in Harris Todd's newest musical"—he held for applause; there wasn't any—"and by pure luck I happened to be in the theatre for a costume fitting the day that Susan came in for the cattle-call. I went right to Mr. Todd and said, 'Harry, I've found her; I've found our Clytemnestra.'" The truth was that they were both rising young stars when they did *Troy, Ahoy!,* and actually it was Susan who had been cast first. Jeremy was still on the upward thrust of his first hit, *The Man Who Knew Mrs. Davenish*, and had been Broadway's newest bad boy— brash, insouciant, rude. Everybody had wanted him. Susan had wanted him, too. "So, as that proves, survival in this business is 90% luck, 10% talent, 20% looks, and 0% math skills. Heh, heh, heh." No one laughed, but after a minute the woman in the jogging ensemble started nodding and pointing and whispering to her husband, who pushed her away. "And then, while I still had half a season left of *Troy, Ahoy!*, Hollywood came calling. Dmitri Lawton"—the director—"came to see the show and the rest, as they say in this business, is history. After the formality of a screen test"—not a formality, really; Sam Geiss, the head of he studio, had insisted on it. He hated the sight of Jeremy and thought that seeing him on film would convince everyone that he had no talent. It didn't—"I was put under contract and I did my first picture, *Lucky Donald*." The large man with the plastic bag applauded and laughed. He kept applauding after a minute had passed, and then another. The *faux*-Gucci ladies sitting in front of him turned in their seats to glare. He didn't stop. He began to hyperventilate. Beside him, close to the wall, a sweaty, turgid woman with a tape recorder on her lap and who had—and it was unfortunate—a sort of a fetus head, stared at him. The pretty girl with the legal pad was writing, filling pages without looking up. "Anyway," Jeremy said, and the man stopped immediately and wiped his brow. Everyone turned back around. "Susan and I had already leased a place together in New York, but I convinced her to come out to L.A., which took some doing"—not really—"and at my insistence she was given the role of Saloon Girl in my next film, *A Horse For Harry Dust.*" This was true. He had used his clout to get her the part, and she went on to receive her first Academy Award nomination. And Jeremy had been very happy for her and even made her pregnant with their son, Alexander (who now wore a dress and was the lead singer of a punk rock band called "Elizabeth Kubler Ross"). When Susan went back to work two years later, she had another hit with *The Marriage Machine,* this time without him. And then she had another. Meanwhile, Jeremy was stuck doing revisionist Westerns for fascist European directors.

The door to the Oak Room was flung open and Jeremy faltered for the tiniest fraction of a second. The door bounced off the wall and slammed shut again. Standing where no one had been standing before was a woman in a tight black skirt, green high heels, and a red tube top that forced her breasts up and out like toaster pastries. Her lips were bright red and her cheeks were artlessly rouged. She wore a scarf combining prints of several species of big cat and a belt with large gold buckle in the shape of the Eiffel Tower. She seemed urgent in a way that made Jeremy wary. This type of woman was not usually allowed at the functions that he attended.

Jeremy knew that this was, no doubt, Laure-Luda. She lowered her head and locked eyes with him. Carefully, slowly, she walked down the aisle, thrusting her hips with every step.

"So, as you can see, luck is the greatest skill you can have in Hollywood," Jeremy said. Laure-Luda moved into the row behind the large man with the bag full of newspapers and sat down.

"The rewards of a career in motion pictures . . . " Laure-Luda got up from her chair as Jeremy spoke and moved to the next one. It squeaked as she sat down. She smiled. She stretched into it, arching her back. The chair screeched under the pressure. She pulled out a large paper fan, snapped it open with a flick of her wrist, and fanned herself with broad sweeps. The air conditioning was stuck on high; the lips of the old man in the jogging suit were beginning to turn blue.

"So don't let the glamour fool you, friends; a career in Hollywood is a lot of hard work. What you have to remember is that show business is a business, and Hollywood is an industry town. It is interested in—and only interested in—producing product. Excuse me," Jeremy said to Laure-Luda, "it's freezing in here. Why do you have a fan?"

"Because I am a fan," Laure-Luda said. "A very big one. It's what I do."

He cleared his throat. Where was he? "Where was I?"

The businessgirl flipped through her yellow pad. "'Hollywood is an industry town. It is interested—'"

"Thank you," Jeremy said. He smiled at her. "Thanks. Yes. Hollywood. Though we try our hardest, it is not always about art. It's not always about fun. It's not really even about friendships. Quite the opposite, really: in L.A., good friends are your worst enemies." Jeremy paused. That was quite good, really. He'd never thought of doing the comedy club circuit before but maybe that was something he should look into when he got back home. "In L.A. loyalties run about as deep as the L.A. River." He laughed heartily, but then saw that he was alone. He realized that the geographic reference was lost on these simple folk. How were they to know that the L.A. River was a bone-dry concrete ditch that ran through the city? Oh, well. He was on a roll.

"Hollywood is a town that values ambition over talent, a town of mansions on stilts on earthquake fault lines, a town where even dogs go to psychiatrists"—the businessgirl in glasses stopped writing and looked up at him. Boy, he had them now!—"and where the livelihoods of geniuses depend on the whims of idiots." He'd waited years for the chance to say that! "Too much of anything is not good, and L.A. has too much of everything. Especially agents."

Jeremy beamed. The room was stunned into silence by his eloquence. What a shame the crowd was not larger, or at least made up of better people. He was on a roll and he hated to waste it.

"Please," he said, "if anyone has any questions, don't hesitate to—" Twelve hands went up. The old couple in jogging pajamas didn't raise theirs, nor did the two teenagers who were hotel employees. The woman with the tape recorder and the fetus head sunk down lower into her chair.

Jeremy smiled down seductively at the nubile woman with the legal pad. "Yes, dear?"

"Can you be a little more positive?"

"Uh . . . "

"Mr. Hatch! Mr. Hatch!" It was the hefty fellow, the one with the newspapers.

"Yes," Jeremy said, pointing at him, "you in the back."

The man giggled and covered his mouth with his hand. "Everyone says I look like you," he said. It wasn't a kind thing to say. The man might have vaguely resembled Jeremy; that is, if Jeremy had abandoned dental hygiene in grade school, had brown eyes instead of blue, and had picked at his left ear until it bled. Then, yes, he would have looked like the man. And if Jeremy had three chins instead of just two, and if he'd worn his pants cinched above the navel. Then the resemblance would have been quite startling.

"Well, um . . . "

"That was a compliment," the man said. He grinned widely and started rocking violently in his chair. Jeremy instinctively tensed—the man was self-comforting. A sure sign of a dependency disorder. And Jeremy should know. Hadn't he himself been cast to play a pathologically dependent man in the ground-breaking and box-office shattering Best Picture nominee, *Borrowed Sorrow*, based on the novel by Guy de Langerouge? He'd been the troubled actor of choice to play all the leading psychos back in the early 70s. That was when movies had something to say.

"Any other questions?" The rocking man jabbed his hand in the air. "Yes," Jeremy said to one of the *faux*-Gucci women, the one with her initials spelled out in rhinestones on the tinted lenses of her glasses.

"You ever thought of doing comedy?" she said. "I like comedy."

What did she think he was doing now? Jeremy snorted and then quickly tried to hide it by faking a sneeze. "*Kiss Me, I'm Jim* was a comedy," Jeremy said thoughtfully. *An uproarious comedy*, actually, according to the New York Times, *with Jeremy Hatch at his edgy, surprising best*. Jeremy continued, slightly peevishly, "*The Moon Zone* was a comedy." Why pay twenty bucks if you didn't know that he'd once been featured on 60 Minutes, introduced by Mike Wallace himself, as "The New American Neurotic"? Why waste your money if you didn't know that "neurotic" was Hollywood shorthand for "self-deprecating comedian"? One would think that the paying of a tuition would presuppose at least a passing interest in the subject under study.

The rocking man pumped his arm in the air.

"Any other questions?" Jeremy said.

"Did you know Steve McQueen?" the rocking man shouted out.

"Yes," Jeremy said and looked away. "Anyone else?"

"Did he do drugs?" the rocking man said.

"Anyone?" Jeremy said. The woman with the legal pad raised her hand.

"Yes," Jeremy said gratefully.

"Do you do Shakespeare?" she said.

Was she mocking him? He couldn't be sure. If this was New York she'd either be mocking him or be stupid. If this was L.A. she'd probably be working for a PR firm. But here in America's Bread Basket it was hard to be sure. One had to be so careful with the slightest inflections. In the baboon world, for instance, inflections meant the difference, literally, between life and death. Two grunts that were indistinguishable from each other to the human ear meant two distinctly different things to the baboons. One meant, "Food is nearby," and the other meant, "I've come to kill your babies." Jeremy should know; he'd slept with the baboon consultant when he was on location shooting *Serengeti Sunrise*.

"Yes," he said, "of course I do Shakespeare. I'm an actor."

"Could you do some?" the woman said. "Only do it like you're drunk."

She *was* mocking him, the little bitch! But the *faux*-Gucci women and the rocking man clapped so persistently that he was forced to acquiesce.

Jeremy took a deep breath, closed his eyes, and bowed his head. He hadn't ever done any real Shakespeare, but he had played Jerry Cruncher in the television mini-series event of *A Tale of Two Cities*. He couldn't remember any of that, though. He exhaled, opened his eyes, and brought his head up. Slurring his words and hiccuping at several well-timed dramatic moments, he recited George C. Scott's speech from *Patton*. He hoped no one would notice.

The room was silent and Jeremy's heart raced. But then all at once they broke into applause; even, grudgingly, the man in Susan Roman T-shirt. Jeremy smiled.

"I think now would be an excellent time to take our break."

The freshly scrubbed young man in the ironed shirt leaped out of his chair before Jeremy could get around the podium. The rocking man, his plastic bag tucked safely under his arm, stomped up and stared at the back of the young man's head.

"You made me want to be an actor, Mr. Hatch," the freshly scrubbed young man said. He looked down nervously and held out his hand. Jeremy took it.

"Nice to meet you . . . ?"

"Stan. Stan Wetchel."

"Nice to meet you, Stan."

The *faux*-Gucci ladies approached and stood three feet away. Jeremy looked at them and smiled. They pulled back quickly and whispered excitedly. The rocking man turned and frowned at them, then turned his focus back to the young man's head.

"My mother was in love with you," the scrubbed boy said. "After my dad left, I mean." The *faux*-Gucci ladies stepped forward again. "She took me to see *September Day* twelve times. No exaggeration. And then *Birds Die* eighteen times. We couldn't afford a VCR."

"That's very moving," Jeremy said. He felt sorry for the boy and wished he had the energy to care more. "Just keep trying. The only way to fail is to give up."

"Thank you!" the scrubbed boy said and grabbed Jeremy's hand. "Thank you! That's brilliant!" It was actually the motto of Jeremy's Brentwood health club.

Laure-Luda waited in her seat until the *faux*-Gucci women wandered away. She pushed herself out of her chair—with a loud wrenching screech—and came up the aisle, sinuously placing each foot directly in front of the other, taking time to shift her weight. She poked her lips open with the tip of her fan. She grinned. Jeremy always found it amusing in a slightly depressing way that at the public affairs where non-industry people were allowed the women would always try to seduce him and the men would try to befriend him or seduce him, thinking . . . what? That he'd pull some strings for them? If he was so good at pulling strings, don't they think he'd pull them for himself? What did this woman, this Laure-Luda, think he was doing giving a seminar in Rondo for twenty per cent of twenty bucks? Is *that* the job she wanted?

" . . . and so in High School I took drama and acted your speech from *Winchester's Men* at assembly"—the freshly scrubbed boy was still talking; the rocking man was getting impatient and started picking his ear—"but I was never in any plays because I had to work after school because my mom was drinking by then—" Laure-Luda angled in and pushed the boy back with her shoulder.

"Mr. Hatch . . . Jeremy . . . Jer . . . I've always dreamed of meeting you face to face." She held out her hand. Jeremy took it. It was hot. Uncomfortably hot. She held on, squeezing. Jeremy pulled his hand back but she had a grip on it. He kept pulling until Laure-Luda released. He smiled his special smile.

"So," Jeremy searched for something to say, "are you an actress?"

Laure-Luda hit him on the chest with her fan.

"You're terrible!" she said.

What had he said? She giggled and rolled her head coquettishly. Jeremy thought that only twelve-year-old girls should act like twelve-year-old girls.

"Well, you're certainly pretty enough. Maybe you should try to get into some community theater here."

"Oh!" she gasped. "You!" She slapped him across the face. Flirtatiously, but a slap nonetheless. The freshly scrubbed man waved at Jeremy and blushed. He walked away quickly.

"If you'll excuse me, Laure-Luda—" Jeremy said. Laure-Luda stopped grinning and became rigid.

"How did you know my name?" she asked.

"Uh . . . "

Laure-Luda narrowed her eyes.

Jeremy faltered. "Miss Larch at . . . uh . . . "

"I knew that you'd know who I was," she said. As abruptly as she had stopped she started smiling again, only this time it was less coy. She dragged the tip of her fan down his chest. "You're terrible," she purred. The rocking man snorted.

"I hope you enjoy the second half of the seminar. Pardon me, but I really have to run and find Miss Larch."

"You better not make me jealous."

"Pardon me," he said and moved past her.

"Mr. Hatch!" the rocking man said, "Mr. Hatch!"

"I'm not kidding," Laure-Luda called after him.

Miss Larch was sitting on the sectional couch in the lobby, counting the money in her cash box.

"Miss Larch," Jeremy said. Miss Larch quickly slammed the lid of the cash box shut.

"Mr. Hatch. I trust everything is going well."

"Yes, thank you. Quite well. I think they're getting their money's worth." Miss Larch's lips became thin. Jeremy continued, "Not a bad crowd."

She looked at him to see if he was kidding. "No. I suppose not."

"What'd we end up with? Eighteen people?"

"Seventeen." Jeremy had counted eighteen. Still, seventeen at twenty bucks, 20% of that.

"That's not bad," Jeremy said. "Could be worse."

"Yes. Unfortunately it will barely be enough to cover our costs. Printing up the brochures"—which couldn't be that much, considering all the money they'd saved by not hiring a proofreader—"the rental of the Oak Room, your hotel room"—without the key to the liquor cabinet; things were suddenly becoming clear—"the snacks"—the snacks? Miss Larch looked over her shoulder and Jeremy followed her look. His eighteen apostles were huddled around a table that had been set with two huge platters of miniature muffins. The rocking man was putting them into his mouth two at a time. The old couple pretending to be joggers were shoveling them into a paper bag. "We were hoping to pay you an honorarium, but after doing the accounting . . . " Miss Larch said. Marv had specifically said percentage, not honorarium.

Jeremy smiled broadly. "Oh, don't worry about that. I'm just happy to be here."

"Oh, that's so nice."

"But Marv, my agent . . . I believe that you've spoken?"

Miss Larch tried but failed to hide her contempt. "Yes. We've spoken."

"Yes. He asked me, do I give you the receipt for my airline ticket?"

"Oh. I thought Marv said something about you taking care of that."

"Oh. Did he? Oh, then that's fine. He usually handles this sort of thing," Jeremy said, "I'm just happy to be here."

"That's so nice."

"Mr. Hatch! Wait! Mr. Hatch!" The rocking man had spotted Jeremy and was trundling toward him.

"Will you excuse me?"

"Certainly."

Jeremy ducked behind a potted ficus and into the bar. He went to the far corner where the light was dimmest and took a stool. Had it come to this? Had it finally, inevitably, come to this?

"What'll it be?" said the bartender, a burly man with more than a whiff of the Marines about him.

"A Pellegrino with lime."

"No Pellegrino," the bartender said. "Sorry. But we do have the lime."

"Scotch neat," Jeremy said.

"We have Perrier," the bartender said, "and plain old soda water, of course."

"A double," Jeremy said. "Scotch neat. A double."

The bartender grunted. Jeremy wondered if the man knew who he was. He poured the drink and set it on the bar in front of Jeremy. Jeremy looked at him full in the face and smiled. "Thank you," he said. The bartender looked down and backed away.

Jeremy gulped the scotch and breathed quickly through his nose to stop from throwing up. He felt the burning, felt it trickle down past his diaphragm, diffuse and spread, and he knew he'd be all right.

"Excuse me," he said to the bartender. The bartender stepped over, grabbed the bottle, and poured Jeremy another.

"Want fish?" the bartender asked. The man did remember him! Jeremy smiled. That line was from the movie he did with Roland Fletcher called *The Battle Room*. Roland had said that to him in the film's climactic scene— "Want fish?" It had been Roland's last movie before he died.

"Not as long as I have an American breath left in my lungs, Cowboy," Jeremy said to the bartender, because that is what he said to Roland in the movie.

The bartender shrugged. "Suit yourself." Jeremy looked down. The man was holding a small dish of little salty crackers shaped like fish. He tossed them in the trash and went to the sink and rinsed out the bowl.

Jeremy sipped his drink. Where had he gone wrong? Or had he? Maybe the world had just gone wrong, had stopped appreciating the good things like talent and complexity and decency, and instead opted for the unchallenging, the easy laugh, the visceral. The world today didn't want to have to think; the world today couldn't be bothered with romance.

Susan's career, of course, was busier than ever. But there's got to be some sense of emptiness when you become incorporated, when your name is traded on the New York Stock Exchange like pesticides or Kleenex or DNA technology. And, sure, Jeremy could have stayed a success, too, if he'd done every script that came his way, regardless of quality, and then held press conferences to announce that it would be his last movie. Susan had retired—what?—six or seven times now, by Jeremy's count.

Jeremy's glass was empty, but not for long. "Thanks," he said to the bartender.

Maybe he should call her.

The third drink went down much easier than the previous two. Smoothly, as a matter of fact.

Jeremy got up and went to the phone booth in the corner by the cigarette machine. He dialed. A man answered.

"Hello?" It was Sid Poppity. Sid Poppity was Jeremy's old agent and Susan's new husband. The two events had transpired concurrently. Now Jeremy was stuck with Marv, and Jeremy's son, Alexander, had taken Sid's last name as his own.

"Hey, Sid."

"Oh, Christ!"

Jeremy heard Susan's voice in the background: "Who in Christ's name is calling at this hour?"

"Take a wild guess," Sid said, holding the phone away from his face.

"Oh, Christ. You're kidding?" Susan said.

"See for yourself."

"Oh, Christ."

Jeremy heard the phone drop. He sucked in his breath and held it. He changed hands because the phone was sweaty.

"Do you own a fucking watch or did you pawn that, too?" It was Susan's voice, very loud.

"Such eloquence," Jeremy said.

"Didn't that nice judge make it very clear that you'd be violating the restraining order if you ever called here?"

"Susan, believe me, I'm much more than a hundred yards away from you at the moment."

"This counts, Jeremy, you know that. Phone calls count. The judge said so."

"I just . . . I'm in Rondo."

"*Rondo?*"

"North Dakota. I'm . . . I'm giving a seminar."

"Oh, Christ."

"What?" Sid said in the background. Susan cupped the receiver with her hand, but Jeremy could still hear.

"He's in South Dakota giving a seminar," Susan said.

"Oh, Christ," Sid said.

"North Dakota," Jeremy said. "It's North Dakota."

Susan uncupped the phone. "Oh, Jeremy," she said, "a *seminar?* Jesus Christ. It's come to that."

"I only wanted to call because—"

Susan interrupted as though she'd just smelled something. "Have you been drinking?"

"What?"

Susan cupped the receiver again. "He's been drinking," she said to Sid.

"Hang up," Sid said.

"But he's giving seminars," Susan said.

"I don't give a rat's ass. Hang up."

"But, Sid, if I were ever—"

Jeremy hung up. He closed his eyes and felt the pain fill his skull like sulfuric acid. Perhaps if he ate something he might feel better. He walked out of the bar and over to the muffin table. All he found were translucent grease stains on the paper tablecloth and crumbs. He walked back into the Oak Room and quickly up the aisle to the podium and held onto it to keep from falling down.

The rocking man bolted out of his seat and ran up to him.

"I went to an agency that handles celebrity look-alikes"—in Rondo? Jeremy found it astonishing that there would be a great need for celebrity look-alikes in Rondo—"and they said, 'hey, you look like that guy,' but they wouldn't pay me, so I left. And then I went to another agency—"

"In Rondo?"

"—and they said they thought I was you for a minute, but they didn't have a camera, so—"

"You know what?" Jeremy interrupted, "I'm actually going to try to be a little linear now, okay? For the sake of the other people. Okay?"

"Okay, Mr. Hatch," the rocking man said meekly. He went back to his chair and slumped down. Jeremy felt guilty and was surprised that he did considering the severe throbbing in his head.

"It's all right if you call me Jeremy."

"Okay, Mr. Jeremy."

"No. Just Jeremy."

"Okay, Mr. Jeremy." The man began to giggle into his fist and rock violently.

The woman with the tape recorder suddenly jumped to her feet. She looked around her, confused, and quickly sat down again and blushed.

"Excuse me," one of the *faux*-Gucci women said. "Excuse me!"

"Yes?"

"I did your wife's zodiac chart for you," she said, "I do horoscopes. Kind of a hobby, you might say, but I'm thinking of—"

"Thank you," Jeremy said, "but we're divorced now."

"Not according to the Catholic church, you're not."

Was he in hell? It suddenly occurred to him that he might be in hell. He'd auditioned once for a movie where the lead character starts to think that everyone around him was crazy, when it actually turns out he was dead and in hell. What was that movie called? *Seventh Circle? Eighth Circle?* Something Circle.

"That's very nice," he said, "but we're not Catholic."

"I don't care what you say you are."

Jeremy wondered if the people in the room could actually see his temples pounding. He looked down at the old woman in the front row. "Can you see that?" he said. He tilted his head slightly. The woman shifted in her seat. "That," Jeremy said, pointing at his head. "Can you see it?" The woman mumbled something and turned to her husband to see what she should do.

"Mr. Jeremy!" the rocking man called out, "Mr. Jeremy!"

"Will you just shut up, you schiz?"

The *faux*-Gucci women gasped. The surly Susan Roman fan snapped upright out of his slouch. A heavy silence overtook the room. The rocking man pulled his plastic bag to his chest and hugged it. He rocked himself in short, forceful jerks. "I have a disorder."

Jeremy tried to think of something he could say. Instead he rubbed his forehead vigorously.

The woman with the yellow pad looked up at Jeremy. "He has a disorder, you creep."

"Yeah? Well I have a headache."

"I don't think that was a very nice thing to say," one of the hotel employees said.

Jeremy held his breath for a moment and the pulsing came faster in his head. He looked at the man in the Susan Roman T-shirt, glowering at him, challenging him. He looked at the woman with the tape recorder and the fetus head, her pink unformed lips twisting into a frown. The woman with the legal pad scribbled with determination; the rocking man bounced like a piston; the *faux*-Gucci women crossed their arms in disapproval and recrimination.

"All right," Jeremy said and wiped the sweat from his neck. "All right. Let's cut the crap. Surviving in Hollywood? Here you go, here's your twenty bucks worth. And it's surviving in Hollywood, not *the* Hollywood, you morons. Here's the number one rule: you don't. I didn't survive. I'm giving seminars in goddamned Rondo, North Dakota, for Christ's sake! I'd like to see that as survival on anyone's map. There's no survival and no redemption. And there sure as fuck is no mercy. Hollywood is a machine with gears and it chews you up and swallows you and then passes you like bad clams. Movie stars? Like Susan Roman? Just an industry. What you mindlessly worship is a shell, a molded plastic money-making commodity. If there was ever a human being called Susan Roman it's gone now. Hollywood sucks the innocence out of you, sucks the compassion and the honesty and anything else that's good and all that's left is a hunger, a raw, consumptive hunger. *That's* surviving in Hollywood."

The delicate man in the Susan Roman T-shirt stood up, threw his chair back, and stormed out. Jeremy took off his jacket and tried to undo his collar, but only managed to pull the button off. "Do you think Hollywood gives a fuck about the people in the movies? How about the people who watch the movies? I've got news for you, friends: they'd film a blister pop if they thought someone would pay to see it. You're idiots and we all hate you and we all hate each other and we all hate ourselves. Good night and thank you for coming."

The old couple in the front row turned and looked at each other. The man groped around for his cane and his wife wordlessly picked it up and put it in his hand. As the man struggled to get to his feet the woman got her purse out from under her chair, put it on her lap, opened it to make sure everything was there, and, without looking, reached over and grabbed her husband's elbow and hoisted him up. He grunted and started down the aisle ahead of her. "It sure was no Steve Allen, I'll say that," he said, trusting that she was behind him. "Now *that* was a seminar."

The freshly scrubbed boy had turned bright red. He was on the verge of tears. He stood without looking at Jeremy and pushed past the *faux*-Gucci women and left. The *faux*-Gucci women clucked their tongues and shook their heads as they gathered together their scarves and purses and tote bags and jackets.

"Oh, and P.S.," Jeremy said. No one turned around, no one looked up. "We have to pay for our own stars on Hollywood Boulevard, you know."

Laure-Luda looked remarkably unpleasant when angry, or frustrated, or when her stunted needs were thwarted. She looked unpleasant now. She strode up to Jeremy.

"I don't think I like you anymore," she said, her pout no longer a come-on but a threat.

"You never really did, Laure-Luda."

"I think you're fat and your skin has big pores and your eyes are all yellowy."

Jeremy smiled patiently. "All right, Laure-Luda."

"And up close you smell old."

Jeremy sighed. "You're a bit of a lunatic, aren't you? They make a lot of drugs now, you know, that would probably help. May I suggest Clozapine?"

Jeremy walked past her before she had a chance to hit him.

"I was voted Best Hair in the Miss Tri-State Pageant three years in a row, you asshole!" she screamed at him. He kept moving.

He walked quickly through the lobby, past Miss Larch (who looked down at her watch), out the front doors, across the parking lot, through the dumpsters, over the lawn, past the shrubs, and stopped when he reached the walkway that ran alongside the Rondo River. It was chillier than he would have suspected and he'd left his jacket in the Oak Room. He started walking along the river away from the hotel.

What had he actually done with his life? Anything worthwhile? Had he changed the face of the planet even the slightest bit, for bad or for good? He'd certainly frightened a roomful of Midwesterners out of ever going into the acting profession, that's for sure. But had he made a contribution? Jeremy supposed he had brought Alexander into the world, but that could be considered another failure, depending how you looked at it. He was bankrupt, he'd screwed up his marriage, his agent barely spoke to him. He probably had grandchildren by children he didn't even know he had. He'd dedicated his life to what? To make believe. A system where fortunes were made and lost in the time it takes cream to turn. And he'd been one of the lucky ones. He'd at least had a career. There were tens of thousands more or less like him—better looking, less better looking, taller, shorter, more talented, less talented—who'd risked everything for a dream and had failed and died. But what was that dream that they were all chasing, anyway? The dream of having strangers applauding because you can convincingly pretend to feel something? The dream of being prettier, being richer, or that people will like you better because you have more cars? The dream of never having to pump your own gas or cook your own food or hunt for bargains in a mall? What dream, exactly, were they all pursuing?

Ahead of him on the path Jeremy saw a bench and beside that was a phone booth. He went to it. She was going to kill him. He dialed and sat down and hugged himself in the cold breeze. She probably wouldn't even answer. She knew he was still awake.

"Hello?" she answered groggily.

"Hello," he said.

She sighed. Jeremy heard Sid snoring beside her. "How was the seminar?"

"A disaster." He took a breath. "What did you expect?" He was suddenly exhausted, drained, his limbs flaccid and heavy as base metals. He wanted to shut his eyes and go to sleep. "I didn't know who else to call."

"Who else could you call?"

"Exactly."

"I certainly wouldn't want you calling Alexander. The doctors say that they've almost reintegrated his personality."

"I'm glad to hear it."

They were both quiet for a moment.

"We're not like other people, Jeremy," Susan said. "Well, you're a little more like other people than I am, of course."

"Why?" Jeremy said, "How is it we're so different?"

"Why? You think it's luck that we're who we are and they're who they are? That we get to be the stars? Wake up, Jeremy. We're like two different species. You know, like what do they call lichens? Where algaes and funguses live together? Co-dependent?"

"Symbiotic?"

"That's it. We're like that. I mean, can you imagine *living* there? In Rondo? Or those people living here?"

"But we weren't always like this. We were like them once."

"Think back, Jeremy. Can you honestly say that's true? We—you and I, everyone else out here—we were always different. Always. And we always knew it, too. We always felt apart."

And it was true. Jeremy knew it was true.

"But is it right?"

"Right schmright. Is it right that trees grow upward, or that fish swim or that the sky is blue? Right has nothing to do with it. It just is."

"Wow."

"Just come back," Susan said.

"Can I stay at your house? I think I've been evicted."

"No."

"Could you get me a part in whatever film you're working on now?"

"You know what I'm working on now, Jeremy."

"*Glass Mountain?*"

"Yes."

"Will you get me an audition?"

"No."

"Will you at least acknowledge me in restaurants?"

"No. Just come back. It's not good for you there."

"All right."

"You okay?"

"I'm fine."

"Hurry back."

"Will do."

"Okay. I have an early call time tomorrow."

"Okay."

He hung up. He supposed he didn't really have a choice. He started walking back to the hotel, but stopped. He turned around. He took off his shirt and his trousers and his shoes and his socks. He thought a swim might make him feel better.

He looked at the tiny ripples of the Rondo River and put his thumbs into the band of his boxer shorts.

"Don't do it." The voice came from behind him.

"What?" Jeremy turned around. He thought of covering himself, but then he didn't really care.

"Don't do it." It was the robust blond woman from the reception desk.

Evidently her shift was over. "It's not worth it. Things can't be that bad."

"I'm only going for a swim."

"That's what they all say. Don't do it. If you need someone to talk to I can give you a number."

"No, honestly, I just need to swim. To clear my head. It's only a creek, for Christ's sake."

"It could just as well be the Pacific Ocean as far as the Perkins' boy is concerned," she said sternly, "or the Whitlock twins."

"Thank you for your concern." Jeremy turned and inched closer to the concrete embankment.

"I won't let you. We're already at twenty-four suicides this year and that makes us tied with Minot. I'm not going to have Rondo be known as the suicide capital of the Dakotas. I'm sorry. I can't have that happen."

"What?"

The girl pulled out a police whistle and blew on it with the lungs of a farm girl.

"What are you doing?" Jeremy screamed and lunged at her. The girl stepped back and blew harder.

"All right!" Jeremy said. "All right!" He grabbed his shirt and pants and socks and shoes. "Fine. I'll just go back to my room. Maybe I have a gun. I *am* from Los Angeles."

"I'm not worried," the girl said. "You won't do it. You're mad at *me* now. Good night." The girl turned and walked away.

Oh, the presumptuous tart! He should kill himself just to spite her. He climbed back on the embankment. Perhaps suicide wasn't such a bad idea. Where, after all, was his life heading, except further degradation? And if he killed himself it would certainly make Maxwell P. Dressler look like a bastard for all the horrible things he said. And Marv would never be able to forgive himself for the cavalier way he handled Jeremy in the last few months. Susan, too, would no doubt feel pangs of guilt and probably wonder what might have been and maybe even never be able to look at Sid the same way again. But why waste a good suicide on Rondo? Plus he didn't want to have to share the headline with anything, let alone the crowning of Rondo as the new suicide capital.

He dropped his shoes onto the gravel path and stepped into them. He started walking back to the hotel. Maybe he should wait until he got back to L.A. In Hollywood celebrity suicides got the front page. They really knew how to do suicides right; they were used to it, they were set up for it. Who knows, it might even cinch his chances for an honorary Oscar. They had a soft spot for that sort of thing.

Pieces of Delores

HER NAME WAS DELORES, but the people at work called her Dolorous.
But only behind her back, of course.
And they were only kidding.
Sort of.

"Over here, Detective," Patrolman Donder called from the ditch ten
yards away. I was sitting in the squad car to get out of the heat. He was talking to me. Detective Nicky Heart, LAPD.

I put out my cigarette, put my shoes back on, and walked down the
slope through the dry brown scrub. I looked down to where Donder was
pointing. Next to a rock was another foot. Well, *the* other foot. This one,
like the other one, was severed just above the ankle. I picked it up with two
fingers and my handkerchief. It was pretty mangled. Cheap shoes can really
do a number on a woman's feet. I guess you get what you pay for, as my
hair stylist always used to say.

The Wilmingtons, Butch and Rainie, were Mallwalkers. Every morning
at eight o'clock sharp they would walk past the Nature Company and the
Disney Store, deliberately pumping their arms and breathing quickly and
loudly through their mouths, putting on the miles; past the Gap, the Radio
Shack, the Mrs. Fields, the Mrs. See's, and the Colonel Sanders. They
proudly wore their canary yellow T-shirts that had "MALLWALKERS"
appliquéed in block letters across the chest and "RAINIE" (or "BUTCH")
appliquéed on the back.

Not everyone wore one, not everyone got into the spirit of the thing that
made the whole thing worthwhile. Why even do it if you don't want to have
fun? Rainie recollected one girl from a while back—a girl who always

seemed lonely, and there was certainly no surprise in that. This girl only ever walked by herself, never even *trying* to make any friends, never bothering to say a neighborly thing to anyone. Straight, drab brown hair. No make-up. Chewed her nails. Always wore long skirts, too, and never a "MALLWALKERS" shirt. Never even bought one. And she would always just stop without any warning in front of some store window or other and you'd practically have to knock her down. And never an "excuse me."

Rainie didn't much like her. Unfriendly girl. And you're not going to make any friends unless you're friendly back. Butch, well, Butch pretty much got along with everyone.

Butch and Rainie liked the mall at this time of the day, everything all closed up and peaceful, no teenagers. Oh, of course they liked it at other times, too, but early in the mornings, before the kiosks were rolled out and the music was turned on, it was just like it was their very own mall.

We didn't have much to go on. Just pieces. A patch of dull, unconditioned hair that we'd found snagged on a beer can down by the concrete river bank. Brown. The feet, of course. A pair of underpanties that had "Wednesday" silkscreened on the front. It was Tuesday, which meant the evidence was at least seven days old. The parts we found so far didn't look chewed up enough to have been lying around L.A. for seven days, which meant we were looking at a possible torture scenario. Or else our Jane Doe wasn't as diligent with regards to her undergarments as she would have liked known. Either way, not exactly a great send-off.

We had a left ear—which told us that she had a taste for turquoise jewelry from the Home Shopping Channel—and fingers, five so far, three from the left hand and two from the right. A nail chewer, and partial to "Passion Fruit Sunset" nail varnish.

We took our baggies back to the station and Donder ran the fingers for prints.

One Delores Sperrow. Thirty-eight years old; born on February 29. A single gal. Lived at 17 Perdido Road. Worked at Libby, Dorsett, Seldom and Moe. We decided to check there first since it was next door.

Brad looked around the office and wondered when he would get stuck, when his momentum would stop and he would get old. Aging wasn't a process, as we would all like to believe, as advertisers and the makers of dietary supplements would like us to believe. Old age was a toggle switch— you were young, then you stopped being young. You grew a spur that snagged on a particular time; you stopped flowing and started complaining. Then you just stayed there until you died.

He saw it happen to his parents, of course, in the 1950s, and you could pinpoint it to the day that they got married. All forward motion just stopped. His mother's hairstyle never changed again. His dad wore the same shirt, or the same type, in every photograph since Eisenhower was president. Gone forever was the carefree, hope-filled prankster on leave in Dusseldorf that Brad had seen in the pictures taken mere months before his father had tied the knot and grew his spur. Brad saw his older brother, Greg, get snagged in the 1970s, due, basically, to the pot.

The new temp they'd just hired, Loretta, hadn't become stuck. Life was still a prowl for her, all men were still viable targets. She still bought new clothes every week, stylish ones. She wasn't who she was going to be yet. Not like Shirley in accounts. Shirley used to be cute, kind of fun. But Brad watched as she detached from the flow. She began to wear the same set of clothes for days at a time. She began layering her make-up, wearing too much and not properly taking off the old. She stopped going out, stopped talking about dates that she'd had and instead started talking about television shows. She called them, "my shows." She'd talk with real concern about how the characters were coping with their lives, as if they were her friends, all the time not noticing, or not caring, that hems had come loose or collars had become frayed.

And then there was that girl Delores. Brad only remembered her name because they used to make fun of it. They used to call her "Dolorous." Simon in payroll had come up with it, of course, being the only one at the time who even knew what it meant. Simon had also come up with "Deloresque." If something was particularly pathetic, like Delores, they would call it "Deloresque." Once Loretta had called a newspaper article "Deloresque." It was about a lonely, heavy woman (there was a picture) who married a man on death row. She'd never even seen him in person, because he was in solitary, but she had written him letters. On the night before he was executed they were married through a video hook-up. Nobody in the coffee room had seen Delores in the doorway when Loretta had said it. But Delores had only smiled dolorously and turned around and walked to the ladies' room. Delores hadn't been stuck anywhere; she had never been in the flow to begin with.

Brad had been at Libby, Dorsett, Seldom and Moe for three years and hoped to Christ his spur hadn't popped out without his knowing it and anchored him there. He looked down at his blazer, a blazer he had purchased a year ago on sale. It occurred to him that he really hadn't been looking to improve his position in a while. Maybe he should start looking for another job before it was too late. Or join the Peace Corps, although even the thought of that made him want to take a nap. Maybe he should take up a sport. Maybe he should cancel his subscription to TV Guide, which he'd started reading from cover to cover the day each new issue arrived.

It wasn't a good sign. No. Not good at all.

Ruthie Waters picked up the new file. Things went as far as they could go before they got to Ruthie. Not an easily daunted woman, she wasn't trained as much as she was selectively unleashed. Her social skills were not highly developed, and it was for this reason that she excelled at her job. Things could conceivably be bleak for someone like Ruthie. It was very lucky indeed that she had found her niche.

Files came to Ruthie when all the gently worded reminders, when the final notices, when the suspended privileges and the veiled threats all failed to elicit a response. Ruthie Waters was the heavy artillery. Ruthie Waters meant business. You don't pay your Mastercard bill, you deal with Ruthie.

Delores Sperrow's outstanding balance was $149.00. It was strange. Delores Sperrow had always paid off her balance every month, and was never late. But Ruthie had seen that before. She'd seen everything before. Delores Sperrow wasn't picking up her phone, the file said. She hadn't been to work. They said she'd quit. After sixteen years? Ruthie placed the open file down on her desk and cracked her knuckles. No problem. She'd find this Delores Sperrow and have her weeping like a baby inside of five minutes.

The offices of Libby, Dorsett, Seldom and Moe were on the third floor. We were greeted at the reception desk by a bulbous, raven-haired temp with a set of cassavas that were so ripe they were practically jam. Temp: short for "temptress."

"We're here about Delores Sperrow," I said. "This is Donder. I'm Detective Nicky Heart, LAPD."

"I'm only a temp," she said. God, I'm good at my job.

"I'm still Detective Heart. Did you know Delores Sperrow?"

She smiled and fellated the end of her pencil. "What would you want with Delores Sperrow?" She licked her big, red lips; full lips, moist lips.

From behind me I could feel the heat starting to come off of Donder, so I stepped forward. "Which desk was Delores's?"

"Over there," the vixen said, thrusting out her chest and pointing over her shoulder, "next to the janitor's closet."

"Thank you," I said. "Jot down your home phone number. I may have some further questions."

She giggled and started scribbling. Loretta. My nephew's babysitter was named Loretta. Donder and I walked over to Delores's desk. Not a particularly nice place for a desk, next to the janitor's closet. Not after sixteen years with the firm.

The desk top was neat. Not neat in some compulsive or fanatical way—something worthy of finely wrought detective insight—but neat in a boring way. No firecracker, this Miss Sperrow. A gray blotter with coffee rings in the left hand corner. Three pencils and a red pen, also on the left hand side. An ashtray holding the torn corners of envelopes with stamps that had escaped a postmark. A little plaque, like from a novelty store, that read, simply, "Endure." A dusty greeting card. This I picked up.

On the front, surrounded by a border of twined irises and daffodils, were the words, "You're Somebody's Somebody Special." An *amour*? Could lead to something. I opened the card. It said, "So take care of that great smile." It was mass-printed notice from her dentist telling Delores that she needed her teeth cleaned. It was from a Dr. M. K. Singer, D.D.S. Dr. Singer; I made a note of it. I've dealt with my share of dentists in these ritualistic dismemberment cases before. Something in their temperament.

"Excuse me, can I help you?" I turned around. It was a pasty-faced consumptive in last year's suit who looked like he needed some fresh air.

"Who are you?" I said.

"I'm Brad Cox. I'm the office manager. Who are you?"

"Nicky Heart. Detective. LAPD. This is Donder. We're investigating the murder of Delores Sperrow."

"*Murder?*" this Brad said. He would've gone pale, but he was already pale. His right eye twitched. "*Dolorous?*"

"'Dolorous'?" I said, "What's 'Dolorous'?"

He twitched again.

"That's . . . well, it's just sort of a joke. We were only kidding. You know, Delores . . . Dolorous."

"No, I don't know, Dolorous. What's it mean, Dolorous?"

"Dolorous. It means, you know, sort of sad. Dismal."

"And you think that's funny?"

"We were only kidding! We never said it to her face!" Brad looked quickly at the temp, who looked at me and smiled. Oh, those lips! I suddenly wished I was wearing my harmonica costume.

"When was the last time you saw Delores Sperrow?"

"Last Friday." Last Friday. That was the underpanties question settled.

"Was she prone to truancy?"

"What?"

"Was she prone to truancy?"

"Uh, no. Not since I've been here. Never missed a day."

"And how long have you been here?"

"Three years. Before that I managed a restaurant up near—"

"Don't leave town," I said.

"What do you mean, don't leave town?" he said with more spleen than I would've given him credit for. I could understand his frustration. It must be tough to be a closeted homosexual and not make enough money to afford a decent wardrobe.

"Just what I said, Cowboy, don't leave town. Hitch your mount to the post. Set a spell." If I'd seen it once I'd seen it a million times. Our boy Brad was just the type who'd chop up lonely secretaries into their component pieces. He fit the profile. Call it a hunch. Call me a professional.

Delores didn't have any pictures of loved ones on her desk. I'm a cat person, she'd always said.

Delores never actually owned a cat. Have you seen the price of cat food these days, she'd say. So she didn't have any pictures of cats, either.

She did buy a goldfish on a whim, for a dollar ninety-nine, but that wasn't what you'd call a pet. It was more of an ornament, really. She named it Louise, and then Charlie. It didn't make any difference to the fish. Not like it would to a real pet.

Frelene slammed the receiver into its cradle. God Almighty, how she hated inconsiderateness! Delores Sperrow was overdue for her biannual cleaning. Frelene had called last week and the week before, but there was no answer. And this, of course, was after the courtesy notice that Frelene had mailed personally—first class—over a month ago. Frelene had gone to the printer herself, had selected the greeting card style with the special pleasant message. Sure, she could've just chosen some ordinary single-sided cards on inferior stock, but Frelene had always thought that it was important to just go that extra mile to make peoples' lives more sunny. Sure, the greeting cards were more expensive, what with the four-color floral design and all, and hadn't she just *heard* it from Dr. Singer when he'd found the invoice! And in the end what good did it do? On people like that Delores Sperrow, such thoughtfulness was just a waste of time. Why did she even continue to bother with these people? Now she got a recording that Delores's number was no longer in service, and there was no forwarding number. Just plain rudeness. Frelene spent her valuable time trying to make sure these people had healthy teeth and they don't even have the consideration to call when they moved. Frelene hoped that Delores's teeth rotted in her head.

Donder and I went to Delores's apartment next. The Super (an over-statement if ever there was one) downstairs (a bitter child actress from the 1930's. I guess that's what happens when you start drinking when you're twelve) wouldn't let us into the building at first, until I shattered her favorite vase with the butt of my gun and made vague references about a cousin of mine who worked for the Health Department.

Inside the apartment we found no signs of a struggle. Or any passion whatsoever. A bloated dead goldfish floating in a two-pint fishbowl on the window sill. A new, unworn T-shirt draped over the back of the cheaply upholstered sofa. I picked this up. It had "MALLWALKERS" written across the front.

Mallwalkers. Hmmm. I made a note.

On the coffee table was a book. I picked it up. *The Rights of Lefts*. Now, now; maybe our little Delores was a deeper puddle than we'd originally sus-pected. Maybe she did have passions. Something pinko by the looks of things. I wondered what Brad had to do with all of this. Maybe Delores knew too much.

I turned the book over. It was by some Trotskyite named Louis Fremont. Under his picture it said, "They call us sinistromanual—" *Sinistromanual?* What the hell does that mean?

"Hey, Donder!" I yelled to Donder, who was in the kitchen, "What the hell does 'sinistromanual' mean?" Donder came into the living room and shrugged. He turned and went back into the kitchen. I read on: "—and that illustrates just how deeply rooted the prejudices are when it comes to per-sons of left-handedness." Persons of left-handedness? Like I was going to swallow that with a cube of sugar. I opened the book to a page with a folded corner. " . . . my first situation, as a teacher in elementary school. In that class was a student whom I shall call Delores S. She was extremely shy, reticent, and believed by many on the faculty to be mildly retarded." What? I skimmed down the page. Fremontski went on to write that Delores was bullied and "disaffected," whatever that means, until one day it was discovered that she wasn't a retard at all, only left-handed. Someone Fremont wants to call "Sandy W." threw a geometry compass at Delores's head and Delores caught it, right through the palm, with her left hand. Good Christ! These liberal pansies will make a case out of anything to sell a book! What's next— telethons for people with moles?

I tossed the book on the sofa and went to the desk in the corner. There was a receipt for some special order from the Razor's Edge Book Shop (how fitting) on San Vicente. There were also messages on the answering machine. Eight of them; a motherlode of evidence. We detectives dream of things like this. I pressed play.

"Hello there, Delores, this is Frelene from Dr. Singer's office. You're due for your biannual cleaning. I've tentatively set you up for next Tuesday, because I know you like Tuesdays." Likes Tuesdays. Hmmm. I made a note. "Nine a.m.? Please call if that's not a good time for you. Thanks. This is Frelene at Dr. Singer's office."

The dentist connection again. Things were falling into place. I wondered what Brad had to do with this teeth thing.

The machine beeped. Donder came out of the kitchen eating a sandwich. "Miss Delores Sperrow, this is Ruthie Waters from Collection Services. It would be in your best interest to get back to me as soon as you get this. My number is—" I hit the erase. I knew this Ruthie Waters. She was an adversary from way back.

"I found this on the fridge," Donder said with his mouth full. He held up a photo. I grabbed it. It was a picture of Delores and some knob in a party hat. He had his arm around her shoulder and was laughing. Delores wasn't smiling. She was looking down at the floor, looking limp.

The next four messages were from Frelene and chronicled her rapid descent into psychotic paranoia. Apparently Delores's teeth being clean was a big deal with Frelene, and she was downright ferocious in her last message, asserting her lack of concern as to whether or not Delores wound up as a "toothless hag" (her words). The last message was from Ruthie Waters, who growled.

Delores had been born on February 29th and perhaps that was when it all started. She didn't have a birthday every year, like other kids. Sure, they celebrated on March 1st when it didn't happen to be a leap year, which it almost never was. But March 1st was not her birthday.

Also, she was born in a trauma center. She was premature, and the ambulance driver had misunderstood the situation (he thought he had a fat lady with appendicitis) so he took Mrs. Sperrow (who, in the driver's defense, really was a bit jowly) to the closest medical facility. There were no problems, as it turned out, other than the usual ones, and Delores came out relatively healthy. But a trauma center is a place where people generally go when they are dying. It just has a different ambiance, is all.

The driver was later fired after another incident when he drove the ambulance through a florist's window and they found a bottle of rum under the driver's seat.

Mrs. Parlor was having her pins removed today. After three months, thank God.

She hadn't seen Delores from across the hall in days. She was a nice girl, Mrs. Parlor thought. Quiet, perhaps a little too quiet for her own good (not that Mrs. Parlor was complaining), but very nice just the same. Delores had helped Mrs. Parlor along in her recovery after that night when, three months ago, Mrs. Parlor had come hurtling across the hall, screeching in pain, and crumpled at Delores's door.

Mrs. Parlor had gone to the cosmetic surgery lab at Pylex International and had undergone a lipophagous bacterial facelift. The dosage, however, had been miscalculated and things had gone wrong. Quite wrong. Delores had taken it upon herself to care for Mrs. Parlor, who was a widow, and had become something of a whiz at designing menus using only soft foods. But more than just being a source of liquid meals, Delores had also been an invaluable source of solace. She was there as a hand for Mrs. Parlor to squeeze when the pain had been so unbearable; there to read light romances to her when the nights had become too horrible; there to hold Mrs. Parlor's shaking frame when Mrs. Parlor had looked in the mirror for the first time and had seen her face, which kind of sucked itself in under her cheekbones.

But where was Delores today, the big day? Mrs. Parlor was ecstatic and wanted Delores to be with her, to share her joy that everything would finally be all right again. Delores certainly deserved to be there to share the moment.

Mrs. Parlor reckoned that she would call her niece. She didn't live far from Mrs. Parlor, and she had a car. A nice girl, her niece. Still single, which was a pity because she had such a pretty face.

"Did you lock the door?"

"Um . . ." Donder tried the knob. It opened. He reached in, locked the door and slammed it shut. We were no more than two steps down the hall when the door opposite Delores's apartment was flung open. I jumped back. The woman standing there looked like her face had been freeze-dried and then shattered. And then reassembled by a wino. She was peeking around the door frame, watching us. I think she was smiling, though I couldn't be sure.

"You the police?" she said.

Donder stepped behind me.

"Congenital?" I said, nodding sympathetically.

"What?" she said.

"Congenital?" I said, nodding sympathetically. I pointed at her face.

"No," she sighed, "no. I just had the pins out." She stepped forward. "You the cops or aren't you?"

"Nicky Heart, LAPD," I said, "and this is Patrolman Donder. Also LAPD. And you are?"

"Mrs. Parlor. Lotus Parlor."

"Mrs. Parlor," I said, "do you by any chance know what the word 'dolorous' means?"

"Yes," she said, one eye drifting up toward what was either her hairline or a fungal growth, the other sinking down her cheek toward her chin. "It means sad, sort of dismal. Where's Miss Sperrow?"

"May we come in?" I wouldn't have asked, but I'd realized that she didn't have three nostrils but just a really deep dent on the bridge of her nose. Mrs. Parlor held the door open.

Once we were in her little sitting room, sitting on her little furniture, she explained about the pins.

"You see," Mrs. Parlor said, "I went to Pylex International for an experimental procedure they're working on. It's a bacterial facelift. They took that flesh-eating bacteria and modified it, or so they thought. Made some of it what they call lipophagous."

"They call it what?"

"Lipophagous. Little bacterias that like to eat human fat cells. Well, they inject it under the skin at various places under the jaw and below the ears, places they call deposit centers. And these little bacterias just clear away all the fat and it's supposed to make the skin tighter. But it's experimental, you

see. And something went wrong. They—the little bacterias—they got too
hungry, and once they cleared out my deposit centers they ate through my
jaw bone. I had to have pins."

"This is all very enlightening, Mrs. Parlor—"

"The night it happened, the night the bacterias got so rambunctious,
Miss Sperrow saved my life! I don't have anyone, you know. Mr. Parlor died
some years back, and my niece, well, my niece—"

"Uh, Mrs. Parlor—"

"Miss Sperrow took me to the emergency. And for the last three months
she's managed to stop by every night to check up on me and make me
dinners. I must say, she's become quite the little whiz when it comes to full
meals in a blender. But no more puree for me! No, siree! It's steak and garlic
toast and crunchy tater skins from now on! You wouldn't believe the
settlement I got from Pylex! Out of court, naturally."

"When did you last see Delores Sperrow?"

"Last week. Friday, I think. She was supposed to take me to get my pins
out. But I never heard from her, and she wouldn't come to her door. I had
to get my niece, Trudy, to take me. She doesn't live far. And she has a car.
She's a nice girl, Trudy. Attractive in her own way."

"Thank you, Mrs.—"

"It's such a shame what she's done with her hair. I mean, it's certainly
not going to help her find a good husband looking like that. I worry about
her. I think maybe it's the crowd she's fallen in with. I mean, who ever heard
of women driving motorcycles?"

Mitchell could see it the moment he walked into the book store and
looked up to the counter, that look on the clerk's face; the eyes narrowing
and the lips tightening to a thin white line. Mitchell could see that the clerk

was an unhappy man and was bolstering all his unpleasantness, daring Mitchell to approach. Why even work with the public if you're so naturally surly? Mitchell would never dream of acting surly at *his* work, even if sometimes he really wanted to. He got paid to do his job, after all. But lately everywhere he went he saw that this surliness was becoming a service industry standard. Life was becoming just one big source of friction.

"Hello," Mitchell said as pleasantly as possible, as pleasantly as his natural defenses would allow. The clerk pulled his shoulders up to just below the ears and a vein on his left temple began to protrude. Mitchell drew a breath. "I would like to special order a book, if I may."

The clerk shifted his weight and rolled his eyes as if his surliness had been justified. Mitchell had expected that. He had seen it before. Just that morning, in fact, when he'd stopped at a cafe to get a coffee and wound up leaving empty-handed and with the girl behind the counter guffawing. But, really, what else were these clerks there for than to take special orders? What other purpose?

"You have to pay in advance," the clerk said with a superior sigh. "In full."

Blatant abuse of position, thought Mitchell. Mitchell was not entirely happy with his lot in life, either, but he did what had to be done. He felt no compulsion to vent his dissatisfaction indiscriminately.

"But I have never paid in advance before and I often special order." It was less a monetary issue, of course, than one of principle. Mitchell took it all day long when he was on the clerk's side of the counter, and he refused to take it now.

"Listen, Chum, you wanna special order, you pay in advance." The clerk picked up a magazine and leafed through it.

"But I've ordered thousands, well, maybe hundreds, no, actually, probably thousands of dollars worth of books from this store and I've never had to pay in advance. So it's not as though I don't *patronize* this store." Mitchell had let a flippant tone slip into his voice. But Mitchell's newly found mettle

did not win over the clerk. In fact, the clerk met Mitchell's snideness with
that of his own. He'd obviously been waiting for an excuse.

"You wanna see what I got back here?" The clerk was very close to
yelling. This made Mitchell uncomfortable. "I got two hundred bucks
worth of Guy de Langerouge! This little rabbitty broad ordered it. And *she*
was a regular customer, too! I've been calling her all week, no answer. You
ever read that shit? You ever even *heard* of Guy de Langerouge? You tell me
who's gonna buy these now? Huh? *Huh?*"

Mitchell sank back down. "Why don't you send them back?" he offered.

"Cause they won't take them back! Cause they're a *special order!*"

Mitchell coughed nervously. He looked down at the counter top. "Will
you take Discover?"

I pulled over to the side of the road as we were driving down Fountain
and Donder opened the passenger's door and started heaving. We were in
front of a transvestite bar called the Bijoux Lounge where I'd once spent
three weeks dressed like Joan Crawford in order to collar a check forger.

Never eat the luncheon meat of a murder victim who's been missing for
more than two days. If I told him once I told him a million times.

Louis Fremont sat on a folding chair on the stage, one in a row of folding
chairs that were arranged in a semi-circle behind the podium. He covered
his mouth with his left hand and swallowed hard. He looked out into the
auditorium but with the stage lights in his eyes he could only see outlines,
no faces.

The name of the symposium was "On The Other Hand." It was an
assembly of educators whose purpose was to promote left-handedness aware-
ness and to eliminate prejudice. The three previous speakers had alluded to

the archaic connection with witchcraft, so Louis, in a panic, hurriedly truncated his speech. He would start, then, with the anecdote, then touch on the barbaric practice of forced ambidexterity in the schools (and maybe even flesh that out a little to fill in the extra time) and then finish with a rallying cry for the abolishment of the word "sinistromanual."

The swell of applause signaled Louis that he was up. He cleared his throat on the way to the podium and graciously let the applause subside before he started. He was pleased to notice copies of *The Rights Of Lefts* on quite a few laps in the front row.

"In my book," several loud whistles and some sporadic, enthusiastic clapping. Louis smiled appreciatively and held up his hand. "In my book, I detail the early life of a student of mine. This was back when I was teaching elementary school. My very first term, as a matter of fact. This student, I'll call her Delores S., was so tremendously shy and frightened that I never heard her speak for the first two weeks of classes. She would always turn in her assignments blank, not even signing her name. When I brought up the subject of Delores with the other teachers, they explained that she had been held back, that there was the possibility that she was functionally challenged." A general empathetic murmuring, a clucking of tongues and a shaking of heads in recognition. "I, too, was at a loss. I was convinced as well that perhaps Special Ed might be the wisest recommendation. If it weren't for the class bully, I'll call her Sandra S., hurling a compass at Delores, and Delores deflecting it with her left hand, she might well have been shuffled aside, forgotten about in some remedial classroom down in the janitor's basement . . ."

Donder and I parked the car on San Vicente and as I got out I was nearly knocked over by a guy mumbling, "Goddamned uppity clerks! Service industry, my balls! Abuse of power is what it is! Goddamned abuse of position by insignificant powerless shitheads with no lives and small penises! Goddamn!"

I grabbed this lunatic by the back of his coat. "Excuse me, but you just disturbed my peace."

He turned and got up into my face. "Yeah? Why don't ya protect and serve me from the piss shit clowns who are flushing this whole society down the toilet? That badge means you have a big penis, right?" Not a healthy move.

"Cuff him," I said to Donder, who did. They both looked at me.

"Throw him in the back of the car." Donder did. "And roll up the windows."

"Wait—!" the man said as Donder slammed the door shut.

"Come on," I said.

The Razor's Edge Bookstore had a bell over the door to wake up the clerk, a reptilian gnome with the disposition of a wasp. He must have been doing community service. I can't imagine anyone actually paying this turd. Before we were even halfway to the counter his sneer was pulled halfway up his face.

"Yes?" he said in a tone that could only be interpreted as assaulting a police officer.

"You ever hear of Delores Sperrow?" I said.

"What'd she write?"

"Your name on a confession claiming that you were an accomplice in an armed robbery. Detective Heart, LAPD. This is Donder. Same thing. Now answer the question."

"Never heard of her."

I grabbed the runt by his shirt and lifted him off his feet. "Listen, Chuckles, we can make this easy, or we can make this hard." I slapped him once across the face and he whined like a school girl. "Don't make me let Donder here get ugly. Uglier."

"Didn't you assholes learn anything after Amnesty International came in and busted you guys?"

"How well did you know Delores Sperrow?"

"I told you, I've never heard of her!"

"Then what's this, then?" I dropped him and pulled out the receipt for the special order and stuck it in his face.

He looked confused, but then his face lit up. "Her? That bitch! Yeah, I know Delores Bitch Sperrow! She ordered two hundred bucks worth of Guy de Langerouge hardbacks and never picked them up. What's she wanted for? I'll say anything you want to get her locked up. Jesus! *Guy de Langerouge?* You ever *read* that guy? *Hollow Yearning? Borrowed Sorrow? Borrowed Sorrow* . . . what is that? *Poetry?* I'm never going to move those goddamned books! And I can't even ship them back. His publisher doesn't even want them!"

"Thank you," I said, "we'll be in touch if we need you."

"Wait," he said, "can I press charges, too? I want to sue the bitch."

"You can shove it up your ass," I said. As we walked out of the store I tipped over a stack of books with my elbow.

Delores's mother had been quite put off by her daughter's letter. For one thing, it was longer than what she was accustomed to, longer than was necessary. Secondly, it was positively raw. Mrs. Lancer (formerly Mrs. Sperrow) had been quite happy with cursory notes inside of Christmas cards and birthday cards. Mrs. Lancer (when she had been Mrs. Sperrow) had raised her daughter to be a quiet, cautious child. She liked her that way. This newest development was most disconcerting and Mrs. Lancer sincerely hoped that it was merely the result of a mild depression or slight illness. Something that would pass.

Delores's mother was at a loss to explain what was behind her daughter's sudden need to analyze her circumstances and assign blame. The letter didn't really illuminate its impetus. At best the letter was trite; at worst it was petty. For example, Delores had railed on and on about some fellow at work who had merely commented on her beautiful handwriting. Apparently he had said, and was probably only joking, or maybe even flirting, that "people with good handwriting don't have quick minds." Delores had been unduly affected by this. That such an offhand remark had devastated her daughter annoyed Mrs. Lancer. Was her own influence over Delores so paltry that it could all be abandoned at the first callous, and no doubt envious, slur? Mrs. Lancer had always stressed how important good handwriting was. Good handwriting and knowing your place. Keeping your emotions in check. Because it is very unattractive to be sloppy.

Delores had gone on to write that everything she did was ordinary. She wrote that the people in her office didn't like her; that they made fun of her, in fact.

I'm developing habits, she had written, which are increasingly like those of people I pity.

Mrs. Lancer could not understand how anyone could possibly write that sort of thing in a letter.

Donder and I found Dr. Singer's office on Hollywood Boulevard in a poorly lit cave wedged between the Checks Cashed/Donuts and a five-dollar tarot card reader who I was tempted to bust just for the fun of it. There were gaps in the acoustic tiles that paneled the waiting room's ceiling and the floors were sticky. A miserable old-world woman with her arms crossed and wearing tennis shoes sat in the corner in one of the molded plastic seats tilted so that you'd slide out if you didn't have both feet planted on the floor in front of you. An unattended delinquent was carving his initials into the pamphlet rack. The same "Hang-in-there" kitten posters that my own dentist had hanging in his waiting room were collecting dust on the walls. Near the reception desk was a framed poster from the tourist board of Denmark. Denmark. I made a note of it. On the coffee table were raggy old issues of True Crime and True Romance—Gone Bad. Frelene sat at the desk. I knew it was Frelene and not just because she sat at the desk. She looked like her voice. She was shaped like concrete poured into an oil drum, her hair was pincurled tight against her head, she was in her early 50's (though who cares?), and she had radiating lines out from her lips that served as canals for her bleeding lipstick.

Donder sat down and picked up a magazine. True Stories from Forensic Medicine. I walked up to the desk.

"You a dick?" Frelene asked before I could open my mouth.

"You a—" I stopped myself. I smiled. "LAPD. Nicky Heart."

"*Harp?*" she said, squinting.

"No. Nicky *Heart*. With an 'e.'"

"But that would make you Necky Harp."

"No. Heart with an 'e.' Like the pumping organ."

"Oh?" she said, "The heart isn't the first thing that comes to mind when I think of a pumping organ." Her face contorted and she twitched from an intestinal blockage—no, she winked.

"You know," I said, "you look vaguely familiar. Didn't I date your granddaughter?"

She smiled. "I like a dick with a sense of humor."

"I'm not here to entertain you, Ma'am."

"Oh, good! Then you're here on business? I was hoping you'd be here on business." Her eyes were bright and she moved forward in her seat.

I took out my notepad. "I don't want to take up any more of your time than necessary"—or than would put me off my lunch—"so I just have a few questions and then we'll be on our way."

She reached out to touch my hand but I pulled it away just in time.

"Is this a murder?" She shuddered with delight.

"Please, Ma'am, I just have—"

"It's about the murder of Randy Durian, isn't it?"

Randy Durian? "Who's Randy Durian?"

She frowned. "I thought this would be about Randy Durian."

"No. It's about Delores Sperrow."

Frelene huffed. "Oh, please! Who gives a damn about Delores Sperrow! I don't. When her teeth start falling out maybe then she'll think to pick up the phone. But it'll be too late because I just don't care. I wish her all the best if she wants to gum her way through spinsterhood."

"That's not very funny, Miss . . . Frelene."

"Not returning phone calls isn't funny, Mr. Heart."

"Who's Randy Durian?"

"What do you want with Delores Sperrow? What'd she do—bore people to death?"

"No, she—"

"Skip town with library books?"

"She's dead. Delores is dead."

Frelene screwed up her face. "Really?" she said. She didn't believe me.

"Yes, really. Where were you every night for the past three weeks?"

"Who'd want to kill *her*? I mean, who'd even notice her in order to kill her?"

"Maybe you can answer that for me."

Frelene snapped her fingers. "Maybe I can. She tried to steal my August copy of Police Blotter last time she was in. I left a bruise on her arm, let me tell you. It was a really good issue. Remember the West Side Ice-picker? It was all about him. The whole issue. Tell me, how was she found? Strapped to a bed?"

"Thank you for your time." I walked to the door.

"Disemboweled?" she said, standing up behind her desk. "De-eyed?"
I didn't turn around.

"Come on!" Frelene pleaded. "Tell me!"

I looked over to Donder. He was asleep with the magazine open across
his chest. I left him there.

Mallwalkers! Unbelievable! A whole tribe of them, all walking around and
around inside the mall before it opens, all wearing T-shirts like the one I'd
seen in Delores's apartment. And I had to chase these robots past the locked
security gates of the Gap Kids and the Bombay Company and the Pup-On-
A-Stick and the Victoria's Secret. Hadn't they heard of Griffith Park?

"Excuse me," I said to an embalmed old debutante waddling past me on
a pair of dried-out drumsticks. "Excuse me, but do you know this girl?" I
showed her the picture of Delores that Donder had found on the fridge.

"You a cop?"

"That I am, Ma'am."

The powdered monster took the picture. "Nah. Doesn't look familiar."

"She was a Mallwalker."

"I don't care."

She trotted away. Alongside me came another broad who looked like
she'd crawled out of the same crypt.

"Excuse me, Miss," I said, holding out the photo, "do you know this
woman?"

"Fuck off or I'll mace you."

"Charming." I fell back; my regulation police shoes were biting into
my ankles.

"Hello! Hello!"

I turned around. Coming at me with jerking arms and slapping sneakers were a couple of plump spouses. "We're the Wilmingtons," the plump wife said, "Butch and Rainie. I'm the Rainie." She laughed, thinking that she had made a joke.

"Nicky Heart, LAPD," I said as I adjusted my pace to theirs. I loosened my tie.

"We know her. That girl."

I held out the picture. "You know Delores Sperrow?"

"Is that her name? We never knew her name."

"That's her name. How well did you know her?"

"Not well. But we've seen her. Not a very pleasant girl."

"Now, Rainie . . ."

"Well, I don't like to say it, but there—I've said it. She wasn't a very pleasant girl."

"How do you mean," I asked, "not pleasant?"

"Well. She wouldn't even buy a T-shirt," Rainie said.

"We have reason to believe she did," I said.

"No, she didn't! We *all* have our T-shirts! But she would always show up looking . . . looking like . . . looking like she was going I don't know where!" Butch rolled his eyes. It couldn't have been easy for Butch.

Rainie continued, "Never tried to fit in, never a 'hello, how are you?', never a 'nice day, isn't it?' And never, *never* an 'excuse me'! She always used to stop so suddenly, never any warning, just to look at something in one of the windows. And one time Butch here nearly knocked her clean through! She just wasn't a joiner. I guess I didn't much like her. You're never going to make friends unless you're friendly back, I always say. Butch, well, Butch pretty much gets along with everybody."

"Did she have any friends? Any boyfriends?"

"Not so's I could see. She always walked alone, out a ways from everybody else."

"Did you ever see her talk to *any*one?"

Rainie shook her head.

"Thank you for your time," I said and leaned against the wall, panting. I took off my trench coat and tiptoed painfully to the gents.

The toughest part of what I do is the next of kin business.

I buzzed Mrs. Sperrow's apartment from the foyer.

"Yes?" she said over the intercom.

"Los Angeles Police Department," I said.

"What now?"

"It's about your daughter. Delores."

"I knew it'd come to this. Oh, all right." She buzzed us in.

She was a shockingly unnatural blond and still in her dressing gown. She drank gin—regularly, probably, and certainly that morning. "So what'd she do this time?"

"This time?" I said, "I wasn't aware that she had a record."

"A *police* record, no. But certainly a record for frivolity and stupidness."

"May we come in?"

"I suppose so."

Mrs. Sperrow led Donder and me into her living room. She strolled into the middle of the room and turned around and stared at us. No one sat down.

"Well?" she said.

"Uh, Mrs. Sperrow, this isn't easy—"

"No," she said, "not Mrs. Sperrow. Not anymore. Please! Don't you boys do your homework? It's Mrs. Lancer. Well, most recently Mrs. Lancer."

"But it said 'Sperrow' downstairs—"

"Well, it's not. Trust me."

"Mind if I call you Mrs. Sperrow to save myself some paperwork?"

"Yes, I do mind."

"Well, Mrs. Lancer, it's, uh, it's—"

"She's dead?"

"Uh, she's, uh—"

"Out with it! Come on! Dead or not? Is Delores dead?"

She was hardly what I'd call distraught. Hardly the grieving mother. I made a mental note to check the drawers in the kitchen.

"Well, yes. Yes she is."

Mrs. Sperrow-Lancer crossed her arms. "Will that be all, then?"

"Mrs. Sperrow—"

"Lancer."

"Lancer. Pardon me for saying so, but the news doesn't seem to come as any great surprise."

"Death is not a surprising thing, Mr. . . .?"

"Heart. Nicky. Detective. This is Donder." I used the frown I use to let suspects know that I'm unsatisfied. "But your daughter was a young woman. Normally one would . . . you just don't seem to be very dolorous."

"*Dolorous?*"

"It means sad."

"I know what it means, Mr. Heart. I was questioning your usage." She sighed, resigning herself to the fact that Donder and I weren't leaving. She sat down. "To tell you the truth, Mr. Heart, I wasn't very close to Delores. To tell you the truth, I hadn't seen her in years. She wasn't the daughter I raised."

"When did you last see her?"

"Years, I believe I just said."

"But what year exactly?"

"I don't believe I can remember, exactly."

"No phone calls? Letters?"

"No. Yes."

"No yes what?"

"Telephone calls—no. Letters—yes." She got up and made herself a drink. "*Letter*, actually. And, of course, cards from time to time. Birthdays. Christmas. You know."

"When the letter?"

"Recently, if you must know."

"May I read it?"

"No."

"I can make you, you realize."

"With a warrant, yes. Where's the warrant?"

She smirked at me, challenging me. Donder was also looking at me with curiosity. I cleared my throat. "Mrs. Lancer, don't make this unpleasant."

Mrs. Lancer waved her hand like she was shooing flies and made a face. "That letter was embarrassing. For her, I mean. Embarrassing for her."

"How?"

"It was imprudent. Morose. Gushing, if you will."

"I'll ask you again politely—may I read the letter?"

"I hate brutes."

"We have a difference of opinion there."

She got the letter. It *was* sort of embarrassing, for Delores. She complained about her own handwriting, of all things, and about people at work making fun of her name. It was time to bring the menace Brad to fore. Delores also went on to snivel that everything she did was ordinary, and that nothing made her laugh, and nothing made her cry.

It sounded like a suicide note. Though considering how many pieces we had found Delores in, I felt that suicide could safely be ruled out.

"So," Mrs. Lancer said when I handed her back the letter, "do you have any leads?" She smiled. "Actually, I'm just being nice by asking. Obviously you haven't got a clue. Quite literally. Goodness, I can't tell you how long I've been waiting to say that!"

"Well, it just so happens there is a rather suspicious dentist that we're investigating . . ."

Mrs. Sperrow looked horrified. "Not the Savage Dentist of Laurel Canyon!"

"The Savage Dentist of Laur—?" Donder and I looked at each other. How could we have missed that? Donder, panicked, tore through his notepad. I turned to Mrs. Sperrow. She was laughing at us.

"Well, you boys ought best run off now. Off to your dentist. I have an appointment." She walked to the door and held it open.

At the threshold I turned to her. "Call us if you remember anything significant," I said.

She laughed and slammed the door in our faces.

"Check the price on this Vanilla Stripple, would ya?" the cashier said to Ernie—Blade—Leifstom. He hadn't legally changed his name yet, but he let it be known. Blade. Just one word.

"Three ninety-nine," he said and continued packing the groceries.

"Check it!" the scary woman who was buying it said, flashing her yellow incisors.

"It's three ninety-nine," he said and shrugged his shoulders defensively. The cashier turned to Ernie—Blade—and said, "Please." She rolled her eyes in sympathy.

"I saw that!" the scary woman snapped at the cashier. Blade let a jug of bleach fall onto a loaf of bread in the scary woman's bag and headed toward the frozen food aisle.

"You might as well be getting another loaf while you're at it, smart boy," the scary woman screamed at him, "I ain't taking no squished bread!" Blade ignored her.

Vanilla Stripple. Like that Holstein needed any more ice cream. What she needed was some mustache wax. And she sure as hell didn't need that six-pack. Blade wondered what she'd do if he brought back some appetite-suppressing caramel chews instead. God, it'd been just that kind of day. One after the other. Double coupons always brought them out.

He wondered what ever happened to that nice, shy woman who always used to come in, the one who never argued, the one who would never have second thoughts about the salad dressing and leave it in the TV Guide rack at the register; the one who always smiled, who always read his name tag and said, "Thank you, Ernie." Ernie—Blade—had always liked her.

He stopped in the toiletries and waited.

"Hi, Mike," he said to Mike.

"Hi, Blade."

After a moment he headed back. The line at the register now stretched down past the corn chips.

"Three ninety-nine," he said. The scary woman glared at him. Or, rather, around him. He hadn't noticed before that she was wall-eyed.

"Not for the twenty ounce, it isn't!" she gnashed.

"Do you still want it?" the cashier said.

"Not for three ninety-nine!" The cashier set it beside the register.

Blade wondered where that woman was, the nice woman. She hadn't been in for a while. Maybe she'd moved. He hoped that she was all right. She never made a fuss. She even let people go in front of her sometimes, if they only had one or two things. She wasn't exactly what you'd call pretty. But Blade liked her that way. He imagined that he could've gotten along with her. She would've appreciated the name "Blade." He would've liked to ask her out to a movie or something. She probably would've said yes. She looked like she would've said yes.

The scary, wall-eyed woman handed the cashier a fistful of moist coupons. Blade packed the rest of her groceries, squeezing his fingers into a bag of grapes as he did so.

"This coupon's expired," the cashier said, peeling off a dusty Lifesaver that was stuck to it.

"My ass!"

Blade couldn't remember the nice woman ever bringing in coupons.

Donder and I got back to the precinct and I threw down my pad so I could start going over my notes. Donder stood fidgeting. I wanted him to leave so that I could take off my shoes. He checked his watch. Something was on his mind.

"What's on your mind, Patrolman?"

"It's almost four o'clock," he said. I sensed there was something behind this besides his pride in the accuracy of his new Lorus.

"So?" I said.

"Um, well, remember I told you about my vacation time that was going to expire? And that I was leaving for Vegas tonight for three weeks?"

"You told me that?"

"I did, Sir."

"Well, then, I guess you'd better be off."

"Thank you, Sir."

"You'll be missed."

"Thank you, Sir."

He left. I spread everything I had regarding Delores Sperrow out on my desk. My notepad, the coroner's report, her picture, the regulation forms that I'd started to fill out. Just as I slid off my shoes I heard a heavy sigh. I looked up. Standing in front of me was a love-starved redhead who was packed into her aerobics unitard tighter than fish in a tin.

"Hello," I said.

"Hello," she said.

"Can I help you?" I knew I could. In ways that she couldn't yet imagine.

She looked down at my desk. "Perhaps I should find another detective. You seem," she shifted her weight, throwing her shoulders back, "overwhelmed."

I grabbed the papers on my desk and stuffed them into my bottom drawer. "Nah. Don't worry about this. Dead end, anyway. Case closed." It was a horrible thing that happened to Delores Sperrow and a great shame. "What seems to be the problem, Miss . . .?"

"Kenyon. Mrs. My husband's gone missing."

"That *is* a crime." I smiled roguishly. I flexed the muscles around my eyes to activate the tear ducts so that I'd get that twinkle. Mrs. Kenyon suddenly looked concerned.

"Are you all right?" she said.

I let out my breath. "Never been better." I crammed my feet back into my shoes and went around the desk. I slid my arm behind her like a caring uncle. I led her to the door. "Why don't we get out of this stuffy office and go somewhere a little more comfortable so you can tell me your whole story."

"Uh, well . . ." She seemed hesitant, but was pliant enough when I increased the pressure on her waist. "I know a place just down the street. We'll get a nice little table in the corner where we won't be disturbed."

On the window sill of Delores's apartment was a two pint fish bowl. The water had thickened, become cloudy, and had evaporated down to just below the halfway point. Up the insides of the bowl, above the water and to about half an inch below the lip, were striated chalky rings. Little viscous groups of bubbles had formed in clumps at the water line. In the middle of the bowl Charlie floated to the top, her eyes gone milky, her valved mouth wide and distended, her body filled with the nitrogen which had brought her up from the bottom. Her orange color was gone and she was now gray, beginning to go opaque. Some of her scales had loosened and floated to the sides. Her back fin was tattered, having been nibbled on by bacteria and microbes and hungry little creatures that just bloomed there, like magic, like a miracle, like in the beginning of time when life first evolved in the primordial sludge, because life on this planet—it just can't help it—flourishes.

Going Forth

LIFE, INTRINSICALLY, ABOUNDS. Life, by its very nature, flourishes. Salmon know this. Gibbons know this. Aphids—probably more than any other creatures—know this (being partial, as they are, to parthenogenesis).

Terra Gae knew this, too. Lately this nudging to become two, to become whole as only a mother can be, swallowed up her every other concern; like an auk in springtime, or a hyena: she was in estrus, in full, desperate estrus. Though the current fashion for birthing may have had some influence (Terra Gae couldn't, after all, go *anywhere* these days without tripping over some other woman's tots), the tug of her unfulfilment was more unconscious. It was simply a wave of pagan harmonics—the Great Mother Gaia flexing her uterine muscles—that gave Terra Gae her near yeast-like need to reproduce. Whatever the reason, she had grown as acutely aware of her lower abdomen as a farmer is aware of his lower forty. And like an anxious farmer who has let his fields lie fallow to drive the price of turnips up, Terra Gae, too, felt the agitation of her years spent without harvest.

So Terra Gae was looking for a man. Not a whole man, actually, but rather just one single cell of a man.

Terra Gae felt her skin tighten in the draught as she lay immobilized with her feet in stirrups, the paper hospital gown bunched at her groin where it had slid. She let out an impatient sigh and looked straight up at the ceiling, having already tested her eyes by reading the printed labels on all the drawers and having kept her mind sharp by calculating the number of cotton swabs in the glass jars. Soon—well, soon enough—the doctor would arrive with the boisterous little tadpole that would bring Terra Gae comfort in her old age. For now she just had to breathe deeply and disassociate herself from her exposed intimates, to somehow subdue the excruciating humiliation with which her present situation was rife. Modesty was an absurd luxury for a woman lying prone, legs in the air, with her cherished little oven displayed as perfunctorily as sweetbreads on a butcher's counter. She steeled herself and regarded her womb, for the time being, as merely a tool through which she might achieve her noble goal. Biology, she insisted, it's just necessary biology.

Terra Gae had never been of a particularly romantic bent. She had preferred her career to the company of men. She had preferred the opportunity to travel to the company of men. She had preferred the company of women and her dog to the company of men. Yet with Terra Gae it was not simply a case of misandry. She had no smoldering hatred of men as a whole, no axes to grind, no hatchets to bury. Nor did she have a carnal love of woman. It was, rather, a mild aversion to sex in general, and to the male member in particular. She liked her brother. She was fond of her cousin, Earl. But the differences that Terra Gae felt that her sex had with the other were irreconcilable.

It wasn't their fault, really. It was just the way the skin happened to fold itself in utero that made them into little boys. It was in their brains. Along with a penis they also developed a need to aggress, to dominate, to, well, to build bombs. And, God bless them, such forcefulness, such savageness served the species well. In the beginning. But these days such drives, such jungle laws were about as necessary as tonsils. Time to move on. Evolve. Because otherwise it will be the end of us all. So Terra Gae couldn't blame men, not really; it was just in their nature. She just didn't want to have anything with it.

But Terra Gae was no aphid, and unfortunately the only thing she shared with yeast was a motive. So mate she must and she set out along the traditional path of fertilization. She assuaged her distaste with the old saw that the end would justify the means, and that it would be over soon enough. If a man was what was necessary to bring forth fruit, then a man it would be.

Terra Gae, fortunately, was not handicapped by a lack of opportunity.

True, she had seldom been on the receiving end of favorable comparisons to, say, flowers, or small furry animals, but nonetheless she was a hardy woman, correctly formed, and not aesthetically displeasing. Though perhaps she'd never been what might be considered a feminine ideal (except, of course, in some primitive tribes, and during times of war), such regard had always been below the threshold of her concern. She didn't care if and how attractive she was—attraction was not a priority of hers—and it never occurred to her to soften the firm set of her jaw, to bend her posture into something less threatening, or to avert her rather daunting gaze when confronted socially. She was no doubt intimidating to the insecure, however to those in possession of themselves she could be quite captivating. Her skin was good, her blue eyes clear, her blond hair accidentally styled in a complimentary way (if not perhaps a tad severe). To those not insistent upon dominance, she could be rather fetching. And to those with a penchant for submission, she could actually be downright bewitching.

For years the girls at the office (Terra Gae worked as a senior accounts assistant in a mail order leisure-wear concern) had been egging and cajoling Terra Gae to join them after work on their nocturnal foraging through singles bars. At first it had merely been a matter of politeness, an effort toward unity, but then her stubborn refusals had become a matter of intrigue, and then speculation, and finally annoyance. Her private life was too private, which was no fun for anyone else. The girls were getting bored with rumors and suppositions. They wanted facts, and they wanted to be witness to those facts. They wanted to see Terra Gae in action, on the loose, on the prowl. They needed to make Terra Gae one of them.

Their invitations had long since become routine, part of the ceremony, part of the game, so it was met with great astonishment when Terra Gae said that she would go.

"I'll go," she said.

The girls slowly circled.

"You'll come?" Jelline, the girl in charge of the copying supplies, said.

It was business for Terra Gae and she had no time for the giggling and the girlish play. "Yes. You just asked me, didn't you?"

The girls dashed off to grab their coats and purses.

Terra Gae stood by the bar of the Parasol Room sipping a gin. Beside her sat Jelline, who, as far as Terra Gae could tell (judging from the angle of view and the slurping sounds), was being eaten by a man in a loudly patterned tie. Jolly and Brenda—the new girls—were dancing stuporously with two equally stuporous young accountants in the space left open after Lucy had fallen onto a table, breaking three of its legs. Lucy had been sent home.

When Terra Gae had entered the Parasol Room, heads had turned. She was a woman with a purpose and it showed: where the others were self-conscious, coy, desperate, or alcoholic, Terra Gae was a beacon of self-assurance and it made her radiant. After a cursory look around (there wasn't much there to excite her) Terra Gae had planted herself conspicuously on a stool in the center of the oaken bar and told her friends not to worry about her. She could manage just fine. After a while the girls had grown restless and had drifted away to their own pursuits.

Soon a steady parade of priapic men in various degrees of intoxication filed past her. Several proffered well-rehearsed lines, introducing themselves without taking their eyes from her breasts. Without being able to stop herself—and in direct opposition to her purpose for even being there—Terra Gae summarily dismissed each of them in turn with remarks meant to wound their pride and reduce their manhood.

Sexual tension hung in the air like smoke, as did smoke. She was distracted.

Throughout the bar—in cubicles, on stools, in corners—couples were groping, tearing, rutting like sheep. Terra Gae, sure she would not be missed by Jelline or the other girls, pulled her things together and headed for the dim perimeter of the bar to catch her breath.

The conversation with Peter Johnson erupted over his facial scars.

"Christ! What happened to your face?" Terra Gae said.

Peter Johnson had been sitting in the murky shadows by the cigarette machine, away from the crowd. He reflexively drew away from direct lighting, preferring the gloom that took away some of the sting that his surgeries caused. Terra Gae sat down next to him without an invitation and introduced herself. Then she bought him a drink.

As he talked, Terra Gae looked at him and squinted. Everything was in place; there weren't two of anything that there shouldn't be, and it was all in the proper order. But still, he seemed more like an artist's rendering than an actual person.

Peter Johnson had done something very, very bad—though he wouldn't say what—and was now living in the witness protection program. What he had done was so bad, in fact, that merely living in a new home in a new state was not enough to keep him alive. He had had to become a whole new person. He had had to change his name to Peter Johnson (from John Peterson; his very bad deeds had apparently not required a great deal of imagination). He also had to have his face changed. In fact, his plastic surgery was still fresh on the night that Terra Gae met him.

He told all of this to Terra Gae, his survival instinct lax due to the despair or the great quantities of beer or just plain boredom. Terra Gae was fascinated. He was pathetic, hence malleable, and she was ovulating, hence maternal. She liked his body type, very frail—she didn't want to think weaselish, but there you have it—with genes delicate enough to perhaps temper her own admittedly mannish breadth of shoulder and too generous (she believed) buttocks. He could probably father a lovely daughter. She glanced at the crowd, at the strutting and posturing, and then back at Peter Johnson, thoughtful and intense.

"I live nearby."

Her invitation was so perfunctory that it left his newly attached lips operating nonverbally for several seconds.

"How near?"

Terra Gae smiled and rose. "Near enough."

At her apartment she had taken Peter Johnson's seed. The ceremony had been as uncomfortable and silly as she had remembered it. He had left shortly after he had arrived with a smug grin and a false telephone number. Two days later Terra Gae noticed an unusual discharge.

Instead of implanting a baby daughter in her womb, Peter Johnson had sown a colony of non-specific tubal urethritis. Terra Gae had cringed at the doctor's words. Non-specific! She couldn't even give faces to the vicious little intruders. What indignity that her jealously preserved sanctum should serve as a petrie dish for pathogens! And how typical of men that her one tryst, the tryst that ended her long-standing resolve, should only result in her gestating bacteria. She knew that they were only nameless single-cells, but to Terra Gae they felt decidedly male. They acted male. Chewing, infecting, conquering. She should have known. She did know; she'd just ignored her common sense and acted rashly. From that point on she swore off penile semination. With Peter Johnson, her point was proved.

Terra Gae smiled now, even with her feet in the stirrups (stirrups; there you go—it must've been a man who named that one). Impersonal humiliation was eminently preferable to personal. Had she known from the beginning that having babies without fathers was so convenient and affordable, she might have saved herself the glitch on her medical record. But the idea had never occurred to her until she had visited her gynecologist to cover Peter Johnson's muddy tracks. While she had been waiting for the lab results, a young couple, also waiting, had received their good news, courtesy of a laboratory technician. "It's a miracle!" the young wife had squealed, and then crumbled into a heap of sobs. No, Terra Gae knew, the miracle of birth was no miracle. It was simply a matter of mathematics.

Terra Gae had shopped by catalogue before and it was usually a disappointment. Things would never fit right, or the color would be off. But not this catalogue! The fit would be microscopically precise. Evolutionarily precise! Biblically precise!

She sat in the earth-toned reception area of the Andrology Clinic and studied the selection of index cards. Terra Gae had declined the receptionist's offer of coffee and crullers. This was not a social outing.

342-DL. Dean of physics at Princeton University. Lineage traceable back to the Mayflower. Yes. Nice. Pastimes and hobbies? *Chess, Russian Literature (1845-1905), French cooking.* Sports? *Croquet* . . . croquet? Was that a sport? Perhaps a sport for sissies.

343-DL. Award-winning author. On the board of directors of the Metropolitan Museum of Art. Big game hunter. Uh-oh.

344-DL. Computer diagnostician. Copyright holder of the "Happy Face" . . . How did that one get in there?

345-DL. Professor of Cryptoeconomics at Peake University. Cat lover. Terra Gae didn't mind cats, it was cat lovers she couldn't abide.

346-DL. Baggage Handler. Invents board games. 151 I.Q. Did anyone check these claims? Could these guys just say anything they wanted to or did somebody do some research? She sat back in horror. How could she ever be sure?

Terra Gae fanned the stack of cards with her thumb. Oh dear, there were a lot of them. She looked up past the reception desk and down the long hallway with the doors. A lot of doors. She shuddered at the thought that behind each one of these was a man with a magazine handling himself, huffing and snorting, and making deposits. Biology, just necessary biology. Chemical arithmetic. Keys in locks.

386-SK. Actor.

387-SK. Dentist. Breeds racing birds. Incurable romantic. What did that have to do with putting sperm in a cup?

388-SK. Doctor. Well! *Rhodes scholar. Captain of the football team, water polo team, track team.* Yes! An athletic daughter—Hail, Hippolyta! Terra Gae sat back and held up the index card. She pushed the stack of other cards away. Chromosomes for brains and chromosomes for brawn! A daughter who would be a spaniel for no man. Yes. This would do nicely. Mr. 388-SK, meet Terra Gae!

She took the card to her assigned counselor and proudly handed it over. The counselor, an officious yet pleasant woman, smiled back and scanned the card.

"Very good choice. You're lucky, this has been our most popular batch. We're almost out."

"It must be my lucky day," Terra Gae said. "And by the way, I'd like that with a double X."

The counselor tensed up. "What?"

"You know, chromosomes. I'd like an XX instead of an XY."

"I'm terribly sorry, but we don't dispense that way. It's beyond not only our technology but also our morality." A rather arbitrary delineation of

morality, thought Terra Gae, though she didn't say so. Instead she laughed.
"Just kidding!" she said and put her hand on the counselor's forearm.
This intimate gesture, Terra Gae had found, always had a reassuring effect.
The counselor laughed back, though uneasily.

Terra Gae was growing impatient now. The doctor had said, "Just a sec"
and Terra Gae, without having to check her watch for the exact number,
knew that many secs had come and gone. But at last the door flew open,
blowing Terra Gae's paper gown to her bustline, and the brash doctor entered
without an apology. He grinned down at her for no apparent reason, his smile
as gracious as a catheter. He snapped his rubber gloves into place but was
suddenly frozen by the look of horror on Terra Gae's face. His back was to
the open door, as were Terra Gae's open legs. Two orderlies had just parked a
gurney carrying a moaning woman in the hallway and were now standing in
the doorway and staring.

"Whoops. Sorry," the brash doctor said and closed the door.

He seated himself on a rolling stool and positioned himself between
Terra Gae's thighs. "Well, Miss Gage, today is the big day," he said without
looking up past her knees. The nurse arrived before Terra Gae was obliged
to make a reply.

The doctor dropped his grin when he said to the nurse, "Maureen, I'll
need a fresh swab," but he quickly pulled it back up when he leaned over to
face Terra Gae. "Don't be nervous," he said, "we'll have you out of here in
just a sec. It's as easy as sticking gum under a chair."

Another nurse entered with a tray of metal instruments. Terra Gae
searched—in the fraction of a second that the tray was in view—for the vessel
that contained half of her little girl, but she had no idea what to look for.

The doctor adjusted the stool and the nurses fell in behind him.

"All right, Maureen," he said and the nurse named Maureen handed him a glint of steel. The doctor peeked past Terra Gae's thigh and leered at her. "This shouldn't hurt. Just pretend it's that Arnold Schwarzenegger in *The Exterminator.*"

"*The Terminator*," Maureen said.

"Whatever."

Terra Gae wasn't up to arguing. She bit down hard on her tongue as the cold appliance was forced into her.

Terra Gae left the clinic and stopped herself from dancing down the sidewalk. She imagined that she felt the little bastula inside of her belly, already splitting and doubling, bobbing her way down the fallopian tube. Yes, her daughter was nigh! Soon a little Terrina Gae to bounce and raise. It wouldn't be long now. The gears in the ancient and noble circle of creation had begun their slow and deliberate grind.

Terra Gae was right. It took. Terra Gae was gravid. She ran her hand over her midriff. For the first little while Terrina would only be a cylindrical cluster of cells with a tube going through it; just a spongy ball with two puckered holes, one that would grow into a little kissable mouth, the other into, well, an anus. So they couldn't manage an XX deposit, huh? It was early. She had time. The genitals wouldn't even pop through for a while. She could will the gonads to just stay inside. Energy follows thought, she believed, and manifestation followed energy. Heck, if people could stress themselves into having cancer, she could certainly pressure her little embryo into forming a uterus.

The girls at the office had been unusually subdued of late; giggling, as usual, but calmer, less driven. Jelline had started dating an accountant from a good family, Jolly was on antibiotics, and Lucy had been sent to rehab. The office had drifted into the social doldrums. Not that Terra Gae would have noticed. She was as impervious to their nattering as she had been before.

The girls, however, were eventually awakened from their torpor by Terra Gae's increasing glow. Was she in love, they wondered. None of them remembered seeing her leave with Peter Johnson, even though some of them had. They also began to notice that she was getting progressively more chunky. This was always a hot topic no matter who it was.

When the accountant left Jelline for a flight attendant named Breeze, and Jolly's infection cleared up, and Lucy had dried out, the girls again began their after-work trawlings, and again began hectoring Terra Gae with renewed vigor. She definitely had a secret. They could smell it.

Jelline caught Terra Gae alone one day when Terra Gae had to copy some monthly ledger sheets and Jelline was replacing the toner.

"We're all going out tonight. C'mon," Jelline said. It was like saying "hello."

"No. Thank you," Terra Gae replied and hit the collate button and pressed "START."

"C'mon," Jelline said, wiping her hands clean on a paper towel. "Come out for a drinkie-poo."

"No. Really. I can't." Terra Gae took her ledger sheets and left.

"Course you can! You had fun the last time!" Jelline pursued her down the hallway. "We *saw* you have fun! Just ask Brenda!"

Terra Gae stopped and turned to her. "No. I can't. I'm going to have a baby."

Jelline's blood left her head and her mouth fell open. She stared at Terra Gae without a trace of intelligence in her eyes. Terra Gae smiled. "So no drinkie-poos for me."

Jelline turned and bolted. Terra Gae expected what she soon saw: Jelline coming back, leading the pack of girls jogging down the hallway and stumbling to a halt in front of her.

"Tell them!" Jelline demanded.

Terra Gae sighed. "I'm going to have a baby."

The girls erupted, shrieking, laughing, gripping each other.

"You are soooo lucky!" Brenda said. Terra Gae wanted to tell her that there was very little luck in this world.

"When?" Jelline said. "When, when, when?"

Jolly pushed her out of the way. "Is it a boy or a girl?"

Terra Gae thrust out her chest. "A girl."

"Who's the father?" Brenda said.

"Yeah, who's the father?"

Terra Gae smiled. "There is no father." She turned and walked away before the girls could regroup.

Terra Gae sat in the waiting room, her hand massaging her distended abdomen. She could hardly wait to get her first glimpse of her little Terrina. Her soon to be firm jaw, her soon to be erect spine! Under her fingers Terra Gae imagined she could actually feel the mitosis, feel the little parts forming in the bubblings and gurglings. Little fingers, lengthening cell by cell, reaching up to grasp her own. (She was well past meditating during the critical sex determination phase.) Minuscule digits that would never serve coffee in a restaurant or hold a secretary's pencil. Fingers that would clutch a test tube holding a Nobel Prize-winning cure; fingers jotting down thoughts that would eventually win the Pulitzer; fingers that would glide along a Carnegie Hall keyboard.

Terra Gae didn't even tense as the nurse spread the cold jelly over her belly. The brash doctor flipped the switch on the ultrasound and roughly placed the transmitter on Terra Gae's abdomen. She watched the grainy screen. The doctor scanned over her taut flesh and an orb jerked onto the screen. The doctor's face knotted and Terra Gae felt a spike of fear. The doctor moved the scanner more urgently. Terra Gae could make no sense of the blurs on the screen, so she watched the doctor's eyes. They didn't bode well. Terra Gae could not speak.

After several rapid adjustments, the doctor's crescendo of panic melted and a relieved grin spread across his face. "Whew!" he said. "For a minute there I thought your baby had a leg growing out of its forehead! Congratulations, Mrs. Gage! Your husband will be very happy. You have a robust set of triplets!"

Triplets? Terra Gae's newly regained sense of well-being evaporated. Triplets? What she'd had in mind was more of a one-on-one sort of bonding. One little Terrina to guide and enlighten.

Triplets? Three extra beds to make. Three bottoms to powder. Three college educations to pay for.

"Triplets?" she asked.

"Yes!" the nurse chimed in, "Three little boys!" She moved to the monitor. "See those little smudges there? Those are their little willies!" She clapped her hands in delight.

"Three *little* boys?" The doctor laughed. The hilarity seemed to be spreading. "Hell! Three *big* boys! Mrs. Gage, you're about to have a healthy start on your own football team!"

Terra Gae walked out of the clinic with her arms held rigidly at her side. Three football captains with cheerleader girlfriends to cheat on. She no longer felt complete, cyclic. She felt invaded. She imagined three little sets of features forming, three lewd little grins, six wife-beating fists. Trigger fingers growing, cell by masculine cell. She walked blindly, wishing there was someplace where she could escape. But she was outnumbered.

Just her luck! And wasn't that just like men? They were always precisely where you didn't want them to be. Like in your womb.

Perhaps she could send them out for adoption. No. The idea made her feel as though she was just a pawn in the male war of domination, as though she was just a baby farm, or a recruiting office. Abortion? She didn't hate men—certainly not enough for that—she just didn't really want to own one.

She continued walking.

Perhaps she could just coddle them. She could give them dolls, teach them to make curtains, make them watch *The Wizard of Oz* over and over again. *Those* boys, after all, were the most devoted children a mother could hope for. Even more than daughters, really.

Terra Gae relaxed, resigned. That was really one of the best qualities of females, wasn't it? It's why women lived longer than men. Why they would probably still be around long after all the men had aggressed themselves into extinction. Adaptability.

repair

"Hello, dear," Mrs. Bitts, his landlady, said.

Graham took pause. He was experiencing some discomfort with that particular "hello, dear." It was not, of course, the words in themselves; he could certainly have no quarrel with the "hello," and the "dear," though unearned, was hardly a cause for alarm. It was the tone with which Mrs. Bitts used them: it was the tone she usually reserved for her cat. Graham Ballard's relationship with his landlady, Mrs. Bitts, could never, even generously, be described as kittenish. "Leonine," perhaps. Even "internecine" on occasion. But it had never been either intimate or affectionate. She's trying to be nice, Graham realized, and grew frightened. He thought the best course of action was to provoke her.

"What the hell are you doing calling me here?" he asked. Why, indeed, was she calling? Because Graham was in Winnipeg while Mrs. Bitts was in Los Angeles. What could have possibly prompted her into making a toll call? "This is long distance," Graham said incredulously.

"Oh, well, dear . . ." Graham was completely off his guard. Normally by this point, considering the tone he had been using with her, the coarse fur would have sprung from the leathery flesh on the back of her neck and she would have drawn her flews back, exposing her pointy teeth. Something has happened; something was wrong. "Something's, well, happened," Mrs. Bitts confirmed, "I'm . . . I'm calling from your phone."

Graham inhaled sharply. His phone? "My phone?"

"Well, yes, dear. There's been a bit of a burglary."

"A . . . bit?"

"Quite a large bit, actually. They sort of cleaned you out, dear."

Graham bit down on the tip of his tongue. The blood drained from his head. His knees gave out. He fell in a seated position on the dolorously patterned sofa in his suite at the Manitoba Motel and Motor Court. Graham was a man who needed the security and sanctuary of a place to call home; a cocoon to protect him from the harsh and mean elements. But now that cocoon had been torn open and he was left exposed like a half-formed pupa drying out on the sidewalk. "Did they damage . . . did they take the paintings?" Over the years Graham had accidentally stumbled across several pieces that had since become relatively valuable.

"No, nothing like that. Basically they just took everything with a plug."

"My stereo?"

"Well, yes. That had rather a large plug, now, didn't it?" Graham now understood why Mrs. Bitts had become so concerned, so uncharacteristically human. She was gloating. She had thrust herself to the forefront of the crime scene because she had wanted to be the first to break the news to him. Sadism disguised as compassion. Graham had seen it before. "I'll get the next flight back. Is the apartment secured?"

"I've closed the door if that's what you mean."

"Did you lock it?"

"Well, there's no lock left, really."

"You haven't replaced it?"

"Well, we're still waiting to decide on whom that responsibility should fall. There's nothing left anyway, except those paintings. No surprise in that." Mrs. Bitts was a Neanderthal whose idea of fine art was the plaster interpretations of bible stories that she'd lugged back from the border of Mexico. Her wardrobe consisted entirely of flammable mu-mus in tropical colors, and she'd eat a wire coat hanger if it was battered and fried.

"I'm calling some friends to come over and get them."

"Oh, now, I don't know about a bunch of people coming and tramping through here . . ."

"Mrs. Bitts!"—she could barely comprehend the elementary sequence of time, how could he possibly expect her to understand abstract expressionism?—"there have already *been* a bunch of people—people carrying out my appliances—tramping through there."

Graham Ballard was in Winnipeg because he thought he'd like to take a week and reclaim some feeling for or from his past. His parents were both dead and he was alone, although neither condition was recent. He hadn't really had a plan when he'd made the reservations, and once he'd arrived he was uncertain as to exactly what he wanted to do. He was hoping for some epiphany, some sudden sense of wholeness from being in the place where his earliest memories were set. But nothing. Just a provincial motel room with a startling lack of TV channels to chose from. And he couldn't get a flight back to Los Angeles until the following day. Unable to focus on any book or newspaper he tried to read, unable to endure another minute of the grizzly bears fishing for salmon on his wallpaper, he decided to, at least, try to salvage some purpose from the trip and went to visit his old neighborhood.

His childhood house was no longer standing but his old school was, so he went there. The raised letters on the side of the building no longer spelled out "General Dooley Elementary School." They spelled out "District Office." But they didn't specify what district it was an office of, nor did they indicate as to an office of what. Graham walked up to the padlocked door and peered inside. He hadn't been at this precise place since the third grade, yet he remembered the name Paul Melville. He couldn't remember the phone number of the apartment that he'd moved out of two years ago. He couldn't remember the name of the first girl he'd ever kissed, or the names of any of his junior high school teachers. He couldn't remember the color of his grandfather's eyes. But he remembered Paul Melville.

And Graham got his memories and they made him cringe. He remembered, for some reason, the green metal electrical shed that stood in the corner of the schoolyard. It was where, probably in second grade, that he and Paul Melville would go at recess to hide from the other children. Later they built a fort there out of cardboard boxes where they would go after school, just the two of them, out of sight from teachers and other students, to plan their marriage. His and Paul's. It was nothing sexual; they hadn't developed enough for that. It was just that in their youthful exuberance and innocence they'd had no idea how to cap their emotions, how to limit their dreams, or how forbidden some feelings were. They'd had no idea that two boys were not supposed to be married. All they knew was that their parents were married, and they seemed to like each other an awful lot. To their untrained little minds that seemed to be the only purpose, apparently, for getting married. Graham felt suddenly ill at the memory. He could only imagine how worried it had made his parents. Bless them. He wondered what had ever happened to Paul Melville. Had he turned out to be a fag? Graham liked to believe, needed to believe, that he hadn't.

"Graham?" Graham was jolted to hear the voice. He turned around. A man his own age was looking at him in astonishment. He looked vaguely familiar in that he looked vaguely ordinary. He could have been a co-worker that Graham had once known in some job. He might have been someone who shopped at the same market. He might be Paul Melville. Good God!

"Yes?" Graham said. He remembered Paul Melville as having black hair. This man was blond.

"Graham Ballard?" Graham found the question annoying. If you approach someone out of nowhere and get their first name right, chances are it isn't luck. Chances are it's the person you think it is. Could this be Paul Melville? He didn't *look* gay, at least.

"Paul?" Graham felt his cheeks get hotter, felt embarrassed at what he had just been remembering. God, he hoped Paul Melville didn't remember second grade recess.

The stranger looked irritated. "No!" he said, "Mark Pasqual."

Mark Pasqual? "Mark Pasqual?"

"We went to school here. Years ago! You, me, Paul Melville . . ."

"Oh, yeah," Graham said with forced *bonhomie*, "I remember . . ." Paul

Melville. He remembered Paul Melville. He had never heard of Mark Pasqual.

"So what are you doing here?" Mark Pasqual said, stepping up to Graham with assumed familiarity.

"Well," Graham said, uneasy with the situation, feeling at a disadvantage, "my mother sort of died and . . ."

"Sort of?" Mark said. He looked concerned.

"Well, she did die, but it was two years ago."

Mark stared at him blankly.

"So," Graham continued, at a loss to explain things to himself, let alone to this interloper, "I don't know. I came back to look around, I guess. I live in Los Angeles. I'm not married. My apartment was just broken into." What highlights of the past 25 years does one wedge into a two minute meeting with someone who, despite having identified himself, is still a stranger? Graham decided to take charge. "What are *you* doing here?" he asked. This Mark Pasqual looked at Graham for a moment, pursing his lips.

"This was our school," he said, as though responding to an idiot.

"Yes," Graham said.

"It isn't anymore, of course," Mark said. "It's a district office."

Graham wondered, yes, but a district office of *what*? "I wasn't told. No one told me."

"I work here now. I'm a regional representative," Mark Pasqual said dreamily, looking up at the bricks of district office. He rocked back on his heels, apparently very proud of his position. Graham wanted to ask what he represented. Mark Pasqual suddenly turned back to Graham. "Remember when you and me and Paul Melville used to go and hide behind that old electrical shed?" Paul Melville *and* Mark Pasqual? Graham vividly remembered Paul Melville and himself, alone. Planning their honeymoon. Hunting tigers in Africa. Graham wondered if perhaps this pathetic Mark might have remembered seeing Paul and him together and decided to insinuate himself into Graham's own memories. Graham felt sad and uncomfortable and wanted to leave. "So, still in touch with Paul?" Mark said, smiling lewdly as though there might be some motive behind the asking besides mere cordiality.

"Uh, no."

"Remember when you and I built a fort out of boxes and went there after school?" he said, smiling more widely.

"No," Graham said, "sorry. Don't remember anything of the sort." Who was this Mark Pasqual? "Will you excuse me?" Graham stiffly walked away in the direction from which he'd come.

"Good to see you again," Mark called out. Graham was out of the schoolyard and walking quickly down the sidewalk toward his rented car. "Keep in touch," Mark Pasqual shouted more loudly, in what seemed to Graham a mocking tone, "I'm listed. Mark Pasqual. P-A-S-Q-U-A-L."

Graham walked up the stairs to his apartment. It seemed so alien, so derelict. He looked down at the plaster on the stairs. The criminals had even managed to crack that. Or had it been that way before?

The screen door was bent and misshapen and creaked in the breeze. The door frame showed signs of gnawing. The new door seemed too bright, vulgar. Impregnable, certainly, but cheap, too. Repellent not only to prospective burglars, but to prospective inhabitants as well. Graham put his hand on the cold, unfamiliar doorknob. It was, of course, locked. He turned and went down the stairs to Mrs. Bitts.

She opened the door, her porcine little eyes wide, almost as wide as a normal person's. "Hold on," she said urgently and shut the screen door fast on Graham. Not that he'd expected to be invited in—and not that he'd have accepted had he been—but his unwelcome was made indisputable when Mrs. Bitts latched the door. Graham put his face up to the screen as she ran, actually ran, to her love seat, grabbed a comforter, and threw it over what looked like his table lamp. She quickly looked back over her shoulder and then walked, slowly, into her kitchen. She came back with the keys.

"This was an unexpected expense," she said. She fitted the key into Graham's new door and ran her hand over the mauve enamel surface. "Didn't expect to be having to buy a whole new door for this place. That wasn't exactly covered in your security deposit." Graham was aghast. Was she wanting him to chip in? For his own violation? Did she want him to say he was sorry? Instead of an apology Graham wanted to give her a shove back down the stairs.

"I've been violated," Graham said before he realized he was speaking it.

"Yeah, well, try being a woman. It's what we feel like every day." Mrs. Bitts opened the door and started to enter. Graham grabbed her sleeve.

"Please," he said, "I really want to be alone."

"Fine," Mrs. Bitts said and flung the door open wide. "Suit yourself. And just remember what I said." She stomped down the stairs. What had she said?

Graham took a breath and stepped inside.

His apartment seemed empty and exposed and unsafe. His couch had been frisked for change, its cushions pulled up and left on the floor. His bookshelves were empty (except for the borders of dust); his walls were bare with ghostly discolored rectangles where his paintings had hung. The cable to his television sat in a coiled pile where it had been ripped out of the back of his television set; the drawers of his desk were open and rifled through, some papers and envelopes were strewn on the floor in front. He pulled the top right drawer all the way open and gingerly felt under the old postcards and dried-out pens. He didn't want to touch anything, and not because he didn't want to mess up any criminal fingerprints—everything the criminals could get their fingerprints on they had already carried out of the front door—but because everything seemed dirty and foreign, like it was no longer his. With the tips of his fingers he poked the far corners of the drawer and found the cigar box and pulled it out. His breath came short. He opened the lid. His passport was gone, as was his birth certificate, his car insurance policy, and his class ring. The naked Polaroids that he and Cynthia had taken on a trip to Kauai were mercifully still there, as was the unredeemed and now expired gift certificate for sky-diving lessons and his gym membership card. He tore the Polaroids up into as small pieces as he could and thanked God that the toilet didn't stop up when he flushed them down.

The radio that had been on the top of the toilet tank was gone. All of his pain relievers and old prescriptions for various minor infections over the years were gone. His Bandaids and cotton swabs and moisturizing lotion were still there, and his mouthwash, too, but he picked this up and dropped it into the waste basket. His blow drier was gone.

They'd also taken his towels.

His clock radio in the bedroom had been taken, as had the lamp from his bedside table (though, mysteriously, the lamp shade remained). All of his clothes had been taken off of their hangers and were left in a tangled clump on the floor that extended from the closet to the middle of the room. His dresser drawers had also been upended directly onto the carpet and the empty drawers stacked upright against the wall. On one of his T-shirts was a footprint. He pulled the shirt from the knot of clothes, and smoothed it out. It was the print of a tennis shoe, by the looks of it, and slightly bigger than his own. He wondered why the police hadn't seized this.

The blankets and sheets had been stripped from the bed and the pillows were uncased, but nothing seemed missing, just searched. The criminals had also gone under the bed in search of booty but had only pulled out three odd socks and an old tissue, something that embarrassed Graham to the point where he thought that he might throw up.

" . . . my toaster, my microwave, my spare watches . . ." Graham was talking to Ireen, one of his very best friends. Ireen and Graham had been together once—lovers, companions—but that had ended. Ireen had wanted to be friends only. It was against his better judgment at the time, but now they were friends, and Graham shared in her happiness, hers and Roy's. Ireen had come by for a visit the day of the break-in and had taken his books for safe keeping because she knew how much they meant to him.

"At least they didn't get your books," Ireen said.

"Yes, thank you. When can I come by to pick them up?"

"Anytime. How are you feeling?"

"It's . . . awful."

"Yes, it is," Ireen concurred. "A violation."

"Exactly! Yes! A violation. I feel like I've been raped." Perhaps he'd gone one step too far on that one.

"No offense, Graham, but I doubt very much that you're feeling anything even remotely like you've been raped. No offense."

He had gone that one step too far. "Sorry. I didn't mean—"

"I doubt very much that you'll be unable to sleep nights because you're worried about infection or pregnancy, or that you'll pull away whenever someone so much as touches you."

Fine, thought Graham, just go ahead and take my victimization away. Might as well steal that from me, too. "You're right. I only—"

"Don't worry about it. So what else?"

"My T.V, of course. My answering machine. My blow drier."

"Your *blow drier*? Good God!"

"I know. Can you imagine?"

"Chad said you were lucky they didn't pull the phone line out of your wall. That happens sometimes, you know. And then the phone company makes you pay for it."

"Chad?"

"Your neighbor," Ireen said. "He was there." In his apartment?

"The gay one?" Graham asked.

"I don't know. Is he gay?"

"Judging from number of times I hear 'Mama's Turn' from *Gypsy* pounding through the wall, my guess would have to be yes." Graham had complained anonymously and frequently to Mrs. Bitts, but only for sporadic and inevitably fleeting reprieve from every original cast recording featuring Ethel Merman since *Girl Crazy*.

"Oh, speaking of which," Ireen said, "at least the criminals left your CDs."

"No! They didn't! They took half!"

"Half?"

"Yes! Half! They only took disc two of *Frampton Comes Alive*."

"Wow. You're dealing with some real psychopaths."

"I know. They took all my Frank Sinatra—well, I only had two—but they left all my Paul McCartney."

"Your Beatles?"

"No. They took all my Beatles, but they left all the plain McCartney."

"Knock, knock."

Graham turned, startled, and saw Chad, his gay neighbor, standing in the doorway and holding Graham's clock radio.

"I gotta go," Graham said into the phone.

"No, please," Chad the gay neighbor said, "I can wait."

"Who's there?" Ireen said.

Graham turned his back and cupped the receiver. "My neighbor."

"The gay one?"

"Really," Chad said, "I don't have to be at work for another hour. Do you have any juice?"

"I'll call you later. Bye," Graham said and hung up. "No," he followed Chad into the kitchen. "They took my food, too."

"Whoa!" Chad said. "Harsh!" He closed the refrigerator door. "Here's your clock."

"Thanks." Graham took it but didn't set it down. He just held it in his arms. He walked back into the living room. Chad followed.

"So they took your Beatles?"

"Yes."

"But left your McCartney?"

"Yes."

"Ouch."

Graham looked over to his mostly empty CD racks and suddenly was very sad. "They also took a bunch of stuff that's going to be hard to replace. Some really early punk stuff. And my Sarah Vaughn songbooks. My Betty Hutton . . ."

"Betty Hutton?" Chad was grinning. Graham was uneasy with this grin of his.

"Yes," he said. "Her greatest hits."

"You own Betty Hutton's Greatest Hits?"

"Owned. Yes. Why?"

"Owned. Sorry. Uh, nothing. It's just that I've only known two other guys who owned CDs by Betty Hutton, and . . ."

"Yes?"

"Well, I just wouldn't have guessed it, is all."

Graham noticed with alarm that this gay Chad was looking more deeply into his eyes than seemed necessary, smiling more welcomingly, and even—Graham could swear—inching his way forward. Why did they always do that? Why did they always assume that everyone was gay? Why couldn't they just be satisfied with their own? God knew, there were certainly enough of them. Why couldn't they just leave Graham and his kind alone to repopulate?

"My girlfriend got it for me. I won't miss it," Graham said, putting to an abrupt halt any little gay ideas this Chad might be firming up in his coifed little head. Graham was lying, though, on both counts. He had bought the CD himself and he would miss it. He liked Betty Hutton and that didn't make him a homo.

"So you didn't see anybody that night? Nobody lurking around?"

"Nope," Chad said. "Just the usual queens behind the dumpster having sex."

Graham had had no idea. He'd thought that they were just homeless people; only just recently homeless, of course, because their Polo shirts were still clean and they still had creases in their khakis. "You don't suppose . . .?"

Chad waved him off. "Honey, the only crime they're interested in is vice. Trust me, they already have their own Sarah Vaughn CDs."

"So you didn't notice *anything?*"

Chad shrugged. "There was no one here when I got home. I saw your door open and I came to see if you were all right. When I saw your place all messed up I had a heart attack! I mean, the last guy who lived here was found trussed up with his tongue down his throat. I was looking for you in the closet when your friend came by."

"Ireen."

"She took your books. I took the clock radio."

"Well, thank you."

"So why don't we meet for a drink later?"

"No, thank you."

"Come on. You seem stressed."

"No. I can't."

"How about any time? It doesn't have to be tonight."

"Didn't you say you had to be at work? It's almost half-past. And traffic this time of day . . ."

"All right," Chad said and walked to the door. "As Ethel always said, you can't get a man with a gun." He left.

Graham took his clock radio into the bedroom and set it down. He didn't plug it in. He went to sit on the bed but at the last minute thought better of it. What he needed was some fresh air, or at least some new air. He went to the window and opened the curtains. Sitting on the window sill was a half-smoked cigarette and a pack of matches. He picked up the matches. On the cover was written, in cursive gold-embossed letters, "The Bijoux Lounge."

Graham stood at the front desk of the West Hollywood Sheriff's Department. "They also took my computer, my stainless steel blender, and my clarinet from high school." He was talking to Detective Derlene Werthy.

"'They'? What do you mean 'they'? How do you know it's a 'they'?"

"I . . . don't."

"Who's this 'they,' then?"

"I don't know! 'They!' Criminals! All criminals."

Detective Werthy grunted. "Did you list all this in your report?"

"Yes, I did. And the spare credit cards they took. My Visa, my Ikea, my American Expresses, my—"

"I see it, I see it." The Detective waved dismissively in Graham's direction and read the paper in front of her. Detective Werthy was not a large woman but she made up for it with her density. She seemed heavier than her size would indicate, like she was made up of isotopes that gave her—subatomically speaking—more gravity. It was evident that she liked having a gun, and that she liked wearing pants. Her hair was tugged away from her face and fastened in the back, and her face was spartanly free of make-up, with the notable exception of her lips, which were painted pink with what looked to Graham like glossy latex house paint. Bright pink. "Betty Hutton?" she said, "It says here Betty Hutton."

"Oh. Well, that's in the list of CDs that they stole. Or whoever stole."

"Okay, okay," Detective Werthy said, and loudly stamped the form—the form which Graham had spent hours meticulously filling out, minutely particularizing the details of the violation that had been done to him—with a red stamp which read "RECEIVED."

"We'll be in touch if we need you."

Graham continued to stand in front of the Detective until she looked up. This took some time. But when she did, Graham smiled broadly and brought his hand up to the inside pocket of his jacket. He'd been saving this for maximum effect. Detective Werthy's hand darted into the top drawer of her desk.

Graham was almost shot through the shoulder before he managed to pull out the matchbook.

"A clue!" he said gleefully.

Detective Werthy exhaled and she relaxed her trigger finger. "We'll be in touch."

"But this is a clue!"

"Yes. Thank you. The Bijoux Lounge. A gay tranny bar. Consider it noted. We'll be in touch."

A gay tranny bar? How sordid. The police didn't seem very surprised; at least Detective Werthy—as their representative, as their public face (as it were)—didn't. They must already be onto this ring of criminal deviates. How dare he, he chastised himself, have even thought for a moment that this woman detective had been curt with him?

"Thank you," Graham said earnestly. Detective Werthy grunted.

A week passed and Detective Werthy did not call. But Graham hadn't really noticed. He had steam-cleaned the carpets and bought new appliances and thrown out all of his old underwear and socks and cutlery. He'd scrubbed the fridge. He'd installed two new deadbolts and arranged his shelves to look like a different apartment. But he thought of Detective Werthy again on the day that he went to get his mail and there, standing in the middle of his mail box, was an envelope from the American Express company.

It was thick, like a packet, like a catalogue of the crimes committed against him. It was so thick that it was able to stand up, on its edge, held upright by its own heft. He didn't worry about having to pay it (well, he didn't worry much); the American Express girl on the phone—Becky—said that when he received the bill he should just ignore it, that his claim had been forwarded to the fraud and forgery department for review. And Graham should have just ignored it. He never should have let the envelope taunt him into opening it. He should have held it in the gas flames of his stove.

But the thickness was alluring. Tempting in that mocking yet irresistible way that was so like what some women have.

Graham opened the envelope and the total at the top of the first page hit him like a bowling ball in his diaphragm.

$7, 253.76.

In one afternoon.

He closed his eyes. He took several deep breaths before he was again able to open them.

$7, 253.76.

He unfolded the sheaves of American Express paper and scanned down the individual amounts.

$525.00 at the Marquise Jewelry Warehouse.

$372.99 at Bullock's Wilshire (beside which American Express had kindly thought to add, to avoid any confusion, "social dress").

$195.97 at Kim & Kim Wholesale Beauty Outlet.

$279.45 at Hollywood Splendor Wigs.

Wigs? It horrified Graham deeply to think that his name would be known to the proprietors of Hollywood Splendor Wigs. Were the criminals planning to disguise themselves for further misdeeds elsewhere, further crimes they were about commit after spending $34.78 of American Express's good money for lunch at Handy's Discount Chicken?

$599.30 at Carina's Lingerie Hide-A-Way.

$457.79 at Le Boodoire Fine Scents.

$275.00 at GAS CIGS SNAX for "incidentals."

"A further clue!" Graham exclaimed, triumphantly holding aloft the bill from the American Express company, as he marched into the West Hollywood Sheriff's Department. He was smiling the smile of a job well done. Detective Werthy's expression was inversely proportionate to that of Graham's: the more he beamed, the more she soured. "Look!" his voice pitched higher, "A trail! A trail of purchases in my burglary case!" He paused, momentarily confused at the lack of enthusiasm to see justice done and wrongs righted. "Do you remember me?"

"Yes, Mr. Ballard, I certainly do."

Graham's zeal was back up and he slapped the top of the counter with an open palm in a gesture meant to indicate camaraderie. "Well!" he said.

Without looking at the American Express bill in front of her—brushing it aside, in fact, with a cavalier flick of her hand—Detective Werthy leveled her gaze at Graham. "Mr. Ballard, we are never going to find the people who took your blow drier." Graham withered.

"It wasn't just my blow drier."

"Do you know how many burglaries are committed each day? How many murders?"

"I only know that this is the one that was committed on me."

"Mr. Ballard, I feel your pain," Detective Werthy lied, "but take my word for it. The perpetrators are not going to be apprehended, at least not for this crime. Your belongings are gone. The people who took them are gone. They are good at their jobs."

"They're certainly better than you," Graham blurted out, recklessly ignoring his long held precept never to insult police officers to their faces. Luckily, Detective Werthy indulged him. "It's time to move on," she said with poorly concealed fatigue.

"You really don't seem to care."

"I care as much as I'm able to care."

"So you're not even going to look?"

Detective Werthy raised her hands, indicating the turrets of unattended files that covered her desk. "Do I look like I'm going to look?"

Graham knocked on Chad's door.

"Hey," Chad said.

"Hey."

They stood a moment.

"Yes?" Chad said.

Graham cleared his throat. "I was just wondering . . . " How to phrase this discreetly? A moment passed as Graham considered.

Chad grinned. "What did you have in mind?"

"Yes, uh, are you gay?" Graham knew that he was, but he thought it was polite not to assume. "No offense."

Well, if the police were going to behave so negligently, then he would have to take matters into his own hands. And it was more than just one man's need for justice; Graham felt that criminals should experience the cold reality of justice, and that Detective Werthy should be shown that if one set one's mind to it, one can do one's part in putting the dampers on society's downward spiral into hell.

"No offense taken," Chad said. He leaned against his door jamb and smiled provocatively at Graham. Graham stared back.

"Well?" he demanded. "Are you?"

Chad stood motionless for a moment, then swung his door open wide. "What do you think?" he said. On his living room walls were large framed posters of, respectively, the musical *Chicago*, a muscley man in low-slung jeans holding two car tires, and a juvenile rendering of Marlene Deitrich done with pastels. There were fresh cut flowers on the end tables and all of his furniture was chartreuse.

Graham squirmed. "I don't know! How would I know all your little codes? I know you all like Judy Garland, but so does my mother." Graham pulled the match book from his pocket and held it in front of Chad's face. "Where's this bar?" he asked.

"Where'd you get that?" Chad said, taking the matches and giggling.

"The criminals left it. The police don't care. Where is it?"

"Drag queens robbed you? Pride on!"

"Where is it?"

"Really, Graham, I don't think you're ready yet for the Bijoux. She-male hookers go there. Glue sniffers."

"Where is it?"

"I'm not taking you."

"Where is it?"

The Bijoux Lounge was just off El Centro, north of Fountain. A painted automotive repair sign, though long faded, was still visible on the outside wall of the squat brown building. The door was propped open with a wooden wedge, but a heavy leather curtain kept the sun out.

The Bijoux Lounge had been around, or so it was rumored, since there had still been orange trees in the valley, since before gays even thought about being liberated but were happy enough just to be released after shock therapy. And Rayene had been there since the beginning, back when she'd been Raymond. The Bijoux had evolved over the years as fashions changed and new laws passed, and Rayene had evolved, too; her breasts were the double-cupped trophy of thirty-plus years of hard work and tips. And it had taken no small amount of focus and scrimping. Her home was a cubby-hole a block north of Hollywood Boulevard, her wardrobe was overmended and inexpertly let out, and her explosion of roan hair had never fit exactly right, being mis-shapen from prior heads. Six presidents had been elected, served their country, and retired in the time that it had taken for Rayene to become the woman that she was today.

"Hello, Miss," Graham said, having parted the leather curtain and walked up to the bar. On a bench by the pool table was an immobile woolen lump that may have been someone sleeping or may have been a carelessly discarded coat. "I'm looking for what I believe to be a man in a dress."

Rayene thrust her newly augmented boobs across the bar at Graham. "Do you mind if some of the parts are already woman? The plumbing's still pretty butch, though." Rayene grinned widely. Looking at the crumbling, mossy stubs of her teeth, Graham could see that all of her—or his—self-improvement budget had been spent on her—or his—new breasts. And Graham could not deny that they were indeed a very nice pair. He'd give her that. If only they had been attached to the front of a proper woman.

"No!" Graham chuckled at the small misunderstanding. "You don't seem to understand"—how to phrase this delicately?—"I'm not looking for a man-in-a-dress, per se. Not just any old man. I'm looking for a particular man in a dress. One who sings Betty Hutton. Or pretends to, rather." Graham pulled up a bar stool and sat down. "A very special man in a dress.

You see?"

"Betty Hutton? No. No Betty Hutton." Rayene put her elbows on the bar and adjusted herself so that one breast lay on top of her hand. She caressed it in tiny circles with her thumb. "We had quite a spate of Jayne Mansfields recently, and then there was that Hedy Lamar frenzy a couple of years back. And, of course, Rita Hayworth is an annual thing, usually around the beginning of June. But no Betty Huttons."

Graham looked forlorn.

"I'll tell you what," Rayene said, "I did Chita Rivera two Halloweens ago. I could dig that out of the closet and let it out a bit, glue some of the sequins back on . . . what do you say?"

She wasn't getting it. She was not comprehending the cardinal fact that Graham did not, under any circumstances, under any amount of sedation, want to attempt to mate with her. Regardless of the dress. How could he convey that sentiment to her absolutely? "I would rather have sex with a goat," Graham said finally. He had decided on the straightforward, unambiguous approach so as to prevent the need for any further clarification.

Rayene unambiguously got the message. Without Graham seeing it, without him even seeing Rayene's hand go beneath the bar to grab it, Rayene brought a baseball bat down hard on the bar, right where Graham— at the last second—had snatched his hand.

The woolen lump on the bench jerked upwards and then wheezed, proving that was indeed a form of human being. Graham clutched his hand and held it to his chest, as though in prayer, massaging it like it had been touched by something more than just the breeze from the baseball bat. Rayene's rugged fingers tightened on the wooden handle. Her false eyelashes slowly narrowed like a Venus fly trap into which a plump aphid has just flown. Her scarlet lips parted slightly, and she spoke with a clenched jaw. "I think you'd better leave."

Graham, needless to say, thought likewise.

Graham paused outside of Hollywood Splendor Wigs on Hollywood Boulevard. He wasn't sure exactly what he was going to do, or even what he wanted to do. He just wanted to do something. He wondered if he was perhaps being masochistic; if, by expanding the crime scene from his apartment, he was just peeling off the scab instead of letting things heal. Maybe he just wanted to get a clue from the sales clerk; a face, a mannerism, a distinguishing tic. Maybe he just wanted to reprimand her for being so careless. He wasn't sure.

He looked down and was surprised to see his knuckles clenched white around the American Express bill. He also noticed that he was standing on a star on the sidewalk honoring Mister Rogers. He smoothed out the American Express bill and opened the door.

From the floor to the ceiling, shelves displayed heads—strangely vacant heads, even for styrofoam ones—sporting an array of sculpted hair in a variety of heights and colors, from a pink beehive that looked like a tornado of cotton candy to a steely-blue ducktail that had sparkles glued on it. Graham even noticed (on a shelf that also held an adding machine and a sluggish hamster in a cage) several comparatively conservative styles that could actually pass as bad dye jobs and not just novelty items. Three girls, teenagers, were at the far end of the L-shaped counter, giggling and slapping each other as they tried on flapper bobs. A man in a tweed overcoat and sunglasses stood motionless, face to face with a wig form outfitted with a tightly pin-curled gray wig, and on which someone had drawn eyes with an orange marker.

Behind the counter, in the back by the filing cabinets, was a man in his fifties whose canary-colored hair was whipped into a froth around his bald spot and whose tight jeans hugged his less tight buttocks. He was dancing around his workbench styling a wig, brandishing his comb and hair spray as though he was conducting a symphony. Graham inhaled and started toward him.

"Can I help you?" a woman said from behind him. Startled, Graham spun around and saw her. She had been sitting on a foot stool behind the cash register. She was portly, sixty-ish, and was smoking a cigarette.

"Um,"—where should he begin?—"my name is Graham Ballard."

The woman's smile remained but she couldn't hide the caution in her eyes.

"Oh?" she said, waiting for Graham's next move, waiting to see how Graham would manifest his schizophrenia. For some reason—ever since they closed down the state mental hospitals—the schizophrenics on the boulevard all gravitated toward the wig shops. Which was not surprising, really, medically speaking.

"Um, does that name sound familiar?" Graham asked tentatively.

"Well . . ." The woman was tense now, on high alert, prepared for Graham to announce his extraterrestrial lineage, or to implicate her in the covert worldwide conspiracy being waged against him by the CIA.

"The only reason I ask," Graham said, "is that, well, someone has been in here using my American Express."

The woman relaxed, nodded, and took a long drag from her cigarette. "Oh," she sighed, "I get it."

Graham was confused, not getting it himself.

"Get what?"

"Don't worry, Sugar, just call Amex and they'll take care of it." She winked.

"No. They already have. It's just that—"

"Did he come in alone, is that what you're asking?"

How could this woman be so casual? A crime had been committed.

"Yes! Who did he come in with? What did he look like?"

"That's not important now, is it? Just go home and—"

"Not important? It's incredibly important! It's vital!"

"Now, Honey, don't you worry. You're a good-looking fellow. People make mistakes. Just call him. I'm sure he's sorry. Just kiss and make up and put all of this behind you."

"What are you talking about? Kiss *who*? I want that bastard in jail!"

"Oh, Sweetheart, I'm sure it's just a spat, is all. Now, really! *Jail*? Good lord, you guys are *sooo* dramatic!"

Graham stood back. "What guys?"

"You guys. You know, you gays. But it'll be all right. You have some words, and the next thing that happens is he borrows your credit card and goes wig shopping. I see it every day. And believe me, jail time never solves anything. Send him to jail for the night, Honey, and you've lost him forever. Trust me."

"What about . . . what was it? The jewelry place."

"Marquise Jewelry Warehouse."

"What about them?"

Graham and Ireen were having drinks at the Parasol Room.

"I didn't go," Graham said. "I couldn't bear it."

"What about the Lingerie Barn?" Chad said, sitting down with a drink. He was a bartender at the Parasol Room and had just finished his shift. He and Ireen had exchanged phone numbers on the night of Graham's break-in; the lonely night that Graham had spent in a Winnipeg motel room deciding to look for some memories at his old school only to be accosted by Mark Pasqual.

"It's pointless. No one cares. The police don't care. Wig boutique clerks don't care. The American Express secret agents don't care."

"Why do you care?" Chad said. "You're not going to get any of your stuff back. Why don't you just rebuild?" Chad and Ireen had started going

to the gym together, and had gone to two movies, and Chad had even made
her dinner one night. "We didn't think you were home," Ireen had said when
Graham asked her why he hadn't been invited. "Your lights weren't on."

"I care because it happened to me. I care because it isn't right."

"Jesus, honey," Chad said, "a lot worse things happen to people all the time."

"Oh, really?" Graham said. His incredulity was not sincere.

"Yeah. People get murdered and are hit by drunk drivers or are swindled
by telephone solicitors . . ."

"$599.30 at Carina's Lingerie Hide-A-Way?" Ireen said. She was re-read-
ing Graham's American Express bill, which was somewhat tattered now,
with mai tai stains.

"I know I should just be big about this," Graham said, "chalk it up to
the pitfalls of modern urban living and all. But I can't. I can't be satisfied
that just because I've been burglarized means the odds of my being hit by a
bus this year are somewhat lessened. No. This is an awful world if things
like this are taken for granted."

"Oooo!" Chad said, mincing. "A vigilante! I love it!"

"What kind of lingerie costs $599.30?" Ireen said. She turned to Chad
and put her hand on his arm. "Maybe we should check this place out?"

Chad took the bill from Ireen. "Does it give the address?"

Graham thought they looked cute together, Chad and Ireen; better than
Roy and Ireen. They were both blond and clean, nice teeth, in shape. Like
sisters. Roy was a bit on the heavy side, with thick features, and his skin was
prone to rashes.

"It's on San Vicente. Near Fairfax," Graham said. He finished the last
gulp of his drink and got up.

"Where are you going?" Ireen said to Graham.

"Oh, I know this place!" Chad said, excited. "I've driven by it. It's the
place that has the windows with the mannequins set up like they're doing a

porno movie."

"Oh, yeah," Ireen said. "Not far from Sammy Red's Hot Dogs! We could stop by there first for some vegetarian chili."

Graham left.

Graham drove down Fountain, heading to Handy's Discount Chicken for a bite to eat, and reflexively turned his head when he passed the Bijoux Lounge. The leather curtain was drawn back to let out some of the smoke and Graham could see Rayene leaning against the bar shelling peanuts. He crossed El Centro and did a U-turn.

When he walked in Rayene stood up quickly—to a height of six feet six inches in her heels—and squared her shoulders. She hissed through her teeth and reached for the baseball bat.

"Look," Graham said, "I'm sorry. What I said before . . . I was angry and frustrated. I mean, I was just robbed and the police are no help and . . . I mean, you're very attractive. I think you've got the nicest stack I've seen in long time. But I'm straight. So I didn't mean to hurt your feelings."

"So you're straight?" Rayene said.

"Yes."

Rayene let go of the bat but still did not smile. "Well, if you wait a year 'til after my operation, I'll be straight, too."

Graham smiled. "We'll see what happens."

"Want a drink?"

"Sure. A beer?"

"I'll get you a boilermaker."

Graham drank it in a gulp and managed to keep from vomiting by closing his eyes and holding his breath. When he finally gasped Rayene patted his hand.

"Feel better?" she said.

"Much," Graham said.

"You seem kinda down. No luck with your pre-op?"

Graham shook his head. "Well," Rayene said, "enjoy the show. It oughta buck you up. It does me."

The show? Behind Graham a reedy man with a ratty face mounted the wooden stage behind the pool table. He was wearing a green day-glo mini-dress and clear plastic sandals. On his head was an uncombed blond wig that was cut just above his large ears, and on top of that was a rhinestone tiara. His chest was shaved down from his neck in a semi-circle, but stopped about an inch above the neckline of his dress, his thick chest hair giving the impression of a fur trim. A small group of men who looked like they just wanted a dry place to sleep sat on folding chairs scattered around the pool table. Graham heard the needle drop on an old 45 and a scratchy recording of Petula Clark singing "Downtown" played from the speakers in the corners. Graham hated when people acted when they sang, which pretty much ruled out Las Vegas for him, and certainly all drag queens. Graham ordered another boilermaker.

"Yup. It's a bastard cold world nowadays. Yessiree," Rayene said.

"Heartless," Graham said.

"I'm with you; I got no time for the police. Back when I was living with Jimbo and he got liquored up and started breaking my furniture? They didn't even bother to come by when they found out it was two guys."

"They don't deserve the pensions we pay them," Graham said.

"And do you think them cops gave a preacher's fart when I had my purse snatched last April? Not on your goddamned life! They wound up taking me down to the station. For solicitation! There is no respect for us in-betweeners."

"We've lost our humanity," Graham said.

One man clapped as Petula Clark's voice trailed off. Graham glanced toward the stage. Replacing the blond man was a taller man. This new one was wearing a relatively tasteful evening dress of blue tulle which looked as though it had been tailored to him. He was also wearing low-heeled modest white pumps, which also looked new, and understated gold earrings with a matching necklace that looked real. His face sagged a bit in places (the jowls, the brow, the left eye) and he could have used a more recent shave. His wig, which seemed to fit, was a newly shellacked still life of red hair.

The last thing Graham expected to—or wanted to—hear at that moment was a Born-again Christian pop tune about the sweet love of Jesus Christ, which is exactly what this man began to pretend to sing. Rayene, Graham noticed, was likewise taken aback. Songs promoting the Christian lifestyle seemed rather an odd choice for a man in sequins and falsies to be singing to a roomful of inebriated sodomites. There were no gospel singers in the diva pantheon of transvestites. Not even Mahalia Jackson, who one might think would make the drag queen grade. But no, not even Mahalia.

"And He shall come with outstretched ha-and

"And lead us to the promised la-and

"Away from lust and perfidy

"To faith and hope and chastity," the man (who'd obviously wandered about as far off the path of the righteous as is humanly possible) pretended to sing.

"What the fuck is that bitch singing?" Rayene said uncharitably.

Graham generously gave the man the benefit of the doubt and assumed that he had post-modernist motives.

The man finished and took a bow. "Thank you," he said tearfully to the handful of customers who didn't care and were certainly not applauding. "And I thank God as well. And I thank Marquise Jewelry for these modest baubles. And I thank Jesus Christ my personal savior and Hollywood Splendor Wigs for allowing me to be as beautiful as I am today." Graham sat bolt upright. Marquise Jewelry? Hollywood Splendor Wigs? Graham, until recently, had been blissfully unaware that either of these establishments even existed. But now he wasn't, and now they were brought together in the same sentence by this hideous man. Coincidence? He couldn't be sure. Perhaps in this under-world of gender misinformation such concurrences were as natural as the love of a man for a woman in other circles.

The man gracelessly stepped down from the stage. "Sorry," he said as he clattered into a cocktail table, "new heels." Graham watched as the man tried to right himself. New heels, indeed. $123.87 at Atomic Shoe Explosion.

The man's new heels propelled him toward Graham. Graham regarded him baldly and without shame. The man, in turn, gently kissed his finger-tips and patted Graham on the cheek. "Peace of Christ be with you," he said and disappeared behind a water-stained velvet curtain next to the ice machine.

The newly gathered mist from the boilermakers dissipated from Graham's head. Hollywood Splendor Wigs?

He leaped off the bar stool and ran through the curtain and down an unlit hallway. At the end a door was ajar and Graham heard a radio playing. He didn't hesitate.

The tiny room had been hastily constructed with unfinished plywood underneath a concrete stairwell. A lacy scarf draped over a table lamp gave the cubicle a pink glow. Dusty boas, sequined and unsequined bustieres, gloves, hats, and underwear lay in piles on the floor and hung from nails in the wall. Cardboard boxes full of power tools, chipped glasses, and Christmas decorations had been abandoned where they had been dropped. Pictures from movie and porn magazines were taped above the dilapidated make-up table where the man sat. Graham's feet were planted as far apart as his shoulders. His breath was fast and shallow. His hands formed fists.

The man looked up, not only intrepidly, but smiling beautifically. His wig was off and Graham saw now that he had more hair on his arms than on his head. All he was wearing was a natty, discolored bra, a girdle, and a pair of hose with runs. "Peace of Jesus be with you, friend," the drag said.

"Where'd you get that dress?" Graham demanded, pointing at the dress that was balled up on the chair next to him.

"I sense by your tone that your curiosity is not just out of an appreciation of style."

"Where, I said!"

"A little blind lady in Chinatown who channels Edith Head makes them for me."

Graham marched over and picked up the dress that still held the heat from the man's body. He looked at the label. Bullock's Wilshire.

"I'm Graham Ballard."

"Yes," the man said, "I suspected as much." He removed his earrings, then some make-up. "I don't know how this is going to sound to you, but I've found Jesus Christ."

"I'm not surprised. You managed to find my hair dryer."

"I was a different person then."

"And the sandwich grill that even I'd forgotten about."

"I've repented for my sins."

"You're not serious?"

"I've opened my heart to Christ."

"Well you can just repent my goddamned microwave oven back up to my goddamned apartment!"

"I was lost on the tortuous highway of iniquity. I am so sorry."

"Sorry won't do."

"It's all gone. Gone to the demons. I'm so sorry."

"Fuck sorry!" Graham blustered, eyes bulging, spittle flying. "Fuck . . .
sorry!"

"I understand your anger."

"My Betty Hutton CD."

The man shook his head sorrowfully. "I don't do Betty anymore. Too
wanton. I only do Sandi Patty now."

Graham impulsively drew his fist back to strike the man. The man
closed his eyes, placidly offering up his cheek. With barely a whisper the
man mouthed the words, "Forgive him, Father, for he knows not what he
does." Graham's fist arced, the man winced.

But Graham's hand passed the man's face and instead grabbed the wig
off of the table. "This is mine," he said.

The man opened his eyes, confused. It took him only a moment to realize that the strange animal shaking in Graham's hand was in fact his wig.
That wasn't right. He deserved to be punished, that was certain, but to take
away a man's livelihood? "That's not right. No." The man made an attempt
to grab the wig from Graham but Graham neatly yanked it out of reach.
With his other hand Graham grabbed a jar of cold cream off of the make-
up table before the man could block him. Graham tucked this into the crook
of his arm. Graham then lunged for an eyebrow pencil, but the man, evidently roused from his shock, anticipated the trajectory of Graham's arm and
grabbed it first. They both pulled on it. "No!" the man screamed. The pencil
snapped. Graham put his half in his pocket. The man threw himself over the
make-up table, protecting his cosmetics with his body. "Revenge is Satan's
spawn!" he cried.

"Give me the shoes," Graham said sternly. The man didn't respond.
Graham was going to kick him in the leg but the man had already started
weeping. "I want the shoes."

"Fuck off!" the man sputtered. Graham looked around the room.

He grabbed the dress, and a blouse that was hanging from a nail on the wall. He turned to leave.

Graham's sense of triumph was quickly quashed when he saw, standing in the doorway, a very angry Rayene, her bright red wig pulled back and snug like a baseball cap. She had kicked off her shoes and stood with her knees bent, stretching the daisy-sprinkled blue fabric of her dress. She held her baseball bat tightly just above shoulder level. Graham heard the sobbing behind him end abruptly with a gasp.

Rayene pulled her lips back from her teeth and said, in a rumbling baritone, "I knew you'd be trouble from the minute I laid eyes on ya."

Graham's arms went slack, his body preparing for flight, and he dropped the purloined wig, make-up, and accessories. Hadn't he and Rayene gotten over their little rough spot? Hadn't they become something like friends? "Wait . . ." he said weakly.

Rayene drew the bat up closer to her body, the sleeves of her dress slipping off of her taut biceps. "I'll teach you to mess with my sister."

"But . . ." Graham sputtered.

Rayene let out a growl and pounced forward. Graham covered his face with his arms and unlocked his knees.

He braced to feel the smack of the bat across the side of his head and, quite frankly, would be relieved when it came.

The air was knocked out of his lungs as he was shoved sideways. He tripped over a box containing barbells from last years Mr. Bijoux Lounge contest and landed on his side on the floor. He opened his eyes when he heard a screech and saw Rayene swing the bat and smash a large nail file out of the hand of the man who robbed him.

"Not my hands!" the man screamed.

"All right," Rayene said calmly and drew back with her bat and aimed for his face.

"You *bitch*!" the man shrieked. "You fat *bitch*!" He ducked and ran past Rayene and out the door. Graham heard a burst of applause from the bar as the man ran through it unwigged and wearing only underwear. He screamed but his voice was suddenly cut off as the leather curtain fell closed behind him.

Rayene stared out the doorway, her bat still raised. She turned and saw Graham crumpled on the floor by the wall.

"Lucky I got here in time," she said. "You just about had a manicure file imbedded in your ribs."

Rayene set her bat down and walked over to Graham. "I had a weird feeling about her," Rayene said. "She never did Judy. Never. That's just not normal." She reached down and offered Graham her hand. Graham took it.

"So *I'm* your sister?" he said.

Rayene pulled Graham to his feet. "Sorry," she said, "it just sort of slipped out."

"Don't worry about it."

"It's actually a compliment."

"I got that. Thank you."

Rayene poked at the wig on the floor with her stockinged toe. "Did you want this?"

Graham looked down at it and thought a minute. "No. Not really."

Rayene nodded. "I've always found it healthy to just move on."

"I guess you're right."

"Sometimes a wig is just a wig."

"I suppose."

"How about a drink?" Rayene said, brightening. "I bet you need a drink."

"Sounds good."

"Do you want to call your friends?"

Graham shrugged. "No. Not really."

Rayene slapped him on the back. "Come on."

Day Job

THE HOLLYWOOD SUN HUNG OVER the Hollywood sign like a cryptic piece of punctuation as it left the Valley, carrying with it a carpet of morning smog that rolled over the lip of the Hollywood Hills like the steam off of a nice hot cup of coffee. On Hollywood Boulevard, near Vine, the Checks Cashed/Donuts was open for business. Inside, behind the counter, Mania Fish sat composing. She was large in the way that made women unattractive.

"I live on Hollywood and Vine." Mania Fish lifted her pencil from the napkin. She liked the line.

She hummed it again: "I live on Hollywood and Vine." Yes. It spoke something. A Grammy, perhaps? Dare she think it? Cher could certainly use a hit right now. So could Tina. Hell, who *couldn't* use a hit right now. Mania wiped her hand down over her forehead, flattening her uneven bangs. She'd never quite imagined herself as the Queen of the Top 40, but it could be an in. If she went double platinum, then she could really get her message out there. She had two choices as she saw it: either she had to get out of L.A. or she had to get into L.A.

There was a tap on the window and Mania looked up.

Outside, over the glass-topped counter on which she leaned, past the empty wood-paneled room whose walls were adorned with framed headshots signed by the extras and lounge singers whose heads they were of, through the sooty windows that gave view to Hollywood Boulevard, Mania Fish saw the bright and round face of Lurene. Lurene was tapping the glass with a toothbrush. Behind Lurene, Mania saw two bobbing sets of buttocks that belonged to Lurene's fellow Star-Washers who were hard at work. Was it really the third Saturday of the month already? They came every month, the Star-Washers. On the third Saturday. With their toothbrushes and furniture polish they would hunch over the sidewalk outside of Checks Cashed/Donuts and polish Barry Manilow's star, removing the dirt and the gum, making it shine. Lurene ("Mandy"), Missy ("Sandra"), and Shelly

("Lola") had gotten there early—to accost as many passersby as possible—
and had been there when Mania had opened up the shop. Mania often
opened up alone, and often closed up alone. But she was never worried—not
even on Friday nights when the hopheads took back the streets—because she
always had Miss Stella with her to protect her.

Lurene was smiling and pulling faces. It was unnerving, that wide, loose
face trying to catch Mania's eye. Just saying hello. Not wanting Mania to
forget that they were out there, working up an appetite. As if! It was days
like this, the third Saturdays, that Mania wanted to introduce Lurene to
Miss Stella; Lurene with her big face, just hanging there, mere yards away.
But it would be too easy. Lurene wiggled her fingers in a wave and bent
down and continued scrubbing.

Mania watched as the three rumps dipped and swayed, clad in bright
synthetics that were stretched to their chemical capacity.

"They wash my star and make it shine . . ." Mania Fish sang, " . . . they
wash my star in salty brine . . ." She set her pencil down on the glass case
and walked over to the cash register. Taped above the keys was a yellowed
piece of newsprint that read, simply, "ENDURE." She opened the cash
drawer and took out a quarter. She went to the pay phone, which was
behind the counter, next to the ice machine.

"Yeah?" Lollie said on the other end of the line.

"Lollie, it's me. Mania."

"Oh, my God! Mania! How are you? I mean, how are you *feeling*?"

"It was quick. I'm okay. It was this morning."

"This *morning*?"

"Well, last night, I guess."

"Last *night*?"

"Yeah. They're open 24 hours."

"24 hours? Christ, you can't even buy beer 24 hours. Well, I'm happy. I mean, I'm sad. I mean, are you happy?"

"I'm relieved."

"Oh good. Then I'm relieved."

"Thanks for the reference."

"No problem, Honey. Did it hurt?"

"No."

"Oh."

There was no sense of loss. There had been no morning sickness, no cravings (other than the usual ones), no maternal glow. There was no little Mania to haunt her dreams. She hadn't even felt pregnant.

"Did you make that bastard pay for it?"

"He doesn't even know."

"Oh, Mania! It was his, too!"

"It wasn't his, too! It wasn't . . . anything. It was nothing."

"Hey! I'm not talking marriage here. Just doctor's bills."

There was a jingle as the glass door opened.

"Where are you?" Lollie said. "Are you at work?"

"Yeah. Where else would I be?"

A balding man in a plaid jacket walked up to the counter and smiled at Mania politely.

"But Mania, couldn't you have taken the day off or something?"

"Why?"

"I mean, go to a movie or something? Go for a drink?"

"Excuse me," the man said, "but I'm in a bit of a hurry."

Mania put a finger in her spare ear and turned her back to the counter.

"At nine a.m.?" Mania said.

"You could've come to my place for a drink. Oh, Christ! What time is it?"

"I don't know. After nine. Ten-ish."

"Ten-ish! Oh, Christ! I've got an appointment at Kerry's this morning!"

Mania rolled her eyes. "What now?"

There was another jingle from the door as the man left. Mania turned back around.

"Calf implants."

Calf implants? What would be left of the old Lollie after that? She'd had her bones shaved, her lips thickened, her buttocks drained of fat, her teeth re-enameled, her breasts balanced, her hairline reshaped, her colon holistically realigned. Mania herself had no such need for the modern renovations of womanhood, not like Lollie and Maxie, though she had noticed lately—when she managed to take the time and pause in front of a mirror—a certain slippage of cheek, a certain gravitational settling of her mass. But what did she—the Voice of the People—need with such plastic amenities?

"Calf implants?"

"The cycling look is in."

"So why don't you cycle?"

"Who has time? Really, Mania, you should treat yourself to a little something. Maybe some tabs or something. Maybe some chest work."

"Listen, Lollie—or should I say 'Gyrene'?—I'm a woman of the people, for Christ's sake! I'm not some blow-up doll! I don't need to get thousand dollar titties just to have them yanked shapeless by some drunk hanging over the side of a mud-wrestling pit! For a five dollar tip!"

"I am a respectable artist! I'm in the union, you know!"

"Then why do you have to call yourself 'Gyrene'?"

"Gyrene is the name I dance with! It's exotic!"

"It's cheap."

"You should listen to Maxie more often."

Oh, yes. Maxie. Her mother. Mania's mother. Now there was a work of art. Maxie hailed from "Beverly Hills adjacent." Sure. In a global sense of the word, perhaps. She lived in Echo Park. The only thing Beverly Hills adjacent about her was her face, because that was where she bought it.

"You know, Mania," Lollie made the effort to speak with a warmer tone; Mania had, after all, been through a tough morning. "When you and her go out together, people think you're sisters."

"Sisters! We look nothing alike! She looks like her surgeon's third wife!"

"Mania, I'm late. Let's talk later. Meet me at the Parasol Room after you get off work, okay? I'll buy you a hurricane. Are you sure you're all right?"

"I'm fine." Mania hung up. She walked over to the counter, pulled out an éclair from the display cabinet, and sat down on her stool. It was nothing, really. It's not like she could even imagine herself being a mother. She picked up her pencil and tapped it on the top of the glass case.

"I live on Hollywood and Vine . . ."

She made the sound of a sweeper on a snare drum through her clenched teeth.

"Tish, tish-ta-tish, tish, tish-ta-tish . . .

"Da-dum, da-dum, da-dum is mine . . ." She took a bite of eclair and resumed tapping.

"Da-dum, da-dum, da-dum, so fine . . ." Where would she even put a baby? She lived in a bachelor apartment. Where would she, Mania, sleep? Where would she wash it? Where would she wash diapers? In the sink? Then where would she put the dirty dishes?

No, no, no. She was a free spirit. She was unfettered. She was a poet. She belonged to *all* people. The earth was her home.

And where would she find room for a doting grandmother? And—oh!—Maxie would definitely dote! And chastise. And ridicule.

"No living eyes have seen me nude," Mania scrawled quickly, "no dum

da da da dum intrude . . . I don't let nobody see . . . what goes on inside of
me." Mania flushed. That was good! "I don't let nobody see . . . what goes
on inside of me." That felt like art. The blessings of the muse were flowing
through her. She was channeling . . . who? Helen Reddy? Yes! She was
being visited!

She set down her pencil. She leaned over to the cash register and peeled
off the yellowing newsprint that said "ENDURE," crumpled it up, and
threw it away. She reached in her purse and pulled out a torn piece of cardboard and taped this up instead. It said, "MADE WITH REAL CHEESE!"

She had come across this piece of inspiration the night before. She had
been in the convenience market and was shopping for food that required no
additional pots or pans, something servable in its own browning box, and
she had seen the words emblazoned on the side of a frozen pizza. "MADE
WITH REAL CHEESE!" It had struck her. When one is of an enlightened
disposition, as Mania was, enlightenment could happen anywhere. One
always had to be on guard. One always had to be ready.

What was that simple, emphatic little sentence actually saying? she'd
asked herself. What were the alternatives? *Pretend* cheese? Suddenly it all
made sense to her. It was what was wrong with the world. What was wrong
with her life, anyway. It should be taken for granted that something like
cheese should be real. It was exactly what she needed. She needed some
real cheese.

She had torn off the corner of the box and then chose a pizza with
pretend cheese (she kept a strict budget) and went to the check-out.

Mania looked up from her handiwork to lock eyes with Lurene. Lurene
rubbed her stomach in a pantomime of hunger. What? Again? They'd
already been in twice that morning, and had twice left with chubby arm-
loads of donuts. Between the three of them they'd gone through six jam-
filleds, three crumbs, and eight day-olds. Mania distractedly brought her
hand up and caressed her own empty stomach.

The bell on the door jingled and Lurene trudged in, knee-protectors affixed over her stretch pants. She was smiling widely, hugely. An eerie light shone from deep within her eyes.

"Hey, Mania! Those jam-filleds sure are fresh today! Yum!"

"Three more?"

"Make it six. Don't want to keep bothering you."

"Fine."

"Did I ever tell you that Barry came to see us once?" Yes. She had. "And that we were on Entertainment Tonight, even?" Yes, she had. The third Saturday of every month for the past year and a half now Mania had, politely at first—rudely, of late—declined Lurene's offer to watch the videotape.

"Yes, actually, you have."

"Debbie's doing Johnny Mathis now. Who does she think she is? Just because Barry kissed her cheek once, now she's trying to lure out Johnny. Fickle bitch! But not us! We're loyal. We're not doing it just for all the publicity. We do it 'cause we love Barry."

"Four-fifty."

"But Debbie! I should've known. She doesn't even own the import of *Barry, Live at the Palace.*"

"Four-fifty."

Lurene pursed her lips and looked thoughtfully over Mania's head. "You know," she said, "I could practically write a script about what's happened to me out there."

"Four-fifty."

Lurene laughed. "We even had this one foreign lady ask us to lift up our blouses so she could take a picture! Can you imagine?"

"Not really. Four-fifty."

Lurene sighed and pulled out her change purse. "Here you go, Honey.

Well, better run! Don't want the girls saying I'm not pulling my weight!"

"Right." Little chance of that.

Mania picked up her pencil.

"I live on Hollywood and Vine . . .

. . . and wine . . .

. . . table scraps and wine." That was it! She had it! Mania Fish, the Pulse of the People! Catchy, yet with a message! It was a blow to the System. A blow for the Republic. Not a solution, mind you, but a blow nonetheless. She had, after all, a responsibility as an artist. The door clanged again and Sol Roe entered. Sol Roe owned Checks Cashed/Donuts, plus the one down on Cahuenga. Mania heard the high-pitched "Hello, Sol's" from the sidewalk before the door glided shut again.

Sol walked over to the cash register and opened it. "Hmmm, the jam-filleds were a good idea." He walked over to the display cabinet and slid open the door. He pinched several maple bars before finally selecting one. He reached beside the coffee pot and took four dairy creamers and lined them up on the counter. He peeled back the foil from one of the little plastic thimbles and sipped it, then he took a bite of his donut.

"Anything I should know about?" he asked.

"No. This place is a machine," Mania said. Sol took another bite. "Barry's girls, you know. Always good for business."

"Hmmm," Sol said. He took another sip and tossed the empty creamer into the trash basket. He peeled back the tab of a second. He looked at the cash register.

"So what's this about real cheese?"

"Nothing. Just inspiration."

"Hmmm. So frozen pizza inspires you?" He took a bite and chewed slowly. "Is this another of your musicals?"

"Maybe."

"Hmmm." Sol Roe went through the door to the back carrying his two remaining creamers and the rest of his maple bar.

Mania pulled the stool up to the counter.

"I live on Hollywood and Vine

"I live on table scraps and wine . . ."

More snare drum. Distorted slide guitar.

"I live in . . . out of a shopping bag

      . . . on change that's spare . . .

"I live in. . . ." The door opened and a dusty, matted man entered and stopped just inside. He smiled sheepishly.

Oh, Christ! "We *sell* the day-olds," Mania said before the man even stepped forward.

"Ain't this Checks Cashed?"

"It's Checks Cashed/Donuts."

"I'd like to cash a check, Ma'am." He strode to the counter, his untied boots clopping. He pulled out a frayed, folded piece of paper. He held it out to Mania.

"Small bills, please, Ma'am," he said. Mania didn't move. She only looked at the man as the beginnings of a sneer pulled at the corner of her mouth. He set the piece of paper on the counter in front of her and smoothed it flat with both hands.

The check was for $64.51. It was signed by Esther Woods. It was made out to the Gas Company.

"What the hell is this?"

"It's endorsed," the man said.

Mania flipped the check over with the tip of her pencil. On the back, in felt marker, was written, "The Gas Company."

"See?" the man said, triumphant.

"We don't cash third-party checks."

"I don't see no sign."

"Trust me."

The pay phone rang. "I'll get it," Mania yelled to Sol in the back.

"Checks Cashed/Donuts, Darlene speaking."

"Mania? It's Buzz." Buzz. She had always loathed men with onomatopoetic names. What had she been thinking? "Mania, I just heard."

Mania sighed. "Heard what?"

"Heard what? What do you think? Lollie just called me."

"Yeah, well, so what?"

Buzz took a moment to think. "I don't know."

"Yeah, so, who cares?"

"Mania, why didn't you call?"

"I was saving my quarters for laundry."

The door opened again and Mania looked up. An older, distinguished man came in and stood behind the dusty man, who waited expectantly.

"I'm busy," Mania said to Buzz.

"I think that donuts can wait, Mania! You've just gotten rid of my son!"

"It wasn't a son."

"It wasn't a son? A daughter?"

"No . . . I don't know. Maybe it was a son. Look, Buzz, it was nothing. And it's none of your business." Lurene now entered, with Missy and Shelly in tow. What was this? They had all day to harass her. Why wait until a line formed? The herd instinct?

"Hey, Sweetheart, get off the Goddamned phone," the distinguished man said. "All I need is a couple of fritters."

"Mania, I'm coming down there," Buzz said.

"Buzz, you're an idiot. I don't want you here. Or anywhere."

The glass door swung open and hit the wall with a reverberant thud.

"Dammit! Open slowly!" Mania screamed. "*Open slowly!* Can't you read?"

A harried man stumbled past the line that had formed and walked up to the counter. He raised his hand, which was in a paper bag, and pointed it at Mania. "Get over here," he said quietly.

"Mania?" Buzz asked. She dropped the phone.

"Gimme the cash," the man sputtered. He had curly hair, glittering eyes, and a small, neat, horizontal scar on his right cheek, just below the eye. He was cute. Cute-*ish*. Mania liked her men with a few flaws. Nothing drastic, mind you, just something small and unobtrusive.

"Gimme the cash, lady, or I'll shoot," the man said, his voice pitching higher.

Yes! Mania thought. This is the real cheese!

"Take me!" she said.

"What?" the man said. Lurene, Missy, and Shelly whispered excitedly.

"Me! Not just the cash! Take me, too!" Mania said. She opened the cash register and pulled out the money, stuffing it into her purse.

"Lady . . ."

"No!" Mania interrupted. "Take me! I'll be a hostage. Here." She handed him the purse.

"What the heck is going on out here?" Sol Roe asked, stepping into the doorway from the back.

"We're being robbed and I'm being taken hostage." Sol dropped to the floor with a thud.

"Wait, lady . . ."

"Hold on! There's more." Mania turned and went into the back. "Excuse me," she said as she pushed past Sol. She went to his desk and kicked the bottom drawer. It opened and she lifted out a cash box. "Just a sec. I'll get

my jacket." She ran and grabbed it off of the ice machine and came around
to the front of the counter. She passed the man and went for the door. She
turned. "Come on!" she said.

"Oh, for Chrissakes . . ." the gunman said. He looked at the line of
people. They stared at him. Sol Roe peeked over the counter. The gunman
turned and ran out the door to where Mania was waiting for him on
the sidewalk.

"Which one is it?" Mania said, looking down the row of parked cars. The
man went around the side of a blue Impala and opened the driver's door.

"Oh, the blue Impala! Perfect!" Mania ran to the passenger's side and
climbed in. "You criminals always drive blue Impalas!" The man started the car
and sped away. Mania, sitting with the cash box in her lap, turned to him
and smiled.

Two blocks down he screeched around a corner and jolted to a stop.
Mania was thrown against the dashboard.

"What are you stopping for? Aren't you supposed to be . . . what is it
you people say? 'On the lam'?"

The man turned and looked at Mania. He threw his gun at her. Mania
opened the bag and pulled out a cucumber. "Oh, how clever!" she laughed.

"Get out!" the man growled.

"No. Wait. Nevada is only four hours away. All we have to do is get on
the Ten . . ." Yes! Vegas! She hadn't exactly imagined herself as the sequins
and feathers type, but it would do. She could do it! And she would transform it! Her message would transform it.

"Get out now."

"Or what?" Mania said. He glared at her. "Or what? I've got the cucumber
now." She glared back. "Just drive."

The man reached forward and turned off the ignition. He rolled down
his window and threw the keys across the street. He smiled. Mania turned

her face fully towards him and pursed her lips. Then she asked, "What's your name?"

The man remained silent.

"Come on! What's your name?"

"John. It's John. My name's John."

Mania smiled. "What's your real name?"

The man closed his eyes and let his head fall on the steering wheel. He giggled, though he could've sobbed. "Why is it that my life has to be a Fellini movie?" he asked. "Tell me, God? Why? Why can't it just be a *regular* movie?"

"Well," Mania said and patted his knee, "I think your name should be Clyde."

Mania turned away, opened the door, and walked across the street to pick up the keys from the gutter. The man looked up and saw her. He opened his door.

"Stay where you are!" Mania yelled from across the street with such authority that the man was stunned. She walked over to the driver's door and yanked it all the way open.

"Slide over," she said.

Mania moved in behind the wheel as the man slid over and opened the passenger's door.

"Don't try it," she said. She had her hand in her purse. She pulled it out holding a shiny chrome revolver. "I'd like you to meet Miss Stella. Lock your door. And put on your seatbelt, Clyde."

The man turned to Mania, pleading. "Look, lady, this was my first job. Really! I'm not a criminal! I'm an actor in real life. Let's just go back to the shop and tell them it was all just a scene study or something."

Mania, driving, was approaching the Hollywood Freeway on-ramp.

"Reno or Vegas?" she asked.

"No. Really. I've got an audition tomorrow. I just had a bad year is all."

Mania lifted the pistol and pushed it into his chest. She looked him in the eye. "So you've had a rough year? I've had a rough morning, Clyde." Her eyes burned. She licked her lips. "Do you think I chose Checked Cashed/Donuts as a career? Do you think I'm going to settle for guys like my Buzz, who boffed me on a dare from his fraternity brothers? Do you think I like being harped on by a mannequin of a mother who . . . do you know what she tells me? She tells me that I'm giving her cancer! She actually tells me that!" Mania's hand, still holding the gun, went to the wheel so that she could maneuver over three lanes into the downtown interchange. "No, Clyde, Nevada's the place for me. They appreciate talent there. It's the entertainment capitol of the world." Mania veered onto the Ten Freeway. She settled in at 70 miles per hour.

She looked at Clyde, sitting there, his eyes getting all puddly. Not the surest footing on which to start a life on the lam. Mania thought she'd better lighten the mood.

"You know, I'm a songwriter." She glanced again at Clyde. She smiled coyly. Clyde was slouched down in his seat, hugging himself. He was looking out the side window. He didn't respond.

"Here's my newest. I just wrote it this morning, as a matter of fact. Here's how it goes," and Mania sang,

"I live on Hollywood and Vine,

"I live on table scraps and wine,

"I use the sidewalk for my bed,

"A shopping bag to rest my head.

"Good, huh?"

Clyde hugged himself tighter. He didn't face her. "I hate it," he said.

"Well, I'm still working on it. These things don't write themselves, you know." Mania looked at him closely as he pouted. Didn't he even realize how lucky he was? The world was changing and he'd been given a place in the new order. He wasn't as cute as Mania had originally thought, now that she got him into the daylight. "It'll grow on you," she said.

"I don't think it's the song that's the problem," he said.

"Don't worry. I'll grow on you, too."

Clyde was silent. Mania watched the road ahead. She exhaled carefully. "We're free, now."